PRAISE FOR ORI(

"Swift and immersive, *Original Twin* is sure to mes... guessing. In her brilliant debut, Gleeson weaves a compelling ne... secrets, lies, and dangerous family drama. This deftly paced thriller is a sinister kaleidoscope of suspense! I dare you to put it down."

—Katya de Becerra, author of *When Ghosts Call Us Home*

"Razor sharp and deftly plotted, Gleeson's debut unfolds like a feature film. The twists hit one after another until reaching a heart-stopping crescendo that left me gasping for breath. I couldn't put it down!"

—Marlee Bush, author of *When She Was Me*

"Paula Gleeson's debut, *Original Twin*, is a clever whodunit loaded with hidden clues and twisted family secrets. This thriller—where no one can be trusted and everyone could be guilty—will keep you guessing until the very last page."

—Ashley Tate, author of *Twenty-Seven Minutes*

"Paula Gleeson will keep you on your toes with every twist and turn. If you love a mystery where each piece of the puzzle calls into question what came before, pick this one up. *Original Twin* is utterly unpredictable!"

—Tracy Sierra, author of *Nightwatching*

"*Original Twin* weaves together twist upon twist, creating a tapestry of intrigue and deceit. Gleeson deftly spins a tale of family secrets, sibling rivalry, and simmering resentment—all laced with her unique brand of wry humor. An effortless, page-turning pleasure read."

—K. T. Nguyen, author of *You Know What You Did*

ORIGINAL

TWIN

ORIGINAL

TWIN

PAULA GLEESON

THOMAS & MERCER

This is a work of fiction. Names, characters, organizations, places, events, and incidents are either products of the author's imagination or are used fictitiously. Otherwise, any resemblance to actual persons, living or dead, is purely coincidental.

Text copyright © 2024 by Paula Gleeson
All rights reserved.

No part of this book may be reproduced, or stored in a retrieval system, or transmitted in any form or by any means, electronic, mechanical, photocopying, recording, or otherwise, without express written permission of the publisher.

Published by Thomas & Mercer, Seattle

www.apub.com

Amazon, the Amazon logo, and Thomas & Mercer are trademarks of Amazon.com, Inc., or its affiliates.

ISBN-13: 9781662519536 (paperback)
ISBN-13: 9781662519543 (digital)

Cover design by Faceout Studio, Jeff Miller
Cover image: © Protasov AN / Shutterstock; © Carolyn Fox, © Miguel Sobreira / Arcangel

Printed in the United States of America

For Mum.
The first one was always for you.

Chapter One

May didn't want to return to her hometown, but funerals always had a way of bringing a person back.

Funeral? *Bullshit.*

How could there be a funeral without a body?

May knew her twin was still alive even if the rest of her town had been eager to move on. One year was all it took for her sister to be officially declared dead.

The afternoon sun hit her face as May scanned their normally quiet street, now crammed with cars and a lonely TV van—here for the reception happening below her.

She turned and surveyed June's room.

The pops of mint-and-lilac decor were exactly what she needed. Her sister had read they were calming colors, and right now May would do anything to feel like the world wasn't squeezing her from the inside.

I need you, June.

The bullshit "funeral" would've been easier if June had been holding her hand and whispering exactly what May needed to hear. June always knew how to make everything okay. Well, not always, but she tried.

The murmuring of the guests from the floor below may as well have been screams echoing around May's brain. Reminding her that life was just one loss after another. First her mother, now June.

Her sister's room wasn't doing enough to comfort her after all.

There's a reason I don't come in here.

May willed the supposed calming colors to wash over her and make her more like her sister. June never let anything faze her—except for that time at the movies, of course.

She could've been the poster child for a teen who had it all together. Instead, June's face was now plastered on social media posts for another reason.

May ran her fingers over the dust-covered photos stuck around her sister's vanity mirror, no longer able to stop the deep sorrow from devouring her. The most famous photo—the one the media loved to flash everywhere of June grinning at the camera and holding up a tennis trophy—had been taken down a year ago, never to be replaced. The photos left behind were of the sisters at various stages of life.

Swaddled babies sharing the same bassinet at the hospital. Timing determined their names when May popped out on May 31 at 11:57 p.m. and June on June 1 at 12:13 a.m.

May and June on their first day of school, their backpacks too big for them. June missing a tooth, its cuteness matching her pigtails. Their mom had run out of time to do May's hair, so it hung limply, with her ears slightly sticking out. May squinted at the sun.

At the beach on a summer vacation. June striking a pose in her bright-blue bikini, while May covered her chubbiness in shorts and a T-shirt. Fourteen years old, with their lives ahead of them. June beamed, while May, again, squinted at the morning sun.

May didn't need to go through them all. She squinted in every photo June had publicly displayed. There were plenty of photos where May looked good, but June thought it was much more entertaining putting up the awful ones. May would've returned the torment if she could find a bad picture of her annoyingly photogenic sister.

She sighed. *June was always prettier than me.*

Locals had pointed this out for most of May's nineteen years—discretion had never exactly found its way to the small town of Harold. And their idea of what classified someone as beautiful was painfully conventional. June had blonde hair, was naturally thin, and hadn't had a pimple in her life. May had black hair, never tanned, and had always been called "the bigger one."

Not anymore. May tugged at the dress covering her dwindling frame, a result of her sister's disappearance a year ago.

There it was. The thing that dominated her every thought.

June's disappearance.

It wasn't uncommon for teenagers to leave without telling anyone. Most turned up within days of going missing and not everything played out like a true-crime TV special, the police had told the family. Instead of investigating, they spent time on other theories and repeated the same questions over and over.

Had she been moody or distant? *Yes, and yes.*

Had she been fighting with anyone? *Me.*

Did she ever threaten to leave before? *Since she was five.*

Running away or having a secret boyfriend got bandied about as if the investigators were offering cake with a cup of tea. May didn't accept what was being offered, especially as days turned into weeks.

That's when their dad, Gary, went to the media—who were happy to help. A beautiful eighteen-year-old white girl missing without a trace was big news in a small town. June's face had become public property. Thankfully, she took a great picture.

May shivered and scratched at her arms, the black wraparound dress she'd taken from her sister's closet stuck to her skin in the airless room. Black was pretty much the only color May wore, but normally it was jeans and heavy sweatshirts because of the chill camped permanently in her bones. She still wore her favorite lace-up black boots—which paired ridiculously with the formal dress that, as soon as today was over, she would never wear again.

The last time she'd worn a dress was in front of the cameras, where she made a plea for her sister's return. The public didn't like that there were no tears. No emotion. None of them understanding May was already a shell of herself without June as her constant companion.

People's fascination with the case turned to judgment. They wanted an identical twin—a June look-alike. Someone with the same popularity, charisma, and beauty. Total bullshit.

That was the last time May appeared in front of the cameras. Willingly.

She wasn't naive; she knew people judged her. Like they were blaming her, somehow, for her sister's vanishing. Or worse, their eyes saying it should have been her and not June.

Then everything changed. May closed her eyes. Taking in deep breaths.

What was found a month or so after she'd gone missing changed everything. June's backpack shoved behind a dumpster at a rest stop. Inside, her phone and the torn clothes she had been wearing that day. There was blood on them—June's blood. Her car had never been found.

Enough. May opened her eyes and yanked the photos from the mirror. If June wanted to freak out about May touching her things, she could come back and stop her.

Willing her sister back into existence was a constant now. Then May could be whole again. Like before. Where smiling didn't hurt. Chocolate tasted like a warm embrace. Fresh rain brought joy. Every plan a possibility.

Better than the blob of dead space she'd become. An ever-widening hole that threatened to consume her from within. Without her twin, she was nothing.

The mirror now empty like May, June's favorite possession reflected back at her. A black stallion statue rearing up, named Magic. May knew June hadn't run away when the police suggested it because she would've taken Magic with her. The horse had been beside June's head wherever she slept since she picked it up at a garage sale when she was eight. Slumber parties, Christmases away, family vacations, even camping trips. June had been adamant it had helped her sleep. Magic was like her favorite blankie, no matter how childish it was or how old she got.

4

The horse was askew like someone had bumped it. Busybodies downstairs snooping in the "dead" girl's room, no doubt.

May walked over from the mirror and picked up the statue. She expected dust to cover her hand, but there was none. Instead, a rolled-up piece of paper dropped from the hole in the bottom.

Had one of the guests left this for her?

No way. A smile surfaced before May could stop it. June had a knack for leaving hidden notes around the house for her to find. Usually asking for a favor, *or four*. Or to swap chores, *she hated vacuuming*. Or to ask a riddle, *I never got them right*.

May scooped up the paper from the carpet and unrolled the well-worn article, which looked like it had been cut out from a newspaper.

LOCAL GIRL GOES MISSING

On Friday, September 2, nineteen-year-old Diana Wells went missing from her on-campus dorm at Bretford University.

Roommate Sharon Hook alerted Diana's parents, Stanley and Pat Wells, that she hadn't seen Diana for three days. Diana's parents immediately notified the police.

Diana is said to be a bright psychology major who never skipped class or missed a call to her parents on Sundays. Police have deemed her absence suspicious.

Diana's boyfriend, Brad Dormer,

```
has  been  questioned  but  isn't  a
suspect,   according   to   Detective
Randall, who is heading up the case.
"Brad has a solid alibi," the de-
tective told the press, but didn't
elaborate further when questioned.

A week has passed since Diana was
last sighted in her dorm, with no
clues or further suspects. The po-
lice are calling for information
from anyone who saw or spoke to
Diana on September 2 or has seen
her since.
```

May reread the article three times.

Questions circled her like a shark. Diana Wells. Their mother. Was this article really about *their* mother? Why had she never mentioned this before? And why had June hidden it in Magic without telling her?

Was this a joke?

May's eyes swept the room, waiting for June to jump out and yell, "Sucker!" The only sounds were from the guests below.

May read the article again, not believing any of it to be true.

The room blurred as a memory stabbed her brain. The second of September.

Today.

Today was the second of September. The exact day one year ago when June disappeared.

The same day as their mother.

Chapter Two

May recoiled like she'd been punched, forcing her to clutch at her stomach. She wanted to gag. Her head spun. She knew this feeling engulfing her. Abandonment had become an unwelcome familiar. Claiming her. Eating her from within.

First her mother, then June. Both gone.

Twins are never supposed to feel alone. *Bullshit.*

The room became a haze of shapes and colors—none of them comforting.

May let the details worm their way into her as she stared at Magic and the newspaper article in her hand.

Like June, her mother had disappeared. She'd never mentioned a thing. Neither had June. Why had her sister hidden this from her? May tried to connect the dots swimming in front of her eyes. Nothing made any sense. She didn't believe in coincidences. And she couldn't ask her mother because her mother died three years ago.

The whole thing had to be a misunderstanding, or her mother would've said something. Wouldn't she? "A silly mistake," her mom would've joked. "I went to a music festival and forgot to tell someone. Can you believe it?" May imagined them laughing about it over hot chocolate, and her insides folded knowing she'd never hear her mom laugh again.

Neither her mother nor her sister was around to answer questions, and her father was a mess. May had already left him downstairs nursing his drink in the corner, while the house overflowed with practically everyone who made up the town.

She instinctively patted her butt cheek for the phone that usually sat in her jeans pocket, but she was wearing the annoying dress. Her phone was in the backpack she'd brought on the bus from the city. Which could be anywhere after Aunty Sue had done a tidy up of the house.

Aunty Sue. *Of course.* Three years younger than Diana, Sue would have been sixteen when (if) this had happened.

May tentatively made her way to the bathroom, where she washed her face. She filled her belly with water, like a camel about to cross the desert. Sometimes it helped fill a void that food couldn't. Sometimes.

Downstairs, faces of people she'd known all her life passed by, offering condolences. Everyone was alien to her, as if she'd stepped into an alternate universe where nothing was real. Grief? Sure. Or maybe it was the fact that she'd left the small town over a year ago and didn't belong anymore.

They gave her pitying looks like they did when her mom died. This was different, though, because May knew her mom was never coming back. With June there was still hope.

"Have you seen Aunty Sue?" May grazed Mrs. Slattery's arm in case she hadn't heard her, which was highly likely. May had always had a soft spot for her eighty-year-old neighbor, who often smelled of roses or bleach, or a combination of the two.

"No, dear, I haven't. How are you holding up?" Mrs. Slattery glanced behind May.

May turned as her dad engulfed her in a hug that almost brought her to tears. His warmth was familiar and should be welcome like when he used to scoop her up as a girl. His touch was now a reminder of how they only had each other.

May pulled back and scanned his ashen face, dark circles now camped under his watery eyes. She wanted to comfort him, tell him it was all going to be okay, but had no idea where to start.

"Hey, love, you holding up alright?" He choked the words out.

"Sure. Just feeling weird, I guess." Did she dare ask him about the article? No, today was not the day to drop another bombshell on him. He was barely hanging on as it was.

He squeezed her arm and tried for a reassuring smile. "I'm glad you're here. I missed having you around."

She should hug her father back. Show him how much she missed him too. Return some of the comfort that he'd always had at the ready for her all these years. Instead she just stood there. A robot inside and out.

"I'll be back in a minute. I need to find Sue."

He wanted her to stay. Talk some more. She could see it written all over his face. Why did she always have to get everything so wrong? June would've stayed, hugged him, told him she loved him. June would have taken his pain away.

Mrs. Slattery lightly grabbed May's hand and leaned toward her ear. "Don't shut everyone out, dear. This past year has not been kind to you, and pushing people away won't help that."

May almost let it all out then. The hurt, the pain, the anger, the blame. Constant companions that she'd neither invited nor understood. She let them simmer inside her. A reminder of how she was still here and didn't deserve anyone's pity. Especially her own.

Some called it survivor's guilt—but June wasn't dead, so May had no name for who she had become. A walking contradiction maybe? One that was impossible to explain. Because how is it possible to be both hollow and possessed with grief?

She squeezed Mrs. Slattery's hand as an answer and walked away before the bubbling volcano inside her burst.

May found her aunty Sue chatting to some ladies from her mom's old book club. They stood in the sun-filled living room, so hot now, sweat carved channels through their foundation. Two of the ladies had handheld fans they flapped so fast it was a wonder they hadn't taken off.

"Sue, I have something to ask you."

"Oh, here she is!" Sue presented May like a game show prize.

The other ladies cocked their heads and raised their eyebrows in obvious sympathy.

May couldn't help but notice the glances up and down her body. *I can't win.* Whatever she looked like, she was never going to be "perfect" like her twin.

"How are you, May? Do you need anything? Have you tried my lemon tarts? They really are to die for." Aunty Sue's hand shot up to her mouth at her poor choice of words. Everyone politely tittered.

"No, I'm okay. I need to talk to you about something. *In private.*"

There was no missing the flicker of annoyance in Sue's eyes, but her pageant smile never left her face. "Oh, pet! This day is so hard for both of us, so it's understandable if you need to *talk.*" Sue said none of this to May, though, but to the ladies surrounding her.

May cringed at the word *pet.* Since when did Sue call her that?

"Why don't you go and hang out with your friends? I'm sure they'd love to talk." Sue's smile was now like a grimace.

Ouch. Sue knew June had been May's only real friend.

"It's so lovely of your schoolmates to come today and show their support."

May followed Sue's eyes to two of the girls from her old high school. What Sue didn't know was that they had been two years below them and were neither her nor June's friends. No doubt just skipping school or fueling gossip on their social media.

All June's real friends who were still left in Harold were down at the local cemetery getting drunk or stoned. That's where they'd hung out when June was in high school, so that's where they wanted to remember her now. May had been invited but couldn't think of anything worse than being stuck with people she'd deliberately lost contact with. That and sitting next to June's freshly placed headstone. Um, no thanks.

"May, how are you? This must be so hard to officially say goodbye to your sister." May turned to the lady who had spoken: Pauline. Red lipstick had made its way onto her front teeth.

Pauline's question encouraged the other ladies.

"Yes, but closure is always good."

"I can't believe they never found her."

"It must be killing you not to know what happened to her, sweetie."

Seriously? Another poor word choice again followed by polite tittering.

May might as well have been a character in one of their soap operas. She glared at Sue, who just nodded along to the questions. Like she cared.

"Excuse me, ladies, but I need to talk to my aunt. *Now.*" May grabbed Sue's arm as she whispered to Pauline, "By the way, you have lipstick on your teeth. Real friends always let you know."

May left their gasps behind, dragging Sue to her father's study to stop her talking to people along the way. The study, where her father had often retreated when there used to be a house full of women, was off limits to guests. They wouldn't be interrupted.

After May shut the timber sliding doors, Sue's facade dissolved.

"What's the problem, May? Can't you see I have *work* to do? Given you and your father can't be bothered to help and, *as usual*, I have to do everything—just like when Diana died." Sue sighed for effect.

May studied Sue's professionally dyed blonde hair, which was in a twisted bun at the back of her head. The dress she wore was her mother's, only it was too tight on her aunt's bust and hips.

"May, we have company." Sue tapped her foot and flicked her eyes to the closed doors and the chatter outside. "What's so important that you had to rudely drag me away?"

"We don't have 'company.'" May did air quotes so Sue couldn't miss her point. "This isn't a party."

"Well, June would've called it a party." Sue stared at her, unblinking. "Plus, my date will be here soon."

"Your date? Seriously?"

"What? Like you would understand. It's just so hard on me, you know? Being left with all this responsibility now that Diana *and* June are gone. Having to care for you and your father is a full-time job—no wonder I had to move in after your mother died." Sue finally took a breath.

"June's not dead." Anger filled May's belly. "So not sure what's going to change around here."

"Regardless, I'll have to look after you and Gary."

"*Me?* I don't even live here. Remember, I moved out over a year ago. Nice to know I've been missed." *It was supposed to be for university, but June changed all that.* May shook the past out of her head. "And Dad isn't exactly screaming for your help."

"I don't need to listen to this." Sue's phone beeped. "My date's here. Gotta go." She spun on her heels, the pageant smile already in place as she went back through the doors.

Great. Nailed it. So much for getting any information out of her aunt.

May stepped behind her father's mahogany desk and sank into the plush leather high-backed chair. May stroked a framed photo of her mother and father on their wedding day. She waited for the tears to come for a family that had halved.

Exhaustion ravaged her bones as the article kept poking at her brain. There was no way it could be true. Her mom would've told them if she'd been abducted. Wouldn't she?

May glanced at the rest of the photos of her family on the desk. *Bingo.*

She knew who would have the answers to her questions.

DIANA

I had a secret.

One I would never share with anyone. This secret was only for me.

Brad sat across from me eating his pasta. I wanted to punch him in the face. The way he slurped his spaghetti into his mouth disgusted me, and other diners were starting to stare. As always, he remained oblivious.

"How is everything here?" I also wanted to punch the waitress in the face. Her crush on my boyfriend couldn't be any more obvious, given the way she flicked her hair and checked on us every five minutes. "Need anything else?"

She was cute. Five foot nothing, curves for days, and a long, black, thick ponytail perfect for flicking.

I wanted to ask her if she would like to sit down and take my place. I didn't think Brad would notice if I was replaced by this stunner. Bonus, her father owned the restaurant, serving the best Italian food this university town offered.

"Some more parmesan would be awesome. Thanks!" Brad had a piece of spaghetti hanging out of his mouth. I bet the waitress thought it endearing.

"Of course! I'll be right back!" She practically bounced off the walls.

No question of her coming right back.

I called after her, "Excuse me!"

The waitress spun around. Her head tilt made me wonder if this was the first time she had noticed me. "Yes?"

"I would like some garlic bread."

"Whoa, I thought we agreed no garlic. There'll be no kissing for you tonight." Brad actually winked at the waitress.

Kiss her then.

"Actually, I'll have extra garlic." I matched the waitress's head tilt, daring her to say something.

She flicked her eyes at Brad, who was too busy glaring at me to notice.

"Sure, I'll be right back." I swear her fabulous ass taunted me as it walked away.

"What's your problem?" Brad took a sip of his soda like he was slurping soup. I swear, he was deliberately trying to annoy me.

"Nothing. I have a craving for garlic bread. It isn't a crime." Technically true, but to Brad I may as well be shoving shit in my mouth.

He widened his blue eyes, like he always did when he wanted me to know he was in charge. "You know how I feel about garlic. It makes me want to gag."

Lately, dating Brad made me want to gag.

No matter.

Soon, I would be long gone.

Chapter Three

Guilt consumed May for bothering her grandmother on the day her granddaughter was officially considered dead—but the way May saw it, she had no choice. She needed answers. More so, she needed to escape.

Her childhood home was now foreign to her. Overrun with people who were more like strangers, no longer speaking of her sister in the present tense. She didn't need the reminder, thanks.

May drove in a haze. Her town a blur. Not that it mattered. Harold was a town stuck in time, and she knew it by heart.

The same businesses had been there for years. Every single one of them lining the only main street through the center of town. It was called Main Street in case there was any confusion.

Main Street had once been a wonderland. A destination. An ice cream as a treat. A small toy with Dad's coins. Mom dancing in the grocery store when an old song came on. Always a warm hand if you reached for it. A promise that this would be forever. Now the cracks were everywhere. In the paint, the sidewalk, her memories. Shadows advancing while the buildings seemingly shrank.

Some said it was a town ready for growth. But the only thing that grew here—thrived here—were the roses. Sometimes blooming, bewitching in their beauty. A ruse from afar. Come closer. Black spot. Everywhere.

Welcome to Harold. Where everything's rotten if you look close enough.

May pulled her mom's car into the empty driveway. Her grandmother's house was only a three-minute walk away, but May knew the one lonely TV van could easily multiply like locusts and devour her with their questions.

The white weatherboard house stood at just over two levels. Far too big a space for an old lady to maintain, but May's grandmother wouldn't leave—until she was dead and smelly, she would remind anyone who listened. Her gout had become too painful for her to access anything but the bottom floor. The upstairs bedrooms lay in sheeted wait for visitors who never came anymore.

May opened the front door without knocking. It remained unlocked no matter how much the family complained about her grandmother's security. Small town or not.

"Pat! Granny Pat, are you here?"

"Yes, child, no need to yell. I ain't deaf . . . yet."

May found Pat in her reading chair, which she rarely moved from. Her floral dress unbuttoned to her flat breasts, which were covered by a beige slip. She fanned herself with a rolled-up magazine, her short grey hair catching some of the breeze. "Why is it like hell out there? It's too early to be this bloody hot."

May gave her an obligatory kiss on the cheek. Her grandma always smelled of scotch. May hated the smell. June had loved it.

"You're just in time to put the kettle on and make this old tart a cup of tea." No mention of June's funeral, which May appreciated. "See you're out of that dress already."

"Dresses suck, Pat."

At their grandma's insistence, the twins called her Pat.

Pat didn't much like *grandma*, tolerated *granny*, and hated *nana*. She said the archaic names implied she had to make cookies. Not something she had done a day in her life.

May put the kettle on the stove and pulled everything down she needed to make the tea. The kitchen was as familiar as her own. The sprawling house and yard, complete with a tree swing, meant many a hiding spot for games of hide-and-seek. The twins had always hoped they would find Narnia in the attic wardrobe. A family of mice was as good as they ever got.

May opened the fridge, then closed it again. Normally there were family photos scattered everywhere on the door. Now there were only the magnets that once held them up. Weird.

"Pat, where are all the photos on the fridge? I hope you didn't throw them away."

"Why would I do a ludicrous thing like that?" Pat barked. "No, I took them down. Your sister gave me the heebie-jeebies."

"What are you talking about?"

"Got the tingles and pulled everything down, didn't I? Felt wretched looking at them. Not right to get down in the dumps when you're slowly dying. Going to put that handsome creature Idris Elba up instead. He sure gives me tingles." Pat chuckled to herself.

May shook her head as she made the tea. She got it. She'd just done the same in June's room. "Where are they? I'm going to keep them if that's alright."

"Of course, child. They're in the drawer with all the bills. Dig a little if it's in a state."

May opened the drawer, which wasn't in a state but neatly arranged. It contained a pile of bills and stationery, but no photos. May fanned the bills, still nothing.

"Not here, Pat. You must've put them somewhere else."

"Like hell I did. I may be old, but I ain't losing my mind!"

"Okay, Granny," May mumbled. No doubt they'd gone in the garbage when Pat was in one of her "cleaning moods." Nothing stood a chance when Pat cleaned.

May brought the tea into the front room, grateful for the afternoon sun shining in and warming the space, even if she was back in her heavy sweatshirt and jeans. The old house always had a chill, even in the height of summer. June had been adamant it was because of the ghosts that lived upstairs in the attic. Although Pat claimed she'd never felt a chill in her life.

"Did you put m' scotch in too?"

"Yes, Pat."

May mouthed the words as Pat said them out loud: "A cup of tea is not a cup of tea without a splash of magic." She wagged her finger in jest. "Good to see you've been listening all these years."

"How could I not? You say it *every* time."

Pat took a sip of her tea and licked her lips with approval. May had put in a little more than a splash; she wanted Pat loose lipped.

"So how you doing, child? A tough day, huh?"

"For you too. You were wise not to come. You would've hated it."

"You get better at making decisions as you get older. June wouldn't have given a fart if I was there or not. And if she did, well then she can bloody well haunt me—I'd be grateful for the company."

May nodded, not having to ask for the same thing. June haunted her every day.

They sipped their tea. May's heart raced, considering how to ask about the article. Pat closed her eyes, either enjoying the sun or covering her tears. May couldn't tell. She saw a lot of herself in Pat. Straight talking and nonaffectionate. June had always been more like her mom, contrary to what everyone thought.

"So what are you doing over here? Had enough of the buffoons in this town, sticking their noses in where they aren't wanted? I imagine Sue is taking Diana's place as hostess with vigor." It wasn't a question. Nothing got past Pat.

May figured now was as good a time as any and pulled a book from her canvas shoulder bag. The book, *Secret Seven Mystery*, had been a favorite of the twins. May had taken it from June's room to keep the article safe. She opened up the page where it lay.

"Actually, I'm hoping you can clear something up for me." She passed the article to Pat. "Can you tell me if this is about Mom? I found it in June's room."

Pat finished her tea and put it down on the coffee table in front of her, along with the article, which didn't even warrant a glance.

"Not this again." Pat sighed heavily. "Your sister was here a couple of years ago with the same bloody thing."

"What?" Confusion swarmed May's face. "Why didn't she show me? What's the big mystery?"

"Oh, child. Life becomes complicated when everyone tries to keep a secret. Remember that. Eventually, those secrets will catch up with you one way or another."

"Why didn't the police ask me about this when June went missing? I mean, did you see the date? It's today. June went missing the *exact* same day as Mom." May stabbed her finger at the date written in the article. "Does Dad know about this?"

Pat stared at her empty cup. "Yes, your father knows. They actually questioned him about it in front of you, and you didn't say a peep. Maybe you don't remember. Not surprising with everything you were going through."

May had blanked out most of the days after June disappeared.

"I'm so confused, Pat. I don't remember anyone mentioning this to me. Tell me what happened to Mom." Dots played in front of May's eyes.

"You don't look so good, love. Make us another cup of tea, would you? Put some sugar in yours. You're in shock. As for mine, forget the tea. I'll just take the scotch."

May did as she asked, and Pat began.

Chapter Four

"Diana couldn't wait to get to university and away from this town. Bit like you, May. She got accepted to Bretford University—you know the one two hours from here—and studied psychology. She wanted to understand people better, help them in some way. Bit hoity toity for me, but Diana seemed to enjoy it."

May chewed her fingernails. She knew this already.

"A real beauty, your mom. Looked a bit like Lynda Carter when she was younger. You know the one, the original actress who played Wonder Woman."

"Pat, get to the point. What happened to Mom?"

"Hold your horses, child. It's all part of the story. Do you want to hear it or not?" Pat's finger wagged again.

May sighed, thankful the sugar had helped and the dancing spots had stopped.

"Diana always had admirers. Couldn't keep track of the boys that would show up on our doorstep. Pa was alive then, of course, and it would drive him up the wall, even if he kept it to himself. Diana had never been serious about anyone, always knowing she would leave this town sooner rather than later. Bit like you—" Pat stopped and glanced over her shoulder toward the stairs. "Did you hear that?"

"I didn't hear anything." May followed Pat's gaze. "You're freaking me out."

The sun now dipping out of sight, May turned on the lights in the living room and the kitchen, then locked the front door—not caring what Pat said.

"I swear, I'm hearing things in m' old age." Pat sipped her scotch.

"Keep going." May sat on the couch facing her grandmother. "If you told June all of this already, then I deserve to know too."

"That's fair." Pat pursed her lips, thinking. "Let's see . . . there was this one kid in Diana's grade at high school who came around more than he should've. William was his name, but he went by Willy. Seemed to have more than a boyish crush on Diana, he did."

May sat forward. "What did he do?"

"Nothing dangerous, just creepy-like. He would follow her home or be sitting on the tree swing out front waiting for her in the morning. Always wanting to walk with her somewhere. He left notes in her schoolbooks that she didn't know how he could've written without her noticing. He gave her candy, flowers, and gifts. It was all too much. At first, Diana tried to be polite, but soon that gave way to frustration."

"Didn't she tell him to back off?"

"We all did. Pa even found his voice and threatened the boy with a knuckle sandwich, which was all bluff, and Willy knew it. That kid couldn't take a hint; he wasn't slow or anythin'. He had all his marbles, but when it came to your mother, he had some kind of obsession."

"So what happened?"

Pat rubbed the top of her cane propped beside her armchair like it was a crystal ball.

"That's the thing. Nothing happened. As quickly as it began, it stopped. Just like that, Willy didn't give Diana another glance."

"Oh." May didn't know why she was disappointed.

"I don't know what was creepier, that kid hanging around or giving up the ghost like he did."

May didn't know how to answer or what it had to do with the article. She knew better than to question Pat, or they would sit in silence for the rest of the night. "So what about Bretford and when she went missing?"

"That bloody university," Pat spit out. "Your mom moved to Bretford after high school. Started up with a boy named Brad. Handsome, but not much going on up top—if you know what I mean? I never met him, mind you, but I got enough from what I heard."

May nodded. Pat had her own way of judging people.

"Diana would call us every Sunday to catch up on the week. *Every* Sunday. Our nonnegotiable. Pa was still alive then, of course, and when Sunday rolled around, he had a skip in his step. He would write out lists on Sunday morning with questions for Diana and stories of what we had been doing. He would try and do at least one new thing every week to have something interesting or funny to say. A good man, your pa. Balls, I miss him." Pat sipped her scotch and went on.

"Sue lived at home with us then, in high school, and hating it. She didn't much care for those Sunday calls. I don't blame her. We weren't exactly shy on our love for Diana."

May didn't say anything. She appreciated Pat talking like her mom could still walk in the door at any moment.

"So, on this one Sunday your pa and I were waiting to hear from Diana. She always called us 'cause her schedule never stayed the same. Only this Sunday, the call never came. We tried her at around eight o'clock at night, 'cause we were worried—or possibly cranky—thinking she had forgotten us. She didn't much care for one of them cell phone things back then, and we got no answer on the landline in her dorm room. I stayed up until eleven o'clock and never heard your pa come to bed. I know he kept trying her, but the phone rang out all night. Odd because Diana had an early class on Monday. Always talking about tucking herself in early to bed on a Sunday night. She had a roommate . . ." Pat paused.

May checked the article. "Sharon Hook, it says here."

"That's right. Sharon. The girls shared the same phone line in the room, so either one could've picked up. Yet neither girl did."

Pat took another long sip of scotch, her hand trembling.

"You alright, Pat?"

"Yes, love, it's hard to remember that time. Bloody awful."

May had still held out hope the article was a misunderstanding. Part of her didn't want to hear any more. "You don't have to tell me anything else if you don't feel up to it."

"No, love. You deserve to know. It's been a long time coming." Pat kept rubbing her cane. For comfort, May decided.

"So the next day, we finally got a hold of Sharon."

May checked the article. "Wait, it says here that she called you."

"Does it? Well, they must've gotten their facts wrong—like they got many things wrong about Diana. Most certainly it was us that contacted Sharon. I was there on the other line, with Pa."

"So what did she say?"

"Not much. Flighty girl. Liked her parties, apparently. Explained she hadn't seen Diana all weekend. Wasn't uncommon. Those girls were in and out of that dorm room like it was a carnival ride. She said she would make some calls and phone us back. So we waited and waited, and it wasn't until the next day she called to say no one had seen Diana since Friday."

May interrupted. "What about her boyfriend? Brad?"

"He'd been at his parents' place a few hours away. So, you can imagine, your pa and I were beside ourselves. It had been four days since anyone had laid eyes on our baby."

"I can't imagine how you both felt."

"I imagine you know good and well, May. What with June being gone for a year now."

May didn't need the reminder.

"I'll leave it be, don't worry." Pat's eyes narrowed. "You doing okay? This has been a big day already. Do you want a break?"

May pulled her lips into a smile that hurt. "No, I'm okay. I need to know what happened. Unless you want to stop."

"If I stop, I face reality. Talking about her makes it feel like she's still here. Some days I forget that we've lost her." Pat rubbed her eyes. "Anyway, we got the police involved. A couple of detectives in Bretford took on the case. Right away, they deemed it suspicious."

"Not like June."

"No, nothing like June. It was a different time back then. People talked more. They paid attention to what was in front of them. Phones weren't glued to faces."

May had to keep Pat on track. "How long was she missing for?"

"Three weeks."

"Okay, so . . . nothing like June."

Pat didn't seem to know how to respond.

May kept going. "What other evidence did they find?"

Pat closed her eyes. Rubbed them. "Diana's purse was found outside her dorm building on the day she went missing. A girl she had a class with kept a hold of it, meaning to give it back to Diana. Of course, she never did. Nothing missing from what we could tell, including her money. So burglary was ruled out."

"Maybe she dropped it?" May offered.

"Maybe, but another thing had always been strange—Diana left a necklace on her desk. One she apparently never took off. An expensive piece of jewelry. A horseshoe necklace made from gold and small diamonds around the shoe. The odd thing was your pa and I didn't know a thing about it."

"That's weird. Maybe Brad gave it to her?"

"No. The police questioned him about it. Brad told them she had it before they were going out. Diana told him we had given it to her for her sixteenth birthday—which was a lie. Your pa and I had done no such thing."

"So where did she get it from?" May sat forward slightly.

"Your guess is as good as mine. Everyone on campus the police talked to said Diana never took it off, even in the shower. Very protective of it, apparently. Her leaving it on her desk was taken as a bad sign."

May chewed on her nails again. "Mom never wore that necklace. Where is it now?"

"It went missing soon after the police had done their search of the dorm room. It should've gone into evidence but never did. Reckon one of the cops took it and gave it to his wife. Bloody disgrace."

"You weren't suspicious something else had happened?"

"No, I wasn't. I hadn't even seen the bloody thing and had to take everyone else's word it existed and meant something to Diana. I wanted to believe it was a fantasy because then Diana hadn't kept something from us." Pat cleared her throat. "That hurt me worse than a missing necklace. We never kept secrets from one another."

May bit her lip. "Sorry, Pat. I didn't mean to upset you."

"I'm getting a little drunk, and I'm tired. Mind if we call it a day?"

"Sure. Of course." May knew her disappointment was obvious. June was the performer, not her. "Do you want me to make you something for dinner? Help you to bed?"

"No, I still have m' legs. All I want now is to close my eyes and forget everything this family has been through." Pat pulled herself up and shuffled across the hall. "Sleep upstairs if you like. Be nice to have a warm body in the house for a change."

May felt a chill run through her as she glanced up the darkened stairs.

Days Mom's been dead: 17.

Hi Mom,
It's me, June!

Don't get too excited because I'm mad at you.
Like SO mad I could kill you.

But I can't because you're already dead.

My therapist told me that it's normal to be angry after someone dies. Yep, I officially have a therapist. I wasn't handling things so great, so this was the solution. But I mean really, how does everyone expect me to be handling things? Swimmingly?

We only have one therapist in town, so ONE guess for who it is. Good guess! Smelly Mr. Milham. Why does his breath smell so much? I think he has serious gum issues because I even gave him like four mints the other day and it STILL didn't help. That's why I do all the talking.

It's weird going to a therapist I've known all my life and is the father of one of my best friends—I mean, it's also how I got in to see him so quickly, so I guess I should be grateful. Yikes, he was even at your funeral. This boring small town. I bet Mr. Milham tells everyone what I say even if he says he doesn't.

That's why I told him the other day that I was pregnant, but either he doesn't believe me or he hasn't told anyone yet. You wait, that rumor will get around in no time. (I'm not pregnant, Mom. I'm only sixteen. Jeez!)

Mr. Milham says it's "normal" to act out while I'm grieving—that's what he calls my lying: "acting out." It seems like everything IS NORMAL when someone dies. Anger, acting out, lying, wanting to kill someone who is already dead.

May isn't doing any of those things. It's like she's pretending nothing happened. Like you didn't JUST die. I mean, she's not even crying. I'm not sure how normal that is! I cry ALL the time, which is probably why she finds me annoying now and likes being by herself.

But so does Dad, and she still hangs out with HIM. I guess Dad has always cried even when it's just sappy commercials on TV, so he's absolutely being normal.

I bet you're wondering why I'm writing to you. I mean it's not like you can read this letter— wherever you are. Mr. Milham says it will help me work out my "feelings." Hah!

How silly does he think I am? As if writing letters to you will help with how I am "feeling." I mean, I don't even know how I am feeling. Sometimes I am angry, then sad, then I feel okay, then nothing. Then we drive past the swimming pool in town, and I remember the day you died and how you slipped, and then there are TOO many feelings! Blah!

Why did you have to die, Mom? WHY?!

Anyway, so here I am writing you a letter. I guess it can't hurt even if you won't answer back. (And, no, it doesn't mean Mr. Milham is a smarty pants.) These letters are just for us. Me and you, Mom.

It'll be where I can share all my secrets and you can't yell at me. Ha ha.

Maybe now I'll find out all of your secrets too. That's usually what happens when someone dies.

Isn't it? ☺

Love, June x

Chapter Five

May couldn't sleep.

No ghosts haunting her. Just the size of the house and its memories, which were maybe worse.

She read the letter over and over that her sister had written just after their mom had died three years ago. She carried it everywhere—like most of June's personal things she'd stolen from her room. June had shown it to her after she'd written it and told her to do the same thing. May tried. Once. But she found writing to her mom didn't help with the pain. Nothing helped.

Had June written more letters to their mom? This was the only one May had ever found. Maybe, like the letter suggested, June had discovered those secrets of her mom's after all.

Her sister's laughter echoed in the single bed next to hers. And if she stared hard enough in the dark, May could make out the glow of the flashlight under a sheet as June read her a ghost story. May was even sure she could smell the sickly sweet perfume her twin wore if she breathed in long enough.

She was officially losing it.

Beating the sun, May slipped out of bed and waited in the kitchen for Pat to get up. Her leg twitched in anticipation of hearing the rest of the story, or it could've been the three coffees she'd already consumed.

Pat called out from the room she slept in—originally a small library but now her bedroom. "Bloody hell, child, I can hear your mind ticking over from here. Let an old woman have her peace, would you? Not all of us are grateful to be alive in the morning."

"Get up, Pat! I'm heading home this afternoon and want to spend some time with Dad before I go."

Pat shuffled into the kitchen minutes later, a bathrobe covering her naked body. May was relieved Pat had bothered to cover herself—not always a regular occurrence.

"Give me some of that coffee, would you? Put in enough sugar to give me diabetes. One more thing that can kill me won't hurt."

May groaned. "Stop talking like that—you're not going anywhere." She helped Pat to the table.

"That's what I'm afraid of. I got a lotta people waiting for me in the land of the dead. If that means I have to live on a cloud and spit rainbows to be with them, so be it. Just don't make me wait too long."

May smiled. She hoped she had an ounce of Pat's spirit when she got to her age. Nothing seemed to faze her—just like June.

May brought over two cups of coffee, Pat's black and sweet and May's straight black. They sat across from each other at the round wooden table.

May couldn't wait any longer. "I want to know what happened to Mom."

"Spit me sideways, you're demanding. Let me have m' coffee, okay?" Pat added more sugar from the bowl in front of her. "While I'm doing that, you can tell me how you've been and why the hell you look so sickly. A woman needs to have some meat with her potatoes. It's what the boys want, you know?" Pat stirred in her sugar and tapped her mug with the spoon. "Or is it girls you like? I'm okay either way as long as you give me grandkids, or is it great-grandkids? It's terrible getting old."

"I'm only nineteen, jeez. It'll be a long time before I give you any kind of kids." It was conversations like this that made May wish she could teleport.

Pat raised an eyebrow. "Promise me you won't wait too long."

"I'm not promising anything." May sipped her coffee.

If only I could teleport to June.

"How's that boy you're seeing? The one with the nice lips."

May spit her coffee back into her mug. "Nice lips? Pat, that's just weird . . . I guess you mean Marcus. How do you know about him?"

"Your father showed me a photo of the two of you."

"Oh. That's right. I forgot I sent it. Marcus and I broke up, though we were never actually dating." May talked into her cup. "Working at the real estate office is fine . . . if you want to talk about that instead."

"One day you'll drink scotch, and I won't be able to shut you up."

"Never going to happen. It smells like paint thinner." May stood, her bones aching. "You want some toast?"

"I don't, but you have some."

May opened the fridge. Closed it. Opened it again. She needed something to do but wasn't hungry.

"Stop fussing, child. Come and sit down and tell me why you sabotaged another relationship."

May stood in front of the kitchen sink. "Don't start with me, Pat. You don't know anything about my relationships. Marcus was no one important."

"Your eyes say different, so he must've been someone special."

Nice one, eyes. May let her hair fall over her face so nothing else would betray her.

"Don't get in the habit of pushing people away just because they might hurt you. Trust me, that just causes more pain." Pat caught May's eye. "Although, I'm not saying there's anything wrong with wanting your own independence, love. You're your own person, after all."

No. I'm May and June. June and May.

Pat flinched as she rubbed her knee. "Sit down and tell me how you really are. You never call me since you became a big shot in the city."

Ouch. May had known Pat's remark was coming. Her dad had been saying the same thing since she got home. She pulled out her chair and slunk into it. How could she tell them that her move had been anything but exciting? That she was far from a big shot. Not even a little shot.

How could she enjoy the city when she was supposed to be there with June? It's all they'd ever talked about. Moving away from Harold. May studying design at university. June becoming a model or actress or reality TV show star—it changed daily. They would share an apartment. Together, they were going to be invincible.

None of that happened, of course.

"I really don't want to talk about me. I'm sorry, Pat. I promise I'll call more, but can we talk about Mom and what happened?"

"Bloody hell, you're as stubborn as me." Pat took a final sip of her coffee.

May stared at her own cup. "I was wondering about that Willy guy. The one that was bothering Mom."

"What about him?"

"What happened to him? Maybe he had something to do with Mom's and June's disappearances. Did you ever think of that?"

Pat shook her head. "That kid had nothing to do with your sister . . . or your mother."

"How can you be sure?"

"I bloody well asked him, didn't I?"

May sat forward. "You asked him? You know where he is?"

Pat chuckled. "Don't get too excited, child. Course I know where he is. So do you for that matter."

"I do?" May struggled to remember someone called Willy in town.

"He goes by Bill now. Makes all of them delicious cakes."

"Wait." May's breath hitched. "Are you talking about Bill the baker? Him? That was Mom's stalker? But he's so . . . so—"

"I'm not sure that you should go around calling him a stalker." Pat tugged at her robe. "A name like that sticks around here."

"You're the one who brought him up! And I don't care what he is. It sounds like he might know something about what happened to Mom. Maybe June too." May stood and gulped down her coffee.

"Leave it, child. Bill doesn't know a thing. It was a long time ago." Pat bit her lip.

May checked the time. "He'll be at the bakery now. I'm going before he leaves."

Pat shook her head. "You're chasing ghosts, child."

"I'll call you later, Pat." May strode to the hallway and grabbed her keys. "Then you can fill me in on the rest."

Pat yelled something, but May was already out the door.

Chapter Six

Having two bakeries in Harold was both a luxury and a pain in the ass. A local couple had run the first bakery, Sweet Tooth, since forever. Then a Vietnamese family, the Nguyens, moved into town and opened their own bakery, simply called Bakery, across the street.

As anyone who lived in a small town could attest, competition between businesses could break up friendships spanning generations, even a marriage or two. The Bakery Saga (as it became known) had been no different.

A truce was established because of June's disappearance, which brought the town together in a way it knew best: sandwiches, cake, and cups of tea. The scout hall was neutral ground and became a refuge for shocked locals who needed to loosen their tongues and fill their bellies.

May had never cared what the locals of Harold thought, and as schoolkids, they could afford only Bakery as an afternoon snack. It also became a safe haven for a secret or two. The Nguyens had no interest in gossip.

It was just a shame that Bill worked at Sweet Tooth. May would have to be discreet if she wanted to talk to him.

The smell of coffee and freshly baked bread filled her lungs as May stepped into the double-fronted shop. One side displayed the bread and sweets and the other a cottagey table and chairs that you could tell the time by, based on which local was sitting there. No one in Harold messed with their daily ritual of when they had their cuppa and sweet treat and when to avoid those they couldn't stand.

It was actually a good time to come. Breakfast rush hour. Most of the tables were full, and there was a queue waiting to be served. May let her hair hang around her face and didn't catch anyone's eye. Most of these people had been in her house yesterday, and she knew it would be small-town gold to be the first to talk to the "sad twin." May knew that's what they called her now.

May could see through the racks of bread into the kitchen. Bill's back was to her, but she knew it was him because of his size. He was short and had the build of a child.

May felt a hand on her arm. Pauline. From yesterday. No lipstick on her teeth today.

"May, it's a surprise to see you in here. I thought you were heading back to the city."

May felt the whole room go quiet, like it was taking a collective breath. "This afternoon. I just needed a coffee."

Pauline's hand stayed on her arm. "Join me for one then. My treat, hey?"

May wanted to run. Or scream. Maybe both at the same time. There were so many eyes on her. She could feel them probing her. Blaming her. Wishing it had been her.

"I actually have to go. Thanks, though." May didn't want to be rude. Her mom had always liked Pauline.

May stepped away from Pauline's hand and dashed out the front door. She had to suck in long breaths as she stepped into the street. What had she been thinking, exposing herself like that?

She ran past the small grocer and then the butcher. Past the hairdresser that was closed more than it was open. She ducked into the thin alleyway between the bricked shops and went around the back. This was the way she should've come to begin with. Either she'd had too much coffee or not enough. Her brain was still a fog from yesterday.

The bakery was easy to find along the fence line because of the empty sacks of flour piled up near the trash. May found the gate unlocked and let herself in.

She slid down against the back wall and closed her eyes, letting the sun warm her where she sat. Everyone knew Bill was a smoker, and she wouldn't have to wait long before he came outside.

The click of the screen door alerted her to his presence before his shadow did. She had no reason to open her eyes or be scared. Bill was smaller than she was. His height and stature perfect for a jockey—everyone always told him so. Besides, she'd give him a hell of a fight if it came to that.

"Whatcha want?" Bill's voice came out scratchy from the smoking.

May let her lids open slowly, the sun now a series of dark dots. "I hear you knew my mom."

"No flies on you. Straight to it, huh?" Bill chuckled. "Everyone knew your mom. Doesn't exactly make me special, does it?"

May blinked, taking him all in as he stood over her on the step. He was pale, red hair, small but all muscle. "What do you know about my mom going missing all those years ago?"

His face gave him away instantly, even if his hands were steady as he pulled out a cigarette. "I dunno what you're on about."

"The way your whole face flushed pink tells me otherwise. Do you know where my sister is?"

He dragged on his cigarette, the smoke coming out in puffs as he spoke. "Out at the cemetery, from what I heard."

May scrambled to her feet, her fists ready.

Bill held up his free hand. "Hey, I'm sorry. That was a shitty thing to say. I don't know why I said it." His voice had shifted, was higher now.

May narrowed her eyes. Everything about him had shifted. Looser, softer. She figured this was the real Bill, Willy. Not the tough guy he'd portrayed moments before.

"I found this." May pulled the article out of her bag. "Tell me what you know."

Bill sucked on his cigarette as he reached for the article. Glitter on the back of his hand twinkled in the sunshine.

Bill followed May's eyes. "Making a unicorn cake. Just about the only order I seem to get anymore."

May nodded like she understood.

Bill read the article slowly or maybe twice. He handed it back to her. "Your mom was a good woman. I always liked her."

"What do you know about what happened to her?" The article shook in May's hands. "To June."

"I don't know nothing about what happened to Di—your mom. I was back here in Harold when all that went down. Those coppers came around and asked me where I'd been. Tell you the same thing I told them—I was working, had a big order for a wedding." Bill stared her straight in the eyes, his truth obvious for some reason.

May broke their gaze first. "Why'd the police talk to you if it happened all the way up at the university, in Bretford?"

Bill flicked his cigarette butt on the ground and let it burn out without stomping on it. "Same reason I reckon you're here. Your grandparents and their big mouths. Guess they'd spread rumors I'd been harassing her."

"Hadn't you?"

"Not like you think. I wanted something. Information. She had something I needed, and I had something your mom needed. We traded, and that was us done. And don't ask what that trade was, because I'm not going to tell you. Just some high school shit that means nothing now."

May sighed. She should've stayed at Pat's. This was a waste of time.

"I gotta get back to work."

"Wait." May took a step toward him. "Were you and my mom friends? More than friends? Did you talk to her after all this happened?"

Bill looked at the article May held up. "No one got near your mom after what happened. Your grandma saw to that. Took her to the city. Then a coupla years later, she came back married to Gary. With you girls too."

May shook her head. "That can't be right. Mom never lived in the city."

"I gotta go."

"Bill, please." May put her hand on the screen door. "I need to know what happened."

"I don't know what happened. All I ever heard was gossip. Saying she made it all up."

"Why would Mom do something like that?"

"I never said I believed it. That's just what I heard."

May took a step back and let him go inside. He had nothing to tell her. It hurt to walk away. Weird.

"May?"

She turned. Bill's small frame leaning against the door.

"Your sister came here as well, asking the same questions. She mentioned something about me being a 'bloody goose' and said only you would understand what that meant." He shrugged. "Thought it was worth mentioning seeing as you need your own information and all."

Bloody goose. Also weird.

June had loved playing the game duck, duck, goose as a child. She had a knack for working out who the kids were going to pick as goose. It drove May nuts that she could never understand how June did it.

But what did this game have to do with Bill? Was May missing something about him that was right in front of her face? What was June trying to tell her?

"Don't worry. No trade necessary," he called out as he went back inside.

Damn. Too late now.

Days Mom's been dead: 121.

Hi Mom!

Well, well, well. I figured I would only write one letter to you and the two of us would never have any secrets to share ever again.

Turns out I WAS WRONG!

Let me set the scene, shall I? It's boring history class. Always after lunch. I'm tired. May is not. As usual.

We have an assignment. Go to the library and see if we can find something on our family's past. The library is two seconds from our school. (I'm not sure why I'm telling you that when you already know. LOL.) So the class all heads over there. May at the front because, did I mention, she is never tired. Even after lunch when EVERYONE is tired. Blah!

My friends try checking out the history of their great-grandparents on this old stuff called microfilm, and it's honestly as boring as it sounds. Plus they are making it go so fast that it's impossible to read and gives me a massive headache.

So instead I check out these old printed news-papers from fifty billion years ago. (When you were born hey, Mom?! Ha ha.) I have to go through them all to see if I can find anything about our family that I don't already know. I'm thinking this assignment is the DUMBEST thing EVER until . . . well, lookee here. If it isn't your name, Mom. Not your name now but your name before you married Dad.

Diana Wells.

(I'm clearly telling you things you already know in case they've wiped your memory wherever you are. You're welcome!)

So here's me, minding my own business and living my life and then BOOM! Diana Wells. Nineteen-year-old student. Goes missing. No one knows where she is. Um . . . GOES MISSING! WTF, Mom? Think you might have mentioned this to us over our cornflakes one day?

I mean now I know why you hated watching true-crime shows about missing girls or why you never opened that copy of Gone Girl I gave you. This really explains a lot. And when I say a lot, I mean nothing. ABSOLUTELY NOTHING, Mom!

Now in case you don't remember, you are dead. Which means I can't go and ask you if this is real or some kind of prank you played. Is this why you were so boring all the time, in our boring little town, with your boring little book clubs, and your boring little dresses? Because you used up all your fun personality at university . . . where you went MISSING?

And, yes, before you ask, I did cut that article out of that old newspaper. Oops! No, I didn't use it for the assignment. No, I didn't tell May (not yet anyway). You bet I asked Pat. Who raved on and on about putting magic in her tea (at least I love the smell!).

She was cagey about what happened after you went missing. Why you didn't go back to school and where you went instead. It's something important, I could tell. Like your disappearance was only part of the story. MUST find out what happened to you AFTER you were found. You're annoying for being dead and not telling me, Mom! VERY convenient, hey?

So then Pat changed the subject and told me about some creeper called Willy, who is actually Bill the baker. Doesn't take a genius to work that out.

Only he never made any of our birthday cakes because you always did that, didn't you, Mom? One for me and one for May because we never wanted the same cake, and we were born on different days. You always made a BIG deal out of that didn't you, Mom?

Love, June x

Chapter Seven

Bloody goose.

Driving home from the bakery, May couldn't shake the sensation that this *had* to be another clue. That June was trying to tell her something. If June had known a secret as big as her mother's, she would've wanted to tell May. Even if she hadn't actually *told* May, June must've wanted her to know. The article hidden in Magic was proof of that.

June had always liked hiding things. She held information and secrets at arm's length, dangling like a carrot. To get it, you had to earn it.

The first time June had left clues for May was when they were nine. June had taken May's new pencil case filled with colored pencils that had May's name embossed in gold on the side of each one. May had earned them by winning a yearlong spelling competition at school. June hadn't come close to winning.

May searched everywhere for her pencil case and pencils, which were always in the top drawer of her dresser. She didn't tell anyone they were missing, or she would never be allowed to get anything again if she couldn't look after her things.

One day, a pink pencil appeared on May's pillow with a note wrapped around it that read: **I ZAP THINGS HOT**.

Treasure hunts were their favorite part of the books the twins read, so May knew the first note was a clue. *Microwave* was the answer. She had to climb on a chair and open the fiddly door before she found a blue pencil and another note inside.

The next clue read: **DAD PUSHES ME**.

Lawn mower. Another pencil stuck in the wheel, with the next note wrapped around it. Eventually May found all her colored pencils and the case. Except for the purple one (her favorite). June never did say where that one went.

Over the years, May would find notes in her schoolbooks and bag, on top of her bicycle seat, and even in her sandwiches. Sometimes they were notes with gossip written on them (like when Sarah Milham started wearing a bra), but mainly they were a series of clues to find something or even nothing (one time the prize was air—not June's finest moment).

May sat in her sister's room in front of June's computer. She'd opened the window, but there was no breeze to calm her. Perspiration trickled down her spine.

The first clue was easy to find—now she knew she was looking for one. After a quick search through June's computer, in her homework folder, she'd found a document file titled: duck, duck, goose.

Bloody goose.

That ridiculous game. June had only told her the secret of how she always figured out who the kids were going to choose as the goose when they had stopped playing the game many years later. "It's *easy*, May. When it's your turn to go around the circle and choose the goose, what do you usually do? As the first thing?"

"Say duck."

"No, silly. You look around the circle, and you decide then who is going to be the goose. Even if you don't think you do, you do. It's instinct. Your body wants to be ready when it's time to run."

"I don't get it," May had said as they sat on the front steps eating Popsicles.

June had rolled her eyes like May was the slowest person in the world. "It's easy, May. The second you get up, your eyes give away who you're going to choose as goose. Even if you don't think they do, they do. Your eyes give away all your secrets—never forget that."

"That doesn't make sense," May had said.

"You don't make sense." June had stuck her purple tongue out and left May alone on the steps.

May opened the document on June's laptop, fully aware that when it came to seeing other people's secrets, she *was* slow. June had that gift. Not May.

June had typed a list:

Magic

Smurfette

Elsa

Butterscotch (My Little Pony)

Pink Teddy

Freaky Clown

Boba Fett

If Magic is it, who will he choose as the goose?

Some of the names were her parents' old hand-me-down toys, which June had claimed as her own, still strewn around the room somewhere.

Why would her sister leave this clue when she knew May would never work it out? How would she know who Magic chose to be the goose?

May studied the document. What had her sister said?

Your eyes give away all your secrets.

May swiveled around to face Magic, the statue horse that held so many clues to June's disappearance. Magic stared at the wall.

May kicked the carpet in frustration. Magic wasn't looking at anything. Why couldn't June make things simple?

The hairs on May's arm stood up as if there were a chill in the room. Dread circulated inside her. Why was June leaving her clues? Did she know something was going to happen to her? Why hadn't she told someone? And why did she want only May to find the clues? Surely going to the police would have been a safer option?

But what if I hadn't picked up Magic and found the article? I would never have known about all of this. Too many questions and no one to answer them.

May stared at Magic. Willing him to give up his secrets.

Then she understood. Magic was looking the wrong way. June had always had him facing toward the mirror so he could see how handsome he was. May had placed him in the wrong direction after she had picked him up.

A flutter of excitement ran through her at actually working something out. She went to Magic, turning him toward the mirror, and crouched in front of him to see what he saw.

June's mirror, now free of photos.

The mirror sat on top of her dressing table, scattered with bottles of perfume, beauty products, and jewelry. A framed photo of their only-ever pet, Cuddles, a cat who did anything but cuddle. Still, May had cried for days after Cuddles was run over in front of their house.

Among the clutter stood a vintage figurine of Smurfette, roller-skating. Of all the old toys of her mom's, this had been May's favorite. Yet no matter what she did, it would always find its way back to June's room.

Smurfette had been on June's list. As she went to Smurfette and picked up the figurine, a familiar surge of adrenaline shot through May at potentially solving another one of her sister's treasure hunts.

The statue fit in May's palm easily, but there were no holes or clues anywhere. Smurfette looked so pleased with herself in her skating pose and pigtails. Her white knickers displayed when May turned her over.

The initials S. S., supposedly for Smurfette Smurf, marked her bottom in red. May couldn't recollect if they were from June's hand or if the letters had always been there.

Back at June's computer, she searched for images of a roller-skating Smurfette. There were plenty, especially from people trying to sell her on eBay. None of these Smurfettes had initials marked on them.

Of course! May struck June's desk with her hand at her stupidity. To be included in the gang, the Secret Seven had to wear the initials *S. S.*

May pulled out her copy of the book *Secret Seven Mystery*, which still held the newspaper article, from the bag at her feet. She flipped through it slowly, searching for any clues from June. It didn't take her long to find a scribbled note on one of the pages.

Silly duck.

Seeing her sister's handwriting was like a punch in the gut.

When had she left this clue? What if I'm too late?

May read the page in the book like June's life depended on it, which it did. Maybe. Unless . . . May shook her head. She couldn't think like the rest of the town; her sister had to be alive.

She *had* to be.

This was proof! Proof that June knew she was going somewhere. That she would need her sister to find her. May knew her twin. This was the start of a treasure hunt. A treasure hunt that would lead her to June.

Her eyes soaked up the page. Hungry for information. For the next clue. It became obvious when she read the paragraph next to June's writing, talking about the clubhouse and the secret password the Secret Seven needed to get in. In this case: mint jelly.

May and June had started their own clubhouse when they were kids. It had been in the sandbox, which was now a vegetable garden. The next clue had to be there.

The front door slammed shut below her, and Sue called out, "Anyone home?"

Her treasure hunt would have to wait.

But not for long.

Because now she knew June was out there.

And May was going to find her.

Chapter Eight

With June's latest clue waiting for her, May canceled her plans to head back to the city on the last bus. Not like anyone was expecting her back for a while at the real estate business where she worked as an office assistant.

Aunty Sue had hung around like an annoying fly all afternoon, so there had been no chance of continuing the hunt. Now the sun had disappeared, her father was home from work, and the vegetable patch stood in wait.

Gary had brought pizza for dinner, so May grabbed plates and napkins.

"Why did you get pizza? You know May and I don't like it." Sue scrunched her nose up at the pizza box in front of her.

"It was June's favorite. I thought we could have dinner in her honor." Gary squeezed May's arm as she went past him with the napkins. "Since when don't you like pizza, May? I thought you loved pizza. I got it with mushrooms, which I know you love."

"I can answer that. May doesn't like anything anymore. Why would pizza be any different?" Sue glared at her slice, pulling off the string of cheese dangling from the base.

May grabbed her own slice, took a big bite, and talked directly to Sue. "I love pizza, Dad. Always have. Always will. Only a psychopath wouldn't like pizza."

"Oh good. I was worried I had screwed up. I seem to be doing a lot of that lately." Gary took a sip of his beer, and then a bite of his pizza.

May didn't need him to say it out loud. They had fought for months about having June's funeral. Someone had sent him a bunch of articles on other missing people who were pronounced dead and given a send-off. He'd liked the idea. Closure was what he'd called it, which May took to mean: stop living in denial.

Well, she wasn't doing that anymore. Because her sister was definitely out there, and no bullshit empty coffin was going to stop May from following what clues June had left for her to find.

Sue sat back in her chair and stuck her bottom lip out like a child. "Well, you did mess up. I don't like pizza."

Gary wiped cheese grease from his chin. "Don't eat it then. There's plenty of leftovers from yesterday—why don't you have something from the fridge?"

"Thanks, but I'm tired of my own cooking. Pizza will have to do . . . I guess."

May smirked at her father. Sue was always different when he was around, not her usual asshole-ness. "You don't have to keep up your fake crap for us, Sue. We know you can't cook."

Sue flung a mushroom onto her plate. "You don't know anything, May. I can cook just fine. I have no trouble looking after your father or any man, for that matter."

Gary choked down his pizza. "Steady on. I don't need looking after."

May stifled a laugh.

"What's your problem? You always have an opinion on everyone and everything, don't you?" Sue glared at May. "Don't be too surprised when you're back in town next and I have a new man on my arm."

"You have a *boyfriend*?" This was news to May.

Sue shifted in her seat. "I didn't say anything about a boyfriend. Not yet anyway. Give me time, though. He'll be eating out of my hands before he knows what hit him."

May shared a look with her father.

"Anyone I know?" Gary asked.

"Doubt it." Sue twisted her napkin. "He works over at the slaughterhouse near Burni Hill. Met him at the bar. Right gentleman, he is. Looker too."

"I'm happy for you, Sue. Let me know when to buy my bridesmaid's dress." May pulled her pizza apart.

"Oh, hardy har har. You don't think I can keep a man, huh? I'll show you. This guy pays attention, asks lots of questions. Really seems to care about me and my life. Even the annoying parts." Sue swilled her wine at May. "And like I'd ever let you be one of my bridesmaids."

"Why are you even here, Sue? Overstayed your welcome, don't you think?"

"Enough, you two. Eat your dinner." Gary covered May's hand as Sue chugged her wine. "It's good to have *you* home again. When do you have to head back to work?"

May had the whole week off but didn't want to tell her father that. Not wanting to hang around Harold longer than she had to. "I was going to catch the bus tonight, but well, that didn't go as planned. I'll get on the bus leaving tomorrow afternoon. Work will be okay with me being gone one more day."

"Why don't you let me drive you home? The bus takes so long. Or you can take your mom's car."

"No way is she taking that car—I need it more than she does." Sue stood above Gary as if she was about to stomp her foot like a child.

"I'm okay—it's only five hours." May resisted the urge to stick her middle finger up at Sue. "Besides, I like the bus. It's quiet."

"You and your 'quiet.' It wouldn't kill you to get out and make some friends."

May didn't take the bait. Sue was good at poking where it stung.

Sue continued. "I heard you went and saw Mom about that article. Showed your face down at the bakery—"

Gary cleared his throat. "You promised you wouldn't bring that up."

Sue laughed. "No, *you* told me to promise, and I told *you* to get lost. So what if she knows about Diana? It's about time."

For once, May could've kissed her aunty. "I wanted to ask you about it yesterday."

Sue wiped her mouth with her napkin. "Look, if you think I know something—I don't. I was back here in Harold with Mom and Dad, and quite frankly, it made my life a living hell. Diana becoming some kind of celebrity overnight and the kids at school giving me grief that she made it all up."

May shook her head. "That's all you remember? How tough it was for you?"

"You have no idea what I went through. Not everything is about my sister, you know. Everyone said she did it to get attention, and she certainly got that. Half of me thinks she made the whole thing up with that kooky boyfriend of hers."

"Enough." Gary sighed. "Sue, you have no idea what Diana went through, so don't be so flippant. Let's drop it."

May noticed something pass between them. "What am I missing here? What happened to Mom? Did she make it up or not?"

Sue leaned toward May. "You know, your sister started asking these questions, and look where that got her."

Gary slammed his empty beer bottle down. "Enough! We are not doing this again. I can't lose anyone else in this family."

"Dad . . ." May's voice came out shaky. "What's going on? What aren't you telling me?"

"Just tell her," Sue groaned.

"Tell me what?"

Gary rubbed his eyes, then kept them closed. His words came out slow, almost rehearsed. "Your mom was taken. She was found walking on an isolated road hours away from the university. She was disoriented, bruised. She didn't remember a thing."

May couldn't breathe. "Who took her?"

Gary opened his eyes, and a tear escaped down his cheek. "We don't know."

DIANA

The detective sat in front of me and waited for my answer.

I couldn't stop staring at the hairs sticking out of his nostrils.

"Miss Wells, it is important we find out who did this to you. We can't help you if you don't help us."

There were two of them. Two detectives just for me.

They were playing good cop, bad cop. The older one, Detective Randall, seemed to be doing all the talking today. He was always bad cop. It didn't take a brain surgeon to know I frustrated him.

The young one, Detective Davis, stood behind him. He ran his fingers over the iris petals in the bunch of flowers my family had given me. He was always the cute cop, so Mom kept saying.

They'd checked me in to the Royal Hospital in the city two days ago, under a pseudonym. Like I was a celebrity checking in to a hotel. The staff had been given strict orders to not allow press or any strangers into my room. For my own safety, I was told.

I pulled the sheets up and tucked them under my armpits. It was the only thing I could think of to protect me from the detectives and their questions.

Randall didn't trust me. He kept asking the same things over and over. He was exhausting. "Miss Wells, did you hear me?"

"I told you before, call me Diana."

I stole a glance at Detective Davis, who was now reading a get-well card that came with the flowers—like I had the flu, instead of what had happened to me. I don't suppose Hallmark made a card for what I've been through.

At least *he* always called me Diana.

Not like the formal one now sitting too close to my bed, smelling of tuna. I shuffled to the other side of the mattress.

"Sorry, I didn't mean to scare you, Miss Wells. I'll move the chair." Detective Randall scraped the plastic seat toward the end of the bed, taking his overweight frame with him.

No more tuna breath. Yay.

"Have you remembered anything since yesterday? Anything at all?" Randall gave me that hopeful look he did by opening his eyes and leaning forward.

I wanted so badly to tell him something. I wanted him to like me, so then Detective Davis would like me. Who knows why I needed anyone's approval right now. It felt important somehow.

"No. I've tried. But I don't remember anything, promise."

Lies.

"Did the counselor come in to help with your recall of events?"

Why did he ask me that when he already knew the answer? I'd heard him and my counselor, Lucy, talking outside my room earlier.

"Yes, she tried to help me, but it's like part of my brain is missing."

Lies.

Randall looked down at his notepad and wrote something inside. Probably how annoying I was.

"The counselor has the best name, don't you think? Lucy Charm. Like Lucky Charms." Guess my quest for being liked or talking crap or whatever the hell I was doing to make them stop asking questions was in full swing.

Did Davis look up from the get-well card?

No.

Wishful thinking.

My mouth kept going. "Reminds me of a My Little Pony or something."

Randall tried to smile, but it came across more like a grimace. He wasn't sure what I was blabbing about. Maybe I wasn't sure either. Or maybe I was. I was a mystery even to myself.

Randall did his best to be polite. "I guess Lucy Charm is a good name. I never gave it much thought."

Ramble, ramble. "I loved My Little Pony dolls when I was a kid. My favorites were Minty and Butterscotch because they are the best ice cream flavors. I had the whole collection, though. I would use my allowance to buy them and line them up on my bookshelf. Every day I made sure I brushed all their manes and tails." I willed the window to fly open and suck me out. That would shut me up. "I don't know what happened to them, though. I think my sister, Sue, sold them or something." Bitch.

"My sister had My Little Pony dolls too. I don't know if she had them all, but she had a lot. She might still have them if you want me to ask?" Detective Davis had finally joined the conversation.

Why was he being so nice to me?

His job, obviously. He has to be nice to me.

I answered with sarcasm because I'm good like that. "I'm too old for them now, Detective, but thanks for the offer."

"Of course. Silly of me." My flowers were his top priority again as he ran his fingers through his hair.

Great. He was just trying to be polite, and I made him look like an ass.

What a jerk. Never getting anything right.

The urge to be alone fell over me like a weighted blanket. Because alone was better than having them in the room, where I was always screwing up or talking too much nonsense.

"Detectives, I'm tired. Can we do this another time?"

"Sure, of course, Miss Wells. I am going to head back to Bretford tonight, but Detective Davis will be here for another day or two. I have something else to attend to, but I assure you, you're in good hands."

Tra-la-la! Finally. Something good.

Detective Randall heaved himself up from the chair and put his notepad into his shirt pocket. He grimaced again, no doubt thinking he was smiling at me and offering me comfort. I would have to teach him the meaning of bedside manner another time.

Davis focused on his boss's back as they headed out. Maybe there was a knife in it I couldn't see, because he was much more interested in looking there than at me.

Like he could read my mind, Davis turned to me. "I'll see you soon, Diana. If you remember anything at all, please call me with the number on the card I left you. The one on the back is my private number."

I didn't need to look at his card to know it was propped in front of a vase of flowers near my head. I had put it somewhere I could easily see; it gave me a sense of peace knowing it was there.

Woosh. The weighted blanket must've flown out the window. Because now I didn't want them to go. Maybe alone wasn't so great after all. That's alright. I knew how to make them stay.

"Detectives, will I ever remember what happened to me?"

They both stopped. Both serious.

"I'm not sure, Diana. I hope for our sake you do, but I hope for your sake you don't. Maybe some things are better left hidden." Davis always knew what to say.

"Yes, hidden," I repeated.

HIDE!

Fuckity fuck. Not this again.

The memory made my stomach thrash about like that lady being eaten at the beginning of *Jaws*. I sat forward in my bed, holding my intestines, which were surely about to fall out.

"Diana, are you okay? Do you want me to call a doctor?" Davis came to my bedside. His regular scent of soap and tobacco flooding me with something I didn't understand. Sadness, maybe?

"No, wait." I panted like a maniac.

The detectives didn't make a peep.

"Take your time, Miss Wells. Is something coming back to you?" Randall had a pen poised, ready to take notes again. Davis stared at me, his eyes telling me nothing.

"I'm sorry. It's gone." I wanted to cry. If only I could stop the flood that toppled over every now and again. If only my brain would shut down and really repress everything.

Life would be so much easier.

"Do you want me to stay a little longer? That okay, boss?"

Don't leave me.

"Fine by me. Better you're here if she remembers anything," Randall said.

"Thank you. I feel a little scared." Not untrue. I was scared of making more mistakes. I had made a lot of them lately.

Randall nodded at Davis; a look passed between them that only they understood. Then he left.

Davis pulled the seat beside my bed toward me. "It's okay. I'm not going anywhere."

We both knew that wasn't true. Soon he would be gone, and I would be alone. Again.

I yawned and pretended to go to sleep. I didn't know what else to do.

Nightmares were easier than real life.

Chapter Nine

May climbed out of bed before the rest of the household woke.

It had been a bizarre night.

Everyone skirting around something she couldn't quite figure out.

Okay, so her mom had been taken. By whom, it was unclear. Diana's memory had gone because she'd repressed the trauma. Pat took her to the city to get away from the media. The whispers of her disappearing for attention. But why?

June must've gone looking for whoever took their mom. That was clear. She must've found something.

No. Someone.

May quietly made coffee and took it outside. Her heart hammered against her chest. A constant bam-bam-bam, telling her she was too late.

Too late too late too late.

The sun edged its way upward, and she glanced behind her to make sure the house remained silent, needing to find the next clue in private. Even if she was too late, she couldn't stop.

May inhaled the fresh morning air as she surveyed the backyard, which adjoined the bushland behind it. Diana had taken great pride in the yard; everything bloomed green because of the grey water system she'd set up. May ached to have her mom by her side, to ask the thousands of questions that kept filling her head. To say sorry for everything she'd gotten wrong.

May left her half-empty coffee mug on the patio table and went down the steps leading to the lawn area.

She didn't have shoes on, and the grass, damp from the overnight sprinkler system, sent a chill through her. The vegetable patch, which used to be their sandbox, lay in the far corner of the backyard.

Do I have to dig the whole thing up to find June's next clue?

May walked around the raised corrugated iron garden bed, hoping something would stick out, but couldn't find anything. The idea of jumping onto the damp earth and searching among the carrots didn't exactly appeal to her.

She had to think like June.

June would've chosen a hiding place that didn't involve the vegetables—or someone would've dug the clue up by now. June wouldn't risk it. She thought of everything.

It had to be around the edging.

The sun had partially risen. The chill now gone, replaced with the warmth of the day to come. With more light to work with, on her next walk around, May spotted it: the initials *S. S.* scraped into the rusted paint.

She wished her sister were there to celebrate her find, and just as quickly dismissed the thought. If her sister were here, there would be no need for a treasure hunt.

She bent down and ran her fingers over the mark. There was nothing obvious. May considered if S. S. *was* the clue again.

It wasn't right. The initials had to be an *X* marking the spot. June would never use the same clue twice.

May edged her fingers under the marking into a small gap between the grass and the iron base. Her fingers didn't fit into the hole, so she grabbed a twig lying in the vegetable patch.

It fit perfectly, and no sooner had May stuck it in than the twig hit upon something. May put pressure on it and dragged it out.

A small piece of tinfoil, folded up many times, came out with the twig. May undid it slowly until she came to plastic wrap, which she also unwrapped. Inside was a small piece of paper that had been protected so well it could've been written on that morning.

In June's handwriting was the message:

Come with me + it is the only way = ?

May flipped the message over, expecting something more. That was it. That was the clue.

"Come with you where? Where are you?" May whispered.

Come with me + it is the only way = ?

There was something about the words that felt familiar, like she should know their meaning.

May sat back on the grass, her jeans soaking through. She didn't know what the clue meant. This was the end. She would never find June.

Come on, tears. You can come now. Wash away this misery. This torture.

A light went on in the house. Her time was up. She had failed June. Her mom. Herself.

"Damn you, June, and your ridiculous clues." May punched her hip and clipped the side of her phone.

Would the internet know what this meant? The words that she should know but didn't.

May pulled out her phone from the back of her jeans and opened the search bar. She typed in: Come with me. It is the only way.

Some songs came up with a variation of those words. Nope. May clicked on "Images," and a GIF of Darth Vader was the first one displayed.

That was it. She knew what the clue meant. Their father had made them watch all the *Star Wars* films. This was from the famous *I am your father* scene. They had reenacted it many times. June was always Darth Vader, and May was always Luke, her hand tucked into her sweatshirt like it had been cut off.

May glanced at the house. The bathroom light was still on. What did this clue mean? *Hurry.*

Come with me + it is the only way = ?

Darth Vader.

Luke.

I am your father.

What did this have to do with June? No. Not June. Her mother. What did this have to do with her mother's disappearance?

The light was off in the bathroom now. Her dad would be in the kitchen soon, knowing May wasn't in her room—because he would look. He always opened the door to make sure she was still there. Maybe abandonment haunted him too.

Not now. *Hurry.*

Why that scene? *What am I missing?*

When they'd watched *The Empire Strikes Back* for the first time, May and June had been in shock at the twist. Their own father had laughed, knowing what was coming. Saying how that scene had also blown his mind when he watched it as a kid.

What had June said that day?

"Imagine finding out you had a father like Darth Vader? The bad guy."

Her eyes had sparkled as she said the opposite of what May had been thinking.

"How cool."

May knew now what everyone had been skirting around. What no one had said out loud. What they wanted to stay hidden.

Why her mom had gone to the city and never said. Why she never mentioned her abduction.

What June had discovered. What she was protecting May from. Who she had been looking for.

Who had her now.

The man who took their mother.

Their real father.

Chapter Ten

Her father sat in front of her.

Bullshit.

May knew the truth now. He had admitted it.

They had escaped the house. And Sue. The Nguyens' bakery, a perfect place for privacy as May and Gary sat among the smell of warming pies and sausage rolls. Both had opted for only coffee, although Mrs. Nguyen had insisted May have a vanilla cupcake too. It sat uneaten in the middle of the table, the yellow frosting slowly melting in the heat of the shop.

It had already been an hour. An hour of awkward silences. Of sentences her dad couldn't finish through tears.

How he had met Diana in the city when the twins were already six months old. She had been struggling to juggle putting the crying twins and the bags of groceries in the car. He had helped. They ran into each other a few more times while shopping. Traded numbers. Began dating. He hadn't known about her past, not then, but it hadn't taken much time to work out that something was wrong.

How her mother had flinched when being touched. Or woken up screaming every now and again. Or looked over her shoulder when they were out at night.

Diana eventually told him. After he proposed. How she had been missing for three weeks, not remembering who had taken her or what she had endured. How she had gone into herself as if none of it had ever happened. Then finding out she was pregnant, so she stayed in the city. In secret. So the media wouldn't put two and two together.

Diana had wanted Gary to know what he was getting into. So he could walk away. He didn't. Stayed because he loved her. And the girls. He had no hesitation in claiming them as his own. They were an instant family, and that kept them all safe.

May could only stare at her coffee cup. Taking it all in. She waited for him to say something. Anything. It was easier than looking at the face of the only man she had ever known as *Dad*. Was he a stranger to her now too?

He wiped sweat off his brow. "I'm so sorry I didn't tell you before now."

"You and Mom should've told June and me ages ago. There's no excuse for it—we had a right to know." May moved on to ripping open sugar packets.

"You're right and I'm sorry. I know your mom would be sorry too. This is not what we wanted for you both." Gary cleared his throat. "Like I said before, I honestly had no idea June had approached Pat with that article. Not until the police questioned me about it after she disappeared. I was more than a little shocked that had been kept from me. I always thought you girls should've known the truth as soon as you were old enough. This family has enough secrets."

May whispered, "I think you mean Mom has all the secrets."

"It must seem like that. I'm annoyed that you found out like this. I shouldn't have listened to anyone and just told you girls myself." Gary reached for May's hand, but she put it in her lap. "Trust me when I say there never seemed like a good time."

"Oh, because now is the perfect time, isn't it?" May could feel Mrs. Nguyen's eyes on her as she raised her voice.

"You're right. Now would have to be the worst time for this." Gary rubbed his thumb between his brows. "Is it bad to say I was personally holding off because I wanted to keep you as my biological daughter for as long as possible?"

Ouch. That made instant sense because of the guilt already swirling inside her. May knew she would never look at her father the same way again. She couldn't even look directly at him now.

Not that she wanted him to know that. "You'll always be my dad. Nothing can change that." May felt as if the walls were closing in on her as she poured sugar from a packet onto the table and drew the same circle, over and over. "This is a lot to take in. I'm not doing a great job of it."

"You're doing much better than you'll ever know." The weight of his eyes were on her. "I'm sorry to say it, but just looking at you is killing me. You resemble her more and more each day."

May didn't know who she was supposed to resemble anymore. "I should go. Can I ask one question before I do?"

"Of course. What is it?"

"Do you know who our biological father is?"

"I don't. I swear to you." Gary paused. "Let it be, May. It's in the past."

May didn't believe that was true anymore. Not with June still out there somewhere.

May's father stood as if he'd aged twenty years overnight, pulling his jacket from the back of his chair. He had a long caterpillar-shaped sweat mark running down the center of his blue shirt.

"Finish your coffee, and get anything else you need." He pulled a twenty-dollar bill from his wallet.

"That's okay. I'm leaving too." May grabbed her bag from the back of the chair, stood, and slid her phone into her back pocket.

In the pile of sugar, her father had spelled out *I ♥ u.*

May followed him to the counter, where he was paying.

I love you too.

"Thanks for the coffee." It's the best she had.

Gary swung his jacket over his shoulder. "Will I see you before you head back?"

Father and daughter caught each other's eyes. They both knew it then. In one question, everything had changed. This would be their future now. Polite. Awkward. A lifetime wiped clean. *Bullshit.*

"Dad?" May's voice cracked.

He looked at her, expectantly. She could do this. She owed him. For everything he had done for them, for being the best father she could ask for. All they had was each other.

"Let's go and visit her grave later. Just us."

He nodded, a genuine smile forming. He didn't need to ask whose. It didn't matter. They were side by side now. Mother and daughter.

May's heart shattered inside her chest. Her whole family was decaying in front of her eyes, and she didn't know if she was strong enough to stop it.

Welcome to Harold. Where everything's rotten if you look close enough.

Days Mom's been dead: Who cares.

Hi Mom,
Well, holy fucking jamoly (and I'm seventeen now, so I can absolutely swear as much as I want to).

Soooo, here I was thinking that you getting abducted was going to be the biggest secret I would ever find... but NO! That was NOTHING compared to what I've now discovered. I KNEW Pat was keeping something from me, and it is a DOOZY!

How could you not tell us, Mom? Talk about self-ish. I always knew something was off in my life, like I didn't quite belong. And now I know why.

I bet you're wondering how I found out. Good question, Mom. Good question. You never thought of me as the smart one, and look at me now. Finding out ALL of your secrets.

Just call me Sherlock fucking Holmes. (Get over it, Mom. Kids swear.)

Have you ever heard of a murder board? Of course you haven't. That would require watching any kind of show that involves a crime or a mystery. We all know you couldn't stand them.

So a murder board is sort of like it sounds. No, not someone being murdered by a board. Jeez! It's where you put up said crime (your abduction) in the middle and have any evidence or photos or whatever coming off that original crime (your abduction). Some people use thread or wool or whatever to connect certain things, but that didn't work for me. It just looked like a giant spiderweb, and I got super confused.

So I listed things like the victim (you), suspects (Brad, Sharon, Dad, Willy/Bill, Aunty Sue—you gotta admit, you couldn't put it past her!), the timeline of events, what we know, what we don't know. Blah, blah, blah. Honestly, if I put this much time and effort into my school projects, I'd be as smart as May.

Not going to lie, I hardly knew anything. Pat, Sue, Dad, and Bill wouldn't give me a thing that was actually interesting.

Here's what I DO know:

- You were missing for three weeks.
- A family found you walking on some isolated road somewhere three hours away from the university.
- You were bruised, disoriented, and couldn't remember anything. (Hmm. Do you KNOW how sus this sounds?)
- Your purse was found outside your dorm on the Friday you went missing, and you left a necklace you apparently never took off beside your

bed—although no one back here had seen or heard of this necklace. (What gives, Mom?)

- You were checked in to the Royal Hospital in the city but didn't return to the university OR to Harold. You STAYED in the city. Ding, ding, ding, ding! Gotcha.

I pressed Pat on this for a LONG time. Why didn't Mom tell us she lived in the city? Why didn't you tell us you lived there with her for a while? When EXACTLY did Dad meet Mom?

You always said you met Dad at university, Mom, and left when you got pregnant . . . but that was a LIE. I know because I checked. It's easy enough to find out if someone went to a school, and Dad was NEVER at Bretford. So that meant you had to have met in the city. Which was AFTER the abduction.

Good. Because that took Dad off the suspect list. Bad. Because it meant the timeline was ALL off.

How could you meet Dad, get married, and then we were born? There wasn't enough time.

Then I did a sneaky and took some of Dad's nail clippings (I know. Gross!) and sent them in for a paternity test. I had to be sure before I told anyone what I suspected.

Well, gee. I WONDER what came back in the results, huh?

You're unbelievable, Mom. Lying to us all these years. Pretending we were just one big happy family, when there was some psycho with our DNA running around out there.

What a bunch of horseshit (no offence, Magic).

Remember how I was mad at you and wanted to kill you after you died? Well, now I just hate you and couldn't care less that you are dead.

Fuck you,

June x

Chapter Eleven

May leaned her head against the bus window as the moonlit landscape flew by.

She was surprised by the surge of inspiration running through her. She had a purpose again. Hope. Hope that she would find June.

Because June wanted her sister to find her. She must have known she had been in danger. That's why she left clues, and May knew there were more. Now she just had to think like June.

This was the only way to get closure. Not an empty coffin.

Her father had been distraught when she left. His eyes had permanent pain in them now. May figured hers did, too, if someone looked hard enough. She wished she could say all the right words and make everything okay again, but that was June's thing—not hers.

May told him she was returning to the city. The lie came easily, and she had a glimmer of understanding why June had done the same to her.

Only, this bus would take her to Bretford. One of many stops along the way across the country.

Bretford. Where her mom had gone to university. Where she had been taken.

May had already called the local police station there and asked for Detective Randall, whose name appeared in the article. She was told he had retired. A Detective Davis had taken his place and wasn't due in until the night shift. May made a decision that she would go to the station unannounced.

She wasn't sure what help the detective would be. From all her research, the police hadn't found anyone of interest in her mother's disappearance. Eerily paralleling her sister's case. But May knew that the only way she was going to find out any real answers was to go back. To where it all began.

It's what June would have done. And she was thinking like June now.

May's head continued to swirl with so many questions but no answers.

Why hadn't June gone to the police if she thought she was in trouble, instead of leaving clues for May? Why didn't she tell anyone what she was doing or where she was going?

When the clues stopped, May would find June. She was sure of it. What she wasn't sure of was what else she would find with her sister. Or who.

◆ ◆ ◆

The small modern police station stood near the town center square, now deserted in the quiet of the night.

May dropped her bag at the front counter and asked the lady behind the clear screen for Detective Davis.

"It's actually Detective *Senior Sergeant* Davis now." The officer opened her eyes wide, like she was telling a state secret.

The officer's face was one of those that instantly made May feel at ease; she didn't know why. Maybe it was because she had an ageless vibe, as something told May she was older than she looked, or maybe it was the smattering of dark freckles on her nose, which made May think of a doll she loved as a kid. Or maybe it didn't matter why.

May's own face softened. "Oh well, lucky him. Is he here? He should be expecting me." He wasn't, but May was too tired to explain herself.

"Is that right? Well, if he's expecting you, then he must be here, huh?" The officer showed her perfectly white teeth in a big grin. It was settled, May liked her.

"Got me there." May didn't exactly grin back, but she thought about it, and that counted. She stretched her back; her whole body felt bruised after the long bus ride.

"And your name?" She picked up the phone.

"It's May. May Simpson."

"Okay, May Simpson. Let me get Detective Senior Sergeant Davis for you then, shall I?" The officer winked like they already shared an inside joke and talked into the phone. "Detective? Yes, I have your appointment, Miss Simpson to see you." She listened into the phone. "She said you're expecting her." Nodding. "That's right, Miss Simpson." Slower now. "May Simpson."

She hung up the phone, her grin back again. "He'll be right out. Guess he was expecting you after all."

"Oh, wow. I mean . . . thanks. Should I sit here?" May pointed to the chairs against the wall, her heart already galloping.

"Sure, hon. I'm about to grab a snack from the break room. If we're lucky there'll still be some chocolate-covered donuts. Want one? Or three? You look like you might fall over if I blew on you."

May chuckled a little as she sat, surprising herself. Remarks about how she looked normally made her want to punch someone. "No, I ate dinner already. Thanks anyway."

"How about a strong coffee, then? We have a fancy machine."

"That would be lovely. Black, no sugar, thanks."

The officer went to get the coffee, muttering about how there better be some chocolate ones left.

If only that was the detective I was coming to see. May pushed down on her knee so her leg would stop with the jittering.

"Miss Simpson?"

May turned to the detective, unaware of the doors behind where she sat. How long had he been standing there staring at her?

He looked exactly like his photo she'd found online, apart from a small dusting of grey over his short brown hair. He was tall, well built, had kind eyes. His jeans and navy polo shirt didn't give off the appearance of a detective, though.

"You're looking at my nonexistent uniform, aren't you? Don't worry, I've got my standard shirt and pants in my locker. Night shifts don't always call for professional attire."

Embarrassment crept up her neck and face like a slow tsunami. *Damn*, he'd caught her checking him out. Sizing him up, more like. This man knew her mom back then, and that meant getting to know who she was dealing with.

"May, uh, Miss Simpson. Did you want to come through?" He waved his hand through the open door behind him.

"Don't you want to know why I'm here?"

"No, June told me you would come. Expected you sooner, that's all."

Chapter Twelve

May sat by the detective's desk, nursing the coffee the officer had left her.

He didn't have an office, just a workspace piled with paperwork, which sat off from other desks that made up a medium-size open-plan design. They were the only ones there, as the officer had returned to the front reception area.

The strong coffee filled her stomach, but it didn't settle her nerves. If the detective had expected her sooner, she was too late.

"So why did June say I would come, Detective?" It was as good a start as any.

"Call me Sam." He had an amused expression on his face, like he knew something she didn't. "I'm very happy to see you again. The last time we met, you were only a few years old."

"Oh . . . well." *Awkward.*

"I'm showing my age now, aren't I, May? Do you mind if I call you May?"

"That's my name."

He chuckled, which May kind of liked.

He thinks I'm funny. Maybe this wouldn't be a complete disaster after all.

The detective cleared his throat. "I heard what happened to your sister and have tried to keep track. I'm so sorry." He appeared genuine. "I take it there are no new leads there?"

May took a breath. "That's why I'm here—June had been searching for someone before she went missing."

Sam confirmed it like June had only been there yesterday. "She was looking for your biological father. The question that drove us all nuts. Me included." He locked eyes with May. "Especially when Diana's kids keep showing up and reminding me I didn't do my job."

May held his gaze. "How could you if Mom didn't remember anything?"

His left eye twitched, but it was so quick, May wasn't even sure she'd seen anything. "I'm sorry about your mom. I tried to get there for the funeral but . . . well, there's no excuse, really."

May sensed something else, but she wasn't sure what. It was like she owed him an explanation, maybe because she was in a police station or something. "It's okay. I don't really remember much of that day anyway."

"Again, I'm sorry, May . . . for everything. With June too. She was bossy when she was here. Came in like she owned the place."

"*Bossy* is a nice word to describe my sister. I imagine you got the grilling of your life when she came into the station, huh?" *I should've been here with her.*

Sam smiled like he was remembering it. "Yes, she had a notebook of questions and theories. Asked to see where we kept our murder boards."

"Murder board?"

"Something that works well in movies, I suppose."

May's eyes narrowed. "When was she here? Exactly?"

"Ah, now you're testing my memory. It was over a year ago. I can't be sure exactly when. I can find out, though, if you need to know. I provided what information I could after she disappeared."

"Where did she go after she saw you?" May's heart pounded in her ears.

"I figured she was going back to Harold. There was nothing here for her. If there was, I would've found it myself." His eyes scanned the room.

"And you let her go?"

"How was I to know she would go missing soon after? What happened to your mom was a long time ago. I had no reason to believe June was in any danger."

"Did *you* take her?" May pushed her chair back and stood above the detective.

He didn't flinch. "No, I didn't, but I don't blame you for asking me. I was one of the last people to see her."

Something wasn't right. It didn't add up.

"Wait. So when did she have time to go home and leave me all these clues?"

"What do you mean, clues?"

"Just sister stuff, so I would find out about Mom. About me and June too." May sat back in the chair.

"Did she tell you to come and see me? Is that why you're here?"

"No. She didn't say anything about Bretford or you. I just figured she would've come here. It made sense."

Sam ran his fingers through his hair. "Your instincts are good. She certainly did come here, but like I said, she didn't find anything."

May shook her head. "I don't believe that. She must've found something if she disappeared soon after coming here. She *must've* found out who took Mom . . . who our father is."

"It's possible, although I'm not one to speculate." Sam glanced at his watch. "May, I have a mountain of work to get through here, but I'm happy to help you in any way I can. Do you mind if we catch up again tomorrow?"

"I'd like that."

"Where are you staying?"

May rubbed her eyes. She was so tired she would sleep on his desk if he offered. "I actually hadn't thought that far ahead. I'm not as good as June at all this impromptu stuff."

"I wouldn't say that's a bad thing." He ran his fingers through his hair again.

"I feel like she would've left me a clue somewhere here. I just have no idea where to look."

He did a tiny shrug. "I can't help you there, I'm afraid."

"I'm missing something. I know I am. She must've planted something where no one else but me would find it."

"If she did, I don't know anything about it." Sam shook his head. "I'm sorry."

"That's okay. Maybe tomorrow, when I'm not so wrecked, we can go over things again. I'm curious to know more about my mom's disappearance."

"Like I said, happy to help any way I can." Sam stood, grabbing a file on his desk. "Look, I won't be home until morning if you want to go to my apartment and crash there."

"Thanks for the offer, but I'll just find somewhere in town to stay."

"We have exactly two hotels, and both of them won't be manned this late at night. Feel free to check." He chuckled. "Other option is staying in one of the cells. Up to you."

She let out her own breathy laugh. "Those are some great options."

Sam shrugged. "My apartment is free. Again, up to you. I usually go out for breakfast before I sleep. I can come and get you in the morning, and we can talk some more. How does that sound?"

May shuffled in her seat. Could she trust this guy? Was this a trap? Something inside her told her she was safe with this man who had helped her mother all those years ago.

"Okay. But only if that won't be weird. I mean, you don't even know me. What if I steal your stuff?"

"If you find something worth stealing, then be my guest." The detective smiled. "And I knew your mother—that's good enough for me. I know she'd want me to look out for you while you were here."

"I'm sure I'll be fine. How would anyone know I'm here, anyway?"

"Given we don't know the circumstances behind your sister's disappearance, it's wise to not presume anything."

May shivered. "Yeah, okay. But just for tonight."

"Done deal."

May yawned.

"You're tired. Let me get Officer Kewa to drive you to my place."

"Wait. Did June ever stay at your house?"

The detective looked around. "No, she didn't."

"Hmm, okay." May was hoping to look for another clue there.

Sam pulled a set of keys out of his drawer and handed them to May. "You're welcome to sleep on the couch. There are fresh sheets in the hall."

"Thanks." May stared at the case file under the detective's arm. "Do you still have one of those for Mom's case?"

Sam followed her eyes. "Sure. Somewhere in the archives."

"You mind if I look at it?"

He shrugged. "Don't see why not. I let June do the same thing."

May sucked in a breath.

That's where she'd find her next clue.

DIANA

Two sets of eyes blinked up at me.

The hospital room was quiet. Only the repetitive sounds of machines, the smell of nothing and everything all at once, and the warmth of my girls in my arms.

Had I made a mistake? Was Mom right?

She'd told me to get rid of my babies. "Give them up for adoption. Separate them if need be. They're fraternal, not identical. More like sisters."

I didn't think that was true. They'd grown together, sharing everything for nine months. That made them special. I know Mom didn't mean to be cruel; she was only protecting me from something so complicated we both didn't know what was right or wrong.

I spoke to them gently. One girl in the crook of each arm. "What am I going to do with you two? I don't know how to be a mom. I'm going to mess it up for sure, and one, or both, of you will end up as unhinged as me."

They blinked away, waiting for me to make the next move. Make all the next moves. I was going to be a parent now, in charge of two little souls who depended on me for everything.

I adjusted them with difficulty, no hands free to do so. As I pulled them closer to my chest, the girls made suckling noises. Together, in unison. My breasts seemed to communicate with them better than I did. I had only just fed them. Now they should sleep. That's what the nurse had told me.

The idea of getting out of bed and preparing them for their nap made me want to scream. Mom should be here to help me.

She walked in as I thought of her. She had a way of doing that.

"Hi, darling. Sorry I'm late. Trying to find parking in the city is like having a heart attack for an hour straight." Mom dropped her handbag on the chair and came over to my bed, her cheeks flushed. "How are you feeling today?"

"I'm okay. Tired and sore, but okay."

"Did you nurse the girls?" Mom gazed down at their tiny squished faces. She was going to an amazing grandma, even if it would take her a while to warm to the idea.

"Yes, they've been fed. Now they should sleep—the nurse told me."

"That sounds about right, but not there they shouldn't. If you fall asleep you could drop or smother one. Or both of them. Never sleep with them when they're babies, no matter how tired you are. Bloody nightmare, otherwise."

Was this what my life had become? Having the ability to kill just by falling asleep?

Mom took one of the girls and placed her in the bassinet near my bed. I wasn't sure which one because they both looked the same to me. It didn't help that they both had identical tiny pink hats on. The teensy hospital bracelets on their wrists were my only way of knowing which one was which. Mom said June was smaller, because she was born second, but I couldn't tell. Bad mother already.

"One of my girlfriends from school smothered her newborn—did I ever tell you that?"

Mom didn't wait for me to answer, swaddling the baby as she spoke. "She didn't mean it, of course. Fell asleep while she was nursing and the next thing, she'd killed it. Like I said, bloody nightmare."

I didn't even want to think about something like that happening. "I heard you the first time, Mom. I promise I'll never sleep with my babies."

Mom gently picked up the other one—May, I read on her ID bracelet—wrapping my baby up like it was no big deal.

What the hell was I doing? Who was I kidding? I couldn't be a mother. I had only turned twenty, for fuck's sake!

Mom may as well have read my mind. "Don't worry, it gets easier. No one knows what they're doing the first time around. God knows, I didn't! No matter what anyone says, being a mother is about as natural as my hair." She patted the ends of her caramel-dyed bob.

Thank god for her.

"Thanks . . . ," I whispered, my mouth suddenly dry. "The whole thing doesn't feel real. I can't believe they're actually mine."

Mom left the swaddled babies and, after moving her bag, sat in the chair near my bed. Memories of the last time I'd been in the hospital flooded back. When it was a detective sitting next to me. I hadn't even known I was pregnant then. I'd thought my nightmare was over. Instead it was just beginning.

"Don't fret. You'll be an amazing mother." Mom patted my arm. "But trust me when I say, when it comes to your children, it'll be a wild ride. I don't know how many times I dropped you, and you turned out okay."

We both laughed in that weird fake way. Mom looked away, and I knew the questions would come again now. They always did.

"Darling, don't you remember anything? Anything at all? You must know who the children's father is. We need to put him away, so he doesn't come back and find them."

I threw my head against the pillow. "Mom, please, this isn't the time. I already told you, I don't remember anything."

Mom shook her head at me like she used to do when I was a child. "How is that possible? The doctor said it was normal to suppress memories when they're traumatic, but you should've remembered something by now."

"Well, I don't. And I don't want to talk about this here." All I'd done was have this same conversation since I'd been found.

"What are you going to tell those girls? They'll want to know who their father is."

"Nothing! I'm not going to tell them a thing. They don't need to know how they came to be in this world. Stop pressuring me, Mom." I wanted to be alone. Totally alone. No babies, no past, no drama. It was times like this I wish I could teleport back to when things were easier. Before I met him.

Mom took two aspirin from her bag, her hands trembling, and swallowed them dry. I always forgot this was hard on her too.

"Sorry, Mom." I paused. "I'm just scared . . . about everything."

"Me too, darling." She sighed and retucked the sheets in where she sat. "I'm sorry. I didn't mean to upset you. You're right—now isn't the time. But soon we need to plan how we'll tell the world about these girls. It won't take a genius to put it all together when they know who you are."

"That's why I'm going to stay here in the city, for as long as it takes. You said that was the best plan." I didn't want to do this alone, but going back to Harold was not an option. "Have you changed your mind?"

"It's the right thing for your girls to stay here—no one knows who you are—and the city is big enough for you to get lost in. Hell, I couldn't even find parking." Mom's smile was forced, and she looked as tired as I felt. "The main thing is keeping your babies safe with that monster still out there. Everything is for them now."

We both looked over at the bassinet with my sleeping babies, for different reasons. I couldn't tell her about the monster. Not now. Not ever.

Mom sat on the edge of the bed. "Your father and I have spoken, and I will stay with you for the next few months. Until you get on your feet. I'll tell everyone I have a sick sister I need to look after."

"Really? That would be amazing! Thank you." It was like whoever had been sitting on my chest had suddenly gotten off. "Hang on, you don't have a sister."

Mom snickered. "Exactly! So when people go snooping, they won't find a damn thing. Then, when the time is right, you can come back to Harold."

I gave laughing a go, which hurt my annihilated stomach. "You're the best . . . Grandma."

"I ain't no one's bloody grandma." Mom puffed out her chest. "They'll know me as Pat. My rightful name. I'll do my best with those girls. I swear I will. You will, too, and that's all a mom can do. You'll learn that soon enough."

I couldn't read her face, which I was thankful for. I had seen enough disappointment from her in the last few months to last a lifetime.

"Sue isn't going to be happy you're leaving her."

"When is your sister ever happy? That child will be the death of me." Mom sighed. "It's your father who isn't happy. He hates being away from you and his new grandchildren, but you know how incredible he is, always doing what's best for the family."

Good to know I wasn't the only disappointment in the family.

Mom went over to the bassinet. "Now, what are we going to call these girls? You aren't really going to stick with May and June, are you? I get that one was born in May and one in June, but it's a little obvious, isn't it?"

"I like their names. Straight from a classic novel like they're my *Little Women*."

"Guess you're right. Although, if my mother had called me February after my birthday month, I reckon I would've had a right fit."

I laughed. Mom smiled and held my hand.

"May and June." I peered across at my sleeping babies, still sharing the same space together. "The Gemini twins."

Chapter Thirteen

"Ready, hon?"

May smiled as an answer to the officer, eager to get some rest.

"Sam's place isn't far from here," Officer Kewa said as she adjusted the seat closer to the steering wheel of the patrol car.

"You mean Detective *Senior Sergeant* Davis?"

"Ha, touché. Yes, him. Won't be long, then you can tuck yourself up in your pj's. Nice of him to let you stay, huh?" A piece of her bun had come loose and stuck up like the raised feathers on a cockatoo's crest.

"Yes, very nice." May pressed her head against the window as they made their way through the streets of Bretford. The streetlamps spotlighted the trees lining them. Blackened restaurants and upmarket coffee shops were a blur.

This is where her mom had gone to school. A world away from Harold. She could've been anyone she wanted here.

"Is it true there's only two hotels in town and they aren't open right now?"

The officer tilted her head, looking confused. "You want to go to a hotel?"

"No, I'm just asking if one is open at this time of night." May hadn't checked herself and wanted to make sure the detective was telling the truth.

"Not now. No. There's a place with cabins outside of town, but I think you have to book ahead to get one. I thought you were staying at Sam's place, or did I miss something?"

"No." May shook her head, wishing she hadn't brought it up. "I was just checking in case I stay on for a bit."

"Copy that." Kewa seemed satisfied. "He's a nice guy, our detective. Still single, you know? Never got married. A few ladies tried, of course. But he wasn't interested."

"Did you ever have a go?"

Kewa chuckled. "Ha! Me? No. Not my type. Besides, this old girl is married. Even if I was single, I have too much respect for a man like that to want anything more. He's an excellent cop. I've been with the force for four years now. Not too bad. Mainly night shifts at the moment. No one tells you how much paperwork's involved. Does your head in . . ."

The officer's chatting lulled May, her eyes growing heavy. Tomorrow she would go back into the station and look at that police paperwork. Her mother's old file.

The strong glow of white lights shooting through a series of treetops broke through the darkness of the night. May rubbed her eyes. "Is that the university over there?"

"No, that's the dorm campus. The university is just behind it. Did you want to take a gander? I'm in no hurry to get back to the station."

"Ye—" May's mouth had gone dry at the thought of seeing where her mom had gone missing.

Kewa signaled left and put her high beams on as they took a smaller, darker road. "This is the back way," she explained as May gave her a quizzical look.

"I was wondering where we were going. Doesn't exactly have a great vibe, does it? Is this really where the students live?" A shiver went through May. The road and the bushland surrounding it were too dark. Ominous.

"The dorms are well lit." The rogue tufts of hair nodded as the officer did. "You'll see. At night, the university is like a carnival of lights."

As the patrol car rounded a corner, the bushland cleared, and a series of old-style brick buildings formed a U shape around a large landscaped area.

They passed a security booth on the way into the complex. A man raised his hand in acknowledgment.

"That's Barry. I used to do his job before I joined the police force. Campus security wasn't exactly a dream come true."

May sat forward in her seat, wanting to take everything in. "Did they always have security on campus?"

"As long as I'm aware. Maybe not as many staff as they have now."

They drove around the perimeter of the buildings, the only road acting as a land-based moat. Bike and walking paths joined all the buildings together, and a lake sat in the middle.

"It's lovely," May murmured. It was like a little village—where her mom had lived once.

"The buildings could do with an update. Like the university had a few years back, but yes, the grounds are lovely. Notice what I mean about the lights? Makes everyone feel a little safer."

May turned to the officer. "My mom used to study here."

"Oh, she did? Must've been a while ago. What was her name?"

"Diana Wells."

Kewa slowed the vehicle to a crawl, examining May's face. "Diana Wells is your mother? I'll be damned." She pulled the car to a stop, twisting her body in May's direction. "I'll never forget that case. It's all anyone could talk about. I was only a couple of years out of university myself then."

May glanced around, not quite sure why she had even mentioned her mom.

Kewa continued. "I found the whole thing fascinating. Sorry to say, but it's true. Nothing ever happened around here, so that's why. My papa locked our windows at night after hearing about your mom's disappearance, thinking it was going to happen again. First time he'd ever done that."

"Should we keep going?" May glanced around. Even with the bright lights everywhere, the grounds were giving her the creeps.

The officer waved her off. "In a minute. I've got the daughter of a celebrity in my car. Diana Wells, huh? Gosh, I remember when they found her. All a big mystery. She had no memory of what happened, did she?"

"So I've been told." May shuffled in her seat.

"You know, a lot of people didn't believe her. Said she made the whole thing up. I've never believed that myself. I mean, where was she for those few weeks and how did she end up on that road so far away with all those bruises all over her body?"

"You have a good memory." Maybe this was why she had mentioned her mom, hoping the officer would tell her something she didn't already know.

"Everyone at the station knows about Diana Wells. She has become the stuff of legends. The mystery case. I hope she's doing well . . ."

May ignored the obvious prompt for information. "What else do you remember? Who were all the suspects?" May chewed one of her nails.

"Suspects? Well, that's putting my memory to the test. Let's see . . . there's that roommate that seemed a little off. I always thought she knew more than she said to—" The officer touched her ear to her shoulder speaker. "Oh, that's me. Hang on, hon."

The officer talked into her shoulder piece. "Officer Kewa here."

"You there yet? You haven't checked in." The detective's concern filled the car via the radio, which the officer had turned up.

"Sorry, Detective, we took a small detour. I'll be at the destination in exactly two minutes."

"Check in when you're leaving."

"Copy that." The officer pulled the vehicle back onto the road. "Guess he's worried about you. Makes sense now . . ." Her voice trailed off.

May put her head on the window. Maybe coming to Bretford had been a massive mistake.

"You never said why you were visiting? You here for a while?"

May yawned, exhaustion winning. "I'm not sure."

Kewa waited for more but recognized May had finished. The lights from the campus faded behind them as they entered the suburbs.

The patrol car pulled up in front of an apartment block with a facade of faded yellow brick and a front yard that had seen better days. A set of stairs separated the four apartments.

"Well, here we are. Told you it wasn't far. I'll walk you up." Officer Kewa already had her door open.

May shook her head. She was going to be escorted to the door whether she liked it or not. She followed Kewa as she climbed the stairs and turned left to the front door of 2A. "This is it—let me get you inside."

The officer held out her palm for the keys and wrestled with three separate locks before the door opened. "Reckon he has gold in there with all that security. Might pay to scout around." The officer laughed, having a peek inside. "He's left a couple of lights on."

"Okay, thanks." May took the keys back from Kewa and swapped places with her in the doorframe. She had a feeling the detective wouldn't want his colleague snooping on his things.

"Rest up." Kewa headed toward the stairs.

"Hey, thanks . . . um, what's your name?"

"Silly me, forgot to give it. I'm Jane."

June?

May shook her head. Great. She was hearing things now.

Chapter Fourteen

May took in the detective's apartment from the door.

The open-concept kitchen and living room contained no sign of a bachelor lifestyle. Not a pizza box or beer bottle in sight. A large blue rug covered the floorboards, with a grey sofa taking up most of the wall space. The sofa faced a floor-to-ceiling bookcase. If he owned a TV, she couldn't see one.

May made her way up the hall, turning on the light as she opened a door to the compact bathroom. She peeked inside. Also clean. No toothpaste or toothbrush sitting on the sink. No wet towels on the floor. Only the faint smell of aftershave.

The only other room was the detective's bedroom at the end of the hall. The bed had been made, but clothes were tossed over a chair in the corner. *So this is where he gets to live a little.*

A desk stood against the wall, and May drifted over to it, curiosity getting the better of her. The top was mainly clean, with a few thriller books piled up, a coffee mug filled with pens, and a closed laptop.

Leaning against the mug was a photo of the younger-looking detective barreling the lens with a wide smile.

He looks so different. Happy.

There was something wrong with the photo. It had been ripped in half. May picked it up, examining it closer. A manicured white hand was hugging his waist. There had been someone else in the picture.

A girlfriend?

Whoever she was, the detective had removed her for a reason.

I'll have to ask him.

May knew immediately she wouldn't, or he'd know she'd come in here. Surely, snooping in his bedroom wouldn't exactly go over well.

She placed the photo back, hoping it was exactly how it had been before. Then scanned the room in case he had a security camera. Nope. Nothing she could see.

May closed the bedroom door and grabbed sheets from the hallway closet. She needed the detective to trust her if she was to get information about her mom, and going through his things wouldn't help that.

She had to see her mom's old case file. June must've found something. Something that the detectives hadn't.

Why hadn't she told anyone? June had always had a flair for the dramatic, but going to look for someone that had hurt their mother, *alone*, was just plain nuts.

June would have had a reason for going alone. She would never put herself in any deliberate danger. That was definitely *not* her style.

Silence filled the apartment in a way that hung heavy on May. She put the sheets down on the couch and peered out onto the street through the blinds. Horror-movie quiet. Not a soul. In fact, May hadn't seen many souls since she'd arrived.

May grabbed her phone from her backpack and put her earbuds in. Queen's "Bohemian Rhapsody" played in her ears. She unlaced her boots and kicked them off. In her socks, she slid on the floorboards to the kitchen. The clock on the microwave read three in the morning. Almost twenty-four hours since May had slept. She opened the fridge, hoping for some inspiration. There wasn't much in the way of food, but a beer would do the trick.

She opened the bottle of some foreign beer she'd never heard of, took a sip, and cringed at its bitterness. Drinking was still a new thing for her, and so far she hadn't found any alcohol she particularly liked.

Sinking into the comfort of the sofa, May let out a deep sigh. The music still pounding in her ears, she reached for her backpack and pulled the *Secret Seven Mystery* book out. First she read the article June had hidden, although now she knew it almost by heart, then flipped the well-worn pages of the hand-me-down book.

May couldn't remember how many times she and June had read this book. Sometimes together. Sometimes separately. They'd read other Secret Seven books, but this one was their favorite for so many reasons. A missing girl who had supposedly run away, the Secret Seven not realizing she was right in front of their faces, horse stables as one of the settings. It had the best mystery to solve out of all the Secret Seven books, and although they already knew the ending, they continued to read it over and over.

May landed on a page, and seeing June's scribbled handwriting felt as if someone had grabbed her insides and given them a good twist. *Silly duck* was still the only clue she could find in the book's pages.

When had June written this? When she first started looking? Or at the end, knowing she would need her sister to find her? May was sure her quota for questions was about to run out.

The book began to feel heavy in her hands, so she swapped it for the beer. May needed the liquid to numb her. It was better than the guilt consuming her.

It was her fault June had disappeared, after all.

Days Mom's been dead: Lots.

Hi Mom,

Big news! Oops. I forgot to say sorry for writing that I didn't care you were dead in my last letter. You know I didn't mean it. Well, maybe I did a little bit, but I'm over it now.

Anyway. Big news! I found out who our father is. I know, I know. I'm amazing. Don't worry, I'm taking a bow now. Ta-da!

Drumroll, please . . . . it's Brad.

Remember him? Some guy you dated in uni for a hot minute. Did you forget him like you forgot what happened to you? Huh?

Why didn't you just tell us about him? He doesn't seem like he's the abducting type, if I'm going to be honest. What's that? How would I know? Well, I went and visited him—of course. Ha ha.

Okay, I can hear you having a meltdown from here. Calm down, Mom. It's not THAT big of a deal. Seriously. Do you want me to tell you the story or not?

Wait. To tell the story of going to see Brad, I have to tell you the story of finding him first. Which means telling you about going to Bretford, seeing that boring detective, having a MASSIVE fight with May. (What's new? That's all we seem to do lately.) Honestly, I don't feel like doing all that. It's all really blah, blah, blah. THEN the good stuff happened!

So!!!!! I went and saw Brad (can still hear you freaking out, Mom. Jeez). Just showed up at dinnertime on his doorstep. Took me hours to get to where he's living now. I took your car, so thanks for that! Anyway, I don't think his wife was too happy about it. I wasn't scared. You would think I would be, but I wasn't. I mean AS IF he's going to chop me up with his wife JUST there, you know?

He has a nice house. Like something in a movie. Has blue shutters and a porch swing on the veranda. I want to live there.

The whole visit was a little bit awkward, tbh. Okay, a LOT awkward. Brad's wife, Jenny, answered the door and had a kid in tow. Thomas, like Thomas the Tank Engine, he told me.

I said I was there to see Brad, and she just knew something was up. I reckon she thought I was having an affair with him. I would have thought that too. I looked good that day (on purpose, of course!). I wore the black wraparound dress everyone tells me I'm hot in and matched it with wedge heels. I did my hair straight and long. I would've sent you a photo, but well, you know . . .

The wife didn't let me in, just called Brad to the door and stood beside him the whole time. It would have made a great picture for my socials, with her holding on to Brad's arm for dear life and the kid hanging on to his mom's leg the same way. They were SUCH an insecure family.

I already knew what Brad looked like from his Facebook photos that I stalked, so won't go into that. What I did notice was that his eyes were bluer than in his photos. They were just like mine!! (May got your eyes, and I got his. Finally it all makes sense.)

Total dad situation!

I told them I was a friend of Diana Wells and was in the neighborhood (like that was ever going to be a possibility! Longest drive EVER!).

Brad's face lit up when I mentioned you. (Don't get a big head, Mom!) He instantly let me inside and gave me a glass of milk like I was a child. They were making spaghetti for dinner, and of course I stayed because what family would be rude enough to let an eighteen-year-old girl starve?

Dinner was boring. Most of it was just looking after the kids, who wouldn't eat and were a pain in the ass. I wanted to ask a thousand questions, but Thomas, who is three, wouldn't eat his food and it was a total drama. The other kid, Jonathan, is only five months, and apparently talking baby crap to him is more important than talking to a new daughter. SO annoying!

Brad asked if I wanted to walk the dog with him after dinner. Thank god he suggested that because I knew Jenny was ready to kick me out. She wasn't exactly subtle that she didn't want me there. I mean, I guess it is kinda weird that some strange girl shows up for no reason but still...

I could hear them fighting in the kitchen before we left with the dog.

"Who is she, and what does she want? I'm not comfortable with you being alone with her." Another blah, blah, blah moment.

Finally, we went for a walk with their big golden Labrador called Sunshine. I didn't hold him, because he was too strong for me and walking dogs in wedged heels is a death trap—everyone knows that. Well, except Dad. Like our real dad. Well not our real, REAL dad but whatever. You know what I mean.

Don't worry, I was ready to run in case Brad turned out to be a total psycho. He wasn't, so that's lucky.

Brad asked about you, and I told him you died. He was sad, so don't ask. Then, I jumped straight into all the juicy stuff, because otherwise: BORING! Asked him about your abduction and then came straight out and asked if he was my father (didn't want to mention May JUST in case he ends up being a serial killer).

He freaked out! I thought he might faint at one stage. Funny thing was he didn't know about me. He said this was the first he'd heard of me being his. He had known you'd had kids but thought I was Gary's. He said after you left school, you didn't want anything to do with him. I can't believe he didn't know you were pregnant!

Drama, Mom. DRAMA!

He realized what I was saying. If he was the father, then he MUST'VE taken you. He denied everything and said not to mention it to his wife.

Poor guy. I actually felt a little sorry for him. (Mom, I can HEAR your eyes rolling from here at how much danger I put myself in, but get over it. I was fine . . . and I'm not as brainless as you think I am.)

Brad didn't know much about what happened to you, just said you were missing for days without any word (no text messages back then because you refused to get a cell phone, which is just totally weird?!! Were you okay?).

Brad admitted he was a suspect but had an alibi (must check if that's totally true). He said he loved you (sigh!) and would never do anything to hurt you. I believed him. He seemed like too much of a wuss to hurt anyone.

They didn't find you for a few weeks. All that time Brad thought you were dead (nice huh?). Said he couldn't help it. Said you had been gone too long to be alive. Wow, you were only gone like three weeks! What a dick!

If I was only missing for three weeks and people were already thinking I was dead, I'd come back and totally kick their asses.

He was wrong anyway because you were VERY much alive. (If you need me to kick his ass for you, just say the word. And we all know what that word is when you're a ghost, don't we? It's BOO, Mom. The word is boo. Sigh.)

I asked about the necklace, and he told me you got it for your 16th birthday from Pat and Pa and you never took it off. (Guess I'm not the only liar, liar pants on fire in the house!)

I asked about your relationship, and he said he wanted to marry you (!!!) but after the abduction, you weren't the same and couldn't even look at him. Um, duhhhhh!

He met Jenny a few years later.

He said he loved Jenny, but you would always be his first true love (awwww!).

Brad ended up being no help really. He was a bit dull, tbh, and I kind of hoped he wasn't really our father, porch swing or not.

I took his used toothbrush (look, it wasn't as gross as Dad's nail clippings) and got another paternity test.

Turns out he IS our father. Which means he took you, didn't he, Mom? Or did something else happen?

I might need to tell May about all of this soon because I'm not sure what to do now that I know who our father is. If only she wasn't being such a bitch and talking about university all the time and getting to act like life is normal while I'm over here risking MY life.

She's going to leave Harold without me, Mom. Yep, that's what she said.

Talk about selfish.

Get over it, Mom. Sisters fight.

Love, June x

Chapter Fifteen

May awoke to the detective standing over her.

"Oops." May rubbed her eyes. "I must've fallen asleep."

Sam picked up the book off the floor. "Anything good?"

"Just an old book June and I used to read." May sat up, cracking her neck. "You'd figure out the mystery in two seconds."

"See you found my beer." Sam put the book on the coffee table and collected the empty beer bottle.

"Sorry." May stood, using the coffee table as support after getting up too quickly. "I'll buy you some more."

"Don't worry about it. Happy you felt at home." Sam trudged to the kitchen, rubbing his shoulder with his spare hand. "You want me to take you out for breakfast?"

"Um, sure. If you're not too tired. Then we can look at the case file like you promised?"

"It'll have to be when I'm on shift later." Sam dropped the empty bottle in the recycling. "I'm starving. Let me change and we can get out of here."

May nodded, hiding her disappointment. She didn't want to wait until later to find her next clue.

Sam changed quickly, and May brushed her teeth, wearing the same clothes she'd slept in. They drove in silence to the café. It was the kind of bonding May preferred.

The café was at the rear of a bookstore, with tables and chairs along a whitewashed brick wall with books on shelves of various sizes and heights. The only other patron was a male student listening to his headphones, engrossed in his computer.

"What do you want?" Sam asked. "I need to order at the counter."

"Just coffee is great. Black."

"Just coffee is not great. I'll get you some eggs on toast."

May didn't have a chance to protest.

She sat at the table for two, perusing the books on the wall at her eyeline. It had been ages since she had read a book from start to finish. She and June loved books. Escaping reality. Creating fantasy worlds once they'd finished a story together. Now words swam on the page if May tried to read anything new. Escaping reality wasn't an option.

The detective returned with their coffees and plonked himself down with an exhausted sigh.

"Long night?"

"Night shifts are the worst." Sam sipped his coffee.

May did the same. "Wow, this is great."

"That's why I come here. And for the books."

"I saw your bookcase in your apartment. Impressive."

"I've always liked reading since I was a boy. My mom encouraged it."

An older lady, dressed in chef's pants and a black T-shirt, placed their meals on the table.

May looked up in surprise. "That was quick."

"I usually come here after work. I'm just a fraction late today." He acknowledged the chef. "Thanks, Julz."

Julz smiled at Sam and nodded in May's direction, before heading back to the kitchen.

Sam said, "Julz is a jack-of-all-trades when it comes to the café. Barista, chef, dish pig. They are my savior after a long shift."

"I'd rather be out here with the books. Books don't ask questions." May spread butter on her toast. "So, do you have any brothers or sisters?"

"What was that about asking questions?" Sam laughed.

"Sorry." May laughed lightly back. "It's none of my business."

"It's okay." Sam squeezed ketchup onto his bacon and eggs. "I have a big sister and a younger brother. Sally and Phil. Sally lives out west and is a stay-at-home mom with two kids." He shoveled in a forkful of food.

"And your brother?"

Sam wiped his mouth. "Phil drowned when he was eight."

May dropped her knife back on the plate. "Oh, I'm sorry."

"It happened a long time ago."

"And your parents?"

Sam washed his food down with his coffee. "Dead. Cancer got them both. Dad's was inevitable, the way he smoked, and Mom followed two years later with breast cancer. I used to be a smoker, too, but gave that up long ago. Wisest thing I ever did."

Neither of them filled the silence as the detective finished his breakfast.

Sam pushed his plate away and sat back in contentment. "So how did it go last night? I hope you slept okay on the couch."

"I must have. I don't even remember falling asleep." May nibbled her toast. "Do you think my sister knew she was in danger? She must have, right?"

"I honestly don't know." Sam finished his coffee. "When I saw her, she acted like she was playing some kind of game."

"That sounds like June. Everything is a game to her." May forced herself to swallow. "How did you know June had gone missing?"

"Your grandmother called me."

"Pat?"

"Yes, Pat. She was also the one who told me about Diana's passing."

His voice broke, and May couldn't help but stare at him. What did he know about her mom's death? It was like he was a little too invested in her mom's case. Or just her mom.

"Were you in love with my mom or what?"

Sam let out a quick burst of laughter. "Are you always this direct?"

"Sometimes." May continued to stare him down. "Answer the question."

His gaze focused on his empty plate. "Diana was one of my first big cases. One that I didn't solve. You get close with some victims in a way that's hard to understand when you let them down. Then they live with you, haunt you."

So I'm not the only one haunted around here.

"Your mom and I go back a long way. Same with Pat. She called me when Diana died because she knew I'd want to know. She called again when June went missing because she needed some police advice. Wasn't happy with how things were being handled."

May chewed her nails, too many questions running around her brain again. "So what did June find? Or who? Do you have any ideas?"

"I don't. I said as much to Pat." Sam ran his hands through his hair. "As much as I would love to believe that the two cases aren't connected, it seems like too much of a coincidence. And I don't believe in coincidences."

"Me neither." May liked that they shared something. "That's why I owe it to both Mom and my sister to pick up where June left off."

"That's not going to happen."

"What, like you can stop me?" May smirked at the detective. "I'm nineteen and don't need a permission slip."

"I know how old you are, May." Sam rubbed his eyes. "You're right. I can't stop you, but well, I can help you."

May waited, a flutter moved around her stomach at the idea of getting help. A good flutter because it meant she wouldn't be doing this alone.

"I have a proposition for you, May."

She took in a breath. "I'm listening."

"I want you to stay here with me until you work out your next move. If you find something, you tell me—no going off by yourself. Deal?"

May rubbed her lips and pretended she was thinking it over. She hadn't wanted to admit it, but part of her had hoped he would ask her to stay. "Deal. On one condition."

"What's that?"

"I'm sleeping on the couch."

"Done. Now speaking of sleep, I need to get some. You coming back to the apartment?"

"No. I'm going to stay here for a bit. I want to have another coffee, check out the town a little."

Sam pushed his chair back. "Righto. There's a tab at the counter, so put anything on that." He picked up the empty plates. "Don't wander too far, okay? You want me to come and pick you up later?"

"No, I remember how to get back to your place. It's not far. I'll walk." May added before he could say the inevitable: "And yes, I'll be careful."

Sam headed off, dropping the plates at the kitchen as he went.

It was like a bag of cement had been taken off her shoulders. Weird, and she couldn't explain it, but May trusted this stranger obligated to her family for all the wrong reasons.

Only maybe she knew why.

This man had been there for her mom during her darkest time. He had helped her once with her greatest secret, and now he could help May find the man who started it all.

If I find him, I find June.

"Excuse me. Sorry to bother you."

May snapped her head up, off in her own thoughts. A woman in her forties or so, with wild hair and a hard face, stood over her, holding a book.

"I didn't mean to startle you. I saw you with Sam. He didn't come and get this from me before he left." She referenced the book she held.

"Sam?" May asked.

"Detective Davis." The woman's voice was gravelly.

"Yes, of course. Sorry. I was millions of miles away."

"I can see that. Penny for your thoughts?"

May shook her head. "You'd need more than a penny."

There was a pause as neither of them spoke. The woman didn't seem like she was in a hurry to leave.

May pointed to the book in the woman's hand. "Do you want me to give that to him?"

"Why would you give it to Sam? Are you staying with him?" The words came out as though from a machine gun.

May twigged to the visit; this woman was being nosy.

"Only for a couple of days. I'm his niece."

Her face lit up, and she appeared ten years younger. "Oh, it's so nice to meet you. I never knew he had a niece."

"So, what's the book?"

The woman presented the cover of a drooling dog's mouth and teeth but didn't hand it over.

"Really? He wanted this?"

"He loves Stephen King, and this one is a first edition. I can't give it to you, of course. It's too valuable."

"No stress." May nodded, waiting for the lady to leave.

"I take it Sam isn't coming back?" she asked, looking around the café.

"No, he isn't, but I'll tell him the book is here."

"That's okay. I'll call him."

"I'm sure you will," May muttered.

"Sorry?"

"Nothing. Just saying, I'm sure he'll be happy it's here."

"Well, maybe I'll catch you around. I hope you enjoy your stay . . . What was your name?"

It came out before May could stop it. "June."

"Pretty name. Have a nice day, June."

"You too."

The woman strode off, holding the book protectively like a baby.

So someone has a crush on the detective, huh?

May would have to tease him about it later.

Chapter Sixteen

Sharon Hook returned to the front counter and placed Sam's book in a paper bag.

Another one, Sharon thought. And lo and behold this one is also called June. *This must be the twin.*

The kids of her old dorm roommate kept showing up, and she had no idea why.

Unlike her smart sister, though, this one has no idea who I am.

Sharon pulled out a pile of books for pricing. The bookstore was hers. A gift from her grandfather who had started the business forty years ago.

It made okay money now that she had opened the café, but the work was mundane. She never admitted to anyone that she didn't actually like books.

Sharon smiled as she had a thought. *Maybe this kid will get smart and finally ask me the right question.*

The only question that matters.

Sharon's smile continued. She highly doubted it.

Not even the dumbass detective had asked her the right question.

Sharon happily hummed to herself.

Yep, it's going to be a wonderful day.

DIANA

"Going out tonight?" I asked.

Sharon's reflection took up most of my wardrobe mirror. She sat on her bed reading a magazine. I had never once seen her studying since we had moved into the dorm together months ago.

"Nope. Just going to hang out." Sharon played with her ponytail. She had worn the same sweatshirt and pants two days in a row.

I, on the other hand, was up to my third change of clothes for the day. Early-run outfit this morning, casual study clothes in the library for most of the day, and I only had to put boots over my skintight jeans, and I was set for my night out.

Crap. And I still had to call Mom and Dad. If I missed a Sunday call, they would totally send out a search party.

"Where you off to now? Out all day and out again tonight. Little Miss Popular, huh?" Sharon didn't bother looking up from her magazine.

"Hardly! I should stay here and study like you . . . oh wait. You don't study either."

"Funny. And I do too study. You're just not here to see it." Sharon put her magazine to the side and lay face down on her bed with her hands on her chin.

"So, who are you hanging out with tonight?"

"Brad. We're going to a movie. Some action flick, probably." I fussed around in the closet, knowing she would see through my lie. I always was a shit liar.

"I don't believe you."

Yep, there we go.

"Why are you hiding in the closet, D.?"

This had been a new development. Calling me D. as if we were friends.

"I'm not hiding. I'm looking for my blue scarf."

"It's around your neck."

I laughed because what else was I supposed to do? "I'm such a ditz! Guess I'm tired."

"You know, I'm always here if you need me."

Oh god, where had that come from? My roomie even seemed genuine for once.

"Thanks, but I don't have anything to tell you. My life is totally uncool. Classes, Brad, classes, Brad. And every now and again I get to sleep. Boring."

"Who's that guy that keeps calling? He won't give his name, but it isn't Brad."

Fuckity fuck.

"No clue. Maybe someone from class wanting notes or something?"

Lie.

"Then why doesn't he say that? He doesn't have to hang up in my ear because it isn't you." Her eyes narrow because she's onto me. "If you'd just get a cell, then your annoying friends could call you directly. Then I wouldn't have to listen to your boring chats with your parents every Sunday night."

"You know I hate those things. Give you brain cancer." I shook my head. "Besides, it's probably just an old classmate from high school trying to freak me out again."

"I hope not! I don't want any psychos coming to our door." Sharon had this weird habit of scrunching up her nose and creating long lines on her forehead. She would pay for that when she was older. "Oh, and speaking of psychos, my brother will be crashing here again while he's in town."

Love it how she never asked if it was okay with me.

"Come on, Sharon. We'll get in trouble if anyone finds him in here. Plus, he snores."

On cue. Nose scrunching. "What's the difference if it's Brad who sleeps over or it's my brother?"

Because your brother gives me the creeps, that's why.

"Do whatever you want, Sharon. Just tell Tony to keep on your side of the room this time."

She jumped up like a spring and crossed her legs. "It'll only be for one night. Maybe two. He'll do as I say. I promise."

Like when you told him to stop putting his hand down his pants as he watched me sleep. That seemed to work so well didn't it, Sharon?

"Let me guess, he lost another job?" I rolled my eyes.

Sharon mumbled something I couldn't hear. I took that to mean yes.

I sighed. "Look, give me some privacy. I want to talk to my parents before I go out."

"Every Sunday, D. You're as regular as my period."

"Nice."

Sharon finally dragged herself out into the hall. A sloth would've beaten her if they were having a race.

The mattress springs stuck into my butt as I sat on my bed. Sharon had changed our mattresses again. What was the point in my parents buying me a new one if my roommate stole it all the time? Fucking Sharon . . . and her perverted brother.

I wiped the handle and mouthpiece of the dorm room phone. Sharon had a habit of sneezing right into it. Ready to dial the number of my parents' house, I stopped myself.

I glanced at the closed door and dialed *his* number instead.

He picked up on the first ring. "Yes."

"It's me. I know I'm seeing you soon, but I needed to hear your voice." My heart skipped around in my mouth.

"You okay?"

His voice could melt a cheese sandwich better than a frying pan.

"Yes, just dealing with some . . ." Another check of the door. "Some roommate issues."

"Tell me when you get here."

"I'll see you soon."

Soon was a lifetime away.

"Hurry. I'm waiting."

The line went quiet, but my body was just getting started. Desire danced through my blood like a disco.

I dialed the number to my parents' house next.

"Darling?"

"Yes, Mom. It's me. Is Dad on the other line?"

"Yes, I'm here, sweetheart!"

"So how are you, darling? Tell us everything."

"Everything is great, Mom. School is busy, I've got a big exam this week . . ."

I talked, but all I could think of was seeing him.

Chapter Seventeen

May was returning emails on the couch when the detective walked into the living room wearing a T-shirt and basketball shorts with half his hair sticking up.

"Morning," she said. "Or should I say afternoon?"

"You gave me a fright. I didn't hear you come in." He picked the sleep from the corner of his eyes.

"Well if that's you getting a fright, I would love to see you watch a horror movie. I figured cops whipped out their guns when they thought they were in danger?"

"Don't exactly have my gun on me, do I?" He glanced down at his sleepwear. "Let me get some clothes on."

May finished the email to her work asking for more time off.

"So how was your day?" Sam called out from the bedroom.

"Okay." May rubbed her cheeks, glad she had someone to talk to again. Solitude was not her friend with all these questions in her head. "Stayed in the bookstore for a while. Some woman came over and chatted—then she kept staring at me. So, I ended up leaving and walking around for a while. I went back down toward the university and had a snoop."

Sam came out of his room, dressed in jeans and a V-necked shirt. "Wow, that's quite a hike. I don't like you walking that far by yourself."

May groaned. "Jeez, you sound just like my dad."

Sam fixed his hair by running his hands through it. "What did the woman want?"

"She had one of your books you ordered. Some first edition or something."

"Oh yeah?" Sam went into the kitchen. "Hey, you want coffee?"

"Sure." May turned around to face him.

"You know which book it was?"

"Some dog book. Had a picture of one on the cover. She wouldn't let me touch it, said it was expensive."

The detective laughed. "*Cujo*? No, it was only forty bucks or so. Not exactly a vintage first edition."

"Well, this woman acted like this was the first edition of the Bible or something. She was a little bit weird, actually." May walked to the kitchen counter divider and hopped up on one of two stools. "Oh, and if you don't know already, she has a crush on you."

Sam opened a few cupboards until he found the coffee cups.

May shrugged. "Sorry about that. I got bored. The kitchen is a little more functional now."

"It was functional before." Sam prepared the coffee, his smile clearly showing he was more amused than upset his whole kitchen had been rearranged.

"Stop changing the subject," May teased. "That book woman has a crush on you."

"Yes, I heard you. She has a crush on anyone who's single. Been married two times already. Don't think I'm open to being her third."

"What happened? She kill them all?"

The detective snorted out laughter. "What? Why on earth would you say that?"

"She just has that vibe about her. Something not right. So did she? Kill them?"

"I believe they are both alive and well, as far as I know. Can't say I drop in on them that often." The detective poured their coffees.

"Well, maybe you should check on that."

Sam saluted May. "Yes, ma'am."

They both laughed without making much of a sound.

"Come on, let's sit down." Sam carried the mugs to the coffee table and sat on the couch. May squatted on the rug.

"So, did she tell you who she was?"

"Who, the book woman?" May blew on her coffee before taking a sip. Sam nodded.

"Nope. She seemed fixated on you, to be honest. Oh, and before I forget, I told her I was your niece! Sorry, I panicked."

Sam wrestled with a cushion. "Good going, kid. Well, she'll know that's a lie. I don't have a niece, only nephews."

"Crap, did I mess up?"

"No. It isn't her business anyway. Although, I'm sure she'll make it hers soon enough."

"Oh, you're so screwed! She has the hots for you something bad." May had a fleeting sense of enjoying herself.

"I have a feeling she was interested in something else besides me." Sam picked up his coffee cup.

"What do you mean? Who is she?"

"She's your mom's roommate from university. Sharon Hook."

May almost dropped her coffee. "No way! I remember her name from the article. Wait, you think she knows who I am?"

"I'd say so. Your sister spoke to her too."

"Crap." May slapped her forehead.

"What?"

"I told her my name's June. I don't know why—it just came out."

"Don't worry. You don't owe her anything." Sam got up and went to the window. "Do you mind if I open these blinds? I like the afternoon sun coming in."

"It's your house."

Orange light streamed into the room as the blinds folded into each other. The sun hit May's face, colored dots appearing in front of her eyes.

"Too bright?" Sam asked, ready to pull the blinds back down.

"No, it's lovely. Just a shock to the system." May let her eyelids close, enjoying the vitamin D.

"Are you staring at me?" May opened an eyelid.

"Busted." Sam sat back on the couch. "Sorry. You look so much like your mother."

"So everyone keeps telling me lately." May blinked the dots away.

"You also share that same maturity I saw in your mother. She was also nineteen when we met."

"I'll take that." The corners of May's mouth turned up. "You kind of have no choice when your twin is the one who gets the attention with all her drama."

The detective chuckled. "Speaking of, Sharon didn't tell you who she was, huh? That surprises me. She normally likes a bit of drama herself."

"Not a thing." May wished she *had* said something. She had plenty of questions for Sharon.

"Let me get more coffee in a thermos. I'll fill you in on Sharon on the way to the station. Prep you before you get to her section in the case file."

Chapter Eighteen

"As far as I could tell, Sharon and Diana weren't exactly best mates. Sharon didn't even report Diana missing, for example."

May sat in the passenger seat, twisted toward the detective in his small Honda hatchback.

"It was really your grandparents who raised the alarm after Diana didn't call them that Sunday. If it wasn't for them, we may not have known about Diana for a lot longer." Sam cleared his throat.

"But what about Brad? He would've known she was missing."

"He'd been at his parents' place a couple of hours away. It was his stepdad's fiftieth birthday."

"Why wasn't Mom with him? Shouldn't she have been at the party too?"

"Brad told us it was just a family thing, and that checked out." Sam sipped his coffee, his eyes never leaving the road.

"So why didn't Sharon notice anything then?"

"Sharon was adamant Diana had been in the room over the weekend. Not uncommon for roommates to miss each other as they came and went, but it was odd Sharon didn't notice Diana hadn't even slept in her bed for days on end."

May picked at one of her nails. "What about the necklace? Wouldn't it be strange for that to be left behind if Mom never took it off?"

The detective hesitated. "Possibly. I don't remember if Sharon noticed it or not."

"Didn't you find fingerprints or something?" May tugged at a piece of skin near her nail.

"It wasn't that simple. Your mom's disappearance wasn't reported until almost a week after she was last seen. The police followed it up but didn't take it seriously because Sharon was adamant Diana had still been frequenting the dorm. You have to understand, students have a habit of disappearing for days sometimes with parties and room swapping, but they usually showed up."

May tore off the piece of skin she had been picking at. "So if Sharon had reported Mom missing earlier, things would've gone differently?"

Sam sighed as he pulled up at a stop sign. "I don't like questions that I can't answer. The truth is, we'll never know."

May stared at the trickle of blood coming from the side of her nail; she liked the pain being isolated to one spot.

Sam glanced at her. "You okay?"

"I'm annoyed. That's all. There must've been other suspects or someone who saw something." May sucked her finger.

"I understand your frustration. It's hard to let unsolved cases go. You only hope that a fresh lead will come from somewhere." Sam turned into heavy traffic.

"Maybe *I* can find that fresh lead." May's voice was high with expectation.

The detective smiled but didn't say anything.

May moved on, a little disappointed he didn't think she could solve the case. "So what's the deal with Sharon? Was she ever a suspect?"

Sam nodded yes. "Not for long, though. There was really no motive or evidence she had anything to do with your mom's abduction. When you get to her interviews, though, you'll notice she mentions thinking Diana had a secret boyfriend. June didn't stop quizzing me on that part, so I figure you will too."

"Really?" May pulled part of the seat belt over her head so she could twist fully in his direction. "Is that true?"

"Not that we were ever able to prove. Diana never said anything, and we couldn't find anyone to corroborate Sharon's story."

Had Mom had another boyfriend that no one knew about? Why would she not tell anyone about him? Great, more questions.

Sam was still talking. "Do you want me to pick you up anything on the way? Food or snacks or anything?"

"You would've made a great parent." May chuckled and leaned back into her seat. "Why didn't you get married or have kids?"

Sam ignored May's comment and focused on the crawling traffic in front of him. Clearly, rush hour in Bretford.

"I'm not going anywhere, so you may as well answer." May tapped her thigh.

He sighed. "It just never happened for me. Work got in the way, I guess."

"Aren't you lonely here all by yourself?"

"No, I'm not," Sam said. "What about you? Anyone special?"

"Fell into that one, didn't I?" May stopped tapping. "Point taken. No more mention of relationships."

Sam stuck his head out the window. "What's going on up there?"

"You think that's who gave Mom the necklace?"

"Huh? Who?" Sam pulled his head back in.

"The mystery guy she was seeing. Could've been a present from him?"

Sam adjusted the rearview mirror. "I'm fairly certain Sharon made the mystery boyfriend up. Like I said, she likes creating her own drama."

"I wish my mom was still here so I could talk to her about this."

"I bet." He glanced at May. "Instead, you got me. Not a fair trade, is it?"

"Not even close." May paused, then laughed. "Actually, you'll do."

The traffic moved, and May stared out through the window. Laughing always brought guilt. She watched the town pass. The setting sun adding a romantic glow to the town compared to when she'd seen it last night.

"You sure you're okay?"

"The million-dollar question." May took in a deep breath. "I honestly don't know anymore. It's just a lot. One minute, I'm burying an empty casket for my sister, and the next I'm here with you. I wish I'd never found that article."

Sam pursed his lips, saying nothing.

"Sorry, that came out wrong. I'm glad we met and everything, but I should be back in the city. Getting on with my life."

What life?

"It's a lot to take in, May. But nothing's stopping you from leaving."

"I need to find my sister." May tucked her arms into her body. "I have no choice now."

Sam turned in to the station. "I know it feels like that, but you always have a choice . . . besides, you might not like what you find. Have you thought about that?"

"Yes," May whispered. "I think about it all the time."

Days Mom's been dead: Too many 😣

Hi Mom,

Oops! I made a mistake.

A big one.

I'm not sure what to do. I really wish you were here helping me with all of this *waves hands around at the mess you left me.*

I thought everything was over. That I'd found our father (Brad) and all I had to do was get him to confess that he had something to do with your abduction.

I was all ready to go back there, to his perfect porch swing and his annoying kids. Crap! I guess they're my brothers now. That's weird.

I was all ready to go, Mom. Drive up to his place again, confront him. Get the real story out of him after I presented the paternity test. I had it all planned.

BUT THEN something happened. Okay, okay. I admit that I'm a little embarrassed I didn't catch this before, but there were so many things on my murder board it was hard to keep up.

Yikes! I'm not making any sense. Sorry, Mom. I am writing this in a hurry before I jump in the car. Before I go and visit this NEW development.

Side note! Speaking of cars, that's what I got for my eighteenth birthday!! Yay!! I forgot to tell you. It's secondhand with questionable air-conditioning, but it's ALL mine! That's right. May and I don't have to share it.

(She didn't want presents, btw. Just wanted everyone to donate to saving the orangutans or pandas or whatever. Mom are you sure I wasn't adopted?!)

ANYWAY. So, when I went and saw the detective, he let me look at your old file. He took all the pictures out (DUN, DUN, DUN!) but left the interviews and police notes. In other words, the boring stuff. I mean, have you read handwritten police notes? It's like reading something a child wrote. What if there was something important there and I couldn't read it?! Yikes!

Anyway, it was totally yawn, tbh. Case files look so interesting in movies, but in real life it's like walking around the museum and having to visit every room when you just want to look at the dinosaurs.

I took photos on my phone of everything to look at later. (Don't tell the detective, or he might get cranky!)

So, ANYWAAAAAY, I finally looked at those screenshots and realized I'd missed something. Something HUGE!

It was where you were found, Mom. Where the family picked you up on that remote road hours away from Bretford. I hadn't seen it before, but the road you were found on. It was called: Old Cemetery Road.

Interesting with a capital I!!!

I'm shaking my head right now, Mom. You always WERE a bad liar. But you were an even worse storyteller. (So is May. I CLEARLY got that special gift because WOW do I tell a good story!)

Do you remember you used to tell us a ghost story about Old Cemetery Road? How there was a man who lived at the end of the street, and he would dig small graves for kids who came and caused trouble at the cemetery. How you warned us to never, ever go into a cemetery at night in case the man was waiting with a shovel to bury us alive when we fell into the graves he dug?

It was honestly a ridiculous story and never ONCE stopped me from meeting my friends at night at the cemetery in Harold. (Shut up, Mom! It was the only place to drink the alcohol we stole from all our parents' cupboards. Ha ha. Oopsie!)

So when I discovered that you were found on Old Cemetery Road AND you'd told us a ghost story about Old Cemetery Road, it got me to thinking . . . what parts of that ludicrous ghost story were ACTUALLY real? The graves that were dug for naughty kids? Or the man that lived at the end of the street? Ding, ding, ding.

Let me repeat that. Ding, ding, DING!

You described his house, Mom. Old. Wooden with flaking white paint. A barn out back that held all of his shovels.

May would crawl under the covers and beg you to stop when you got to that bit. That's because you made it feel like we were really there. You even described the smell of rust and chicken shit. (Well, you never said shit, but we both knew that's what you meant.)

Here's the thing, you made it sound alive, Mom. Like there REALLY was a bad man living in a creepy house at the end of Old Cemetery Road. So, I looked on Google Maps, and there's a house at the end of the road JUST like you described in your "story."

So I guess your stories about the bogeyman WERE real?

Only one way to find out.

Love, June x

Chapter Nineteen

May heard a noise.

She spun around in the foldout chair the detective had given her. The dungeon he'd set her up in was dark and creepy. A desk had been pulled out from the wall for her to work on, along with one reading lamp casting a small circle of light—otherwise the room was pitch black. Even if someone were hiding in the rows of archived boxes, May wouldn't see them.

She shivered. Wishing she'd agreed to open her mother's case file at one of the desks near the detective. Where there was appropriate lighting and the comforting smell of coffee.

Instead she was down in the basement with the stench of musty boxes and automatic lights that only came on when she walked down one of the rows. Rows that were packed with shelves containing cold cases, old evidence, and who knew what else.

May shivered again.

It had been almost an hour since she'd opened her mother's own cold case, containing files of interview transcriptions, police reports, DNA results, and very little physical evidence. Sam had removed any photos, saying they were "off limits."

Her main priority had been finding June's clue. She figured it would be obvious. Another scribbled note or word only she would understand. Maybe something more pronounced, like an underlined name or a location. Or a sign with neon lights telling May where June was would've been great too.

So far, May had found nothing. That meant that either she had missed it or the trail had gone cold.

It *had* to be here. May shifted her butt in the uncomfortable chair and stared at the pile of paperwork she'd haphazardly removed to get to June's clue quickly. She would have to start again, but slower this time.

She began with the DNA reports. That seemed like as good a place as any. It was also one of the slimmest files. There was only one report. For Brad. Her mom's ex. The one who had been away that weekend and had a solid alibi. They'd taken something called a blood card that gave them his full DNA profile. This was matched to things collected from her mother after she was found.

Left and right fingernail clippings and swabs under her nails. Hair fibers found on her jeans and shirt. Blood found on her right shoe and back of her shirt. The list was long, but each item was only a match for her mother's own DNA profile as the source. Or just listed as inconclusive. Or strangely listed as: *the profile is that of an unknown male (Unknown Male #1).*

There were no matches with Brad.

May scanned the items and results, looking for any new name or suspect, but found nothing. And there was definitely no clue left behind from June.

Who is Unknown Male #1? May made a note on her phone and placed the DNA folder back in the box.

She moved to Brad's folder next, which contained multiple interview transcriptions, police notes scribbled on scraps of paper, and a paternity test. She already knew Brad wasn't her father, given his alibi, but that didn't stop her heart from racing.

The paternity form was mainly a series of numbers in two columns. One reading: *CHILD*, the other: *Alleged FATHER*, with Brad's name.

At the bottom of the columns was written: *The alleged father is excluded as the biological father of the tested child.*

Yep, confirmed. *Brad is not our father.* May knew that already.

She rubbed her eyes, tired from all the hard-to-read documents and poor lighting. It would take her days to get through everything in each of the files.

She gulped the dregs of her now cold tea, which she desperately wanted to refill but didn't want to disturb the detective or bring attention to herself. He was very clear about keeping a low profile.

She sighed, and it echoed around her. The silence was so loud she had to cover her ears before she heard noises that weren't there.

May picked through the rest of the files she'd already glanced through. Sharon. The family who found her. Anonymous tips. Bill (or Willy back then). The student who found her purse.

The purse.

May had piled the bagged physical evidence away from the paperwork. Her mom's shirt. Shoes. Jeans. Socks. Underwear. No purse, though.

There was a list containing each piece of evidence, with an item number and description, a section for if anything had been checked in or out at any stage or released. May glanced down the list until she came to her mom's purse, which had been listed as released back to the "victim."

Victim. Her mom had been a victim of a crime. One that she'd never spoken about. How had she kept it in for all that time? Acting like everything was normal. That their family was *normal.*

May felt the tears spring into her eyes. She welcomed them. Hoped that they would finally relieve her of all the pain and guilt now taking up too much space inside her.

She blinked and blinked some more. Nope. They'd stopped. She'd get no relief today.

She rested her head on the evidence-list document. Too tired to care anymore. Too tired of the games and the lies. She would ask the detective if she could take the box of files back to his place. Go through them slowly. Find June's clue that *had* to be there.

June had to have found something in these files. Something no one else had seen. Something that May was missing.

She sat up, her head spinning from exhaustion or too much caffeine. She *couldn't* stop. She couldn't take her time. She had to sit here for as long as it took. June was still out there; May knew she was. There was no question now. Too many clues. Too much of a trail.

Rubbing her eyes again, she looked over the evidence list one more time. There was definitely something missing. The necklace her mom had supposedly never taken off. It hadn't been listed at all. No record of it anywhere.

What had Pat said? It had gone missing after the police had searched the dorm. May couldn't quite remember.

She checked the time. Just after eight p.m. Worth a try.

May grabbed her phone and dialed Pat's number. It picked up on the first ring.

"Whatever you're selling, we don't want it."

Not Pat. Sue.

"What're you doing there?"

"Well hello to you too," Sue grumbled. "Where are you? And don't say back in the city because that's a lie."

Crap.

"I want to talk to Pat."

"And I want to marry Dev Patel, but we don't always get what we want, do we?"

It was May's turn to grumble. "Just get Pat."

Sue sipped something. Probably wine. "She's gone to bed. Brokenhearted from all your lies."

Double crap.

"How'd you know I wasn't back in the city?" No point fighting it now.

Sue scoffed. "Pat wanted to send you flowers. Let you know we were thinking of you. I called your office to get your hours, and they said you'd asked for some extended leave. Didn't take an Einstein brain to work out you'd gone on a wild-goose chase looking for June."

May didn't have to be in front of her aunt to know she had a smug look on her face. Possibly patting herself on the back.

More sipping. "So where are you?"

"In a galaxy far, far away."

"Oh, har har." Sue sighed. "You won't think you're so funny when Pat and Gary get a hold of you."

"How's your boyfriend?"

"Actually good!" Instant mood shift. The change of subject had worked. "Reckon he's gonna make it official soon."

"Oh yeah? That's great." May had heard this before, so who knows how true it was.

"Don't sound too excited. Would it kill you to be happy for me for once?" And back to cranky Sue. Awesome.

May closed her eyes. Time to get on with it. "Tell me about the necklace that Mom wore back at university. What do you know about it?"

Sue laughed. "I knew you were out there thinking you were Miss Marble or something."

"I'm pretty sure it's Miss Marple." There was a thud in the corner of the room behind May. *Ignore it.* "Just answer the question."

"How the hell would I know? I had my own life back then."

"Hmm." May was only half listening as she shone the reading lamp into the darkened room. The light wasn't strong enough to reach the corner where the noise had come from. *Pipes.* It had to be pipes. Or rats. *Definitely rats.*

"What're you doing? Where are you?" Sue didn't sound the least bit concerned.

May wasn't going to stick around any longer. This place was beyond creepy. "Great chat, Sue. Gotta go."

"Don't you hang up on me," Sue spit out. "Think you're so smart, huh? I bet you a million bucks you're in that boring university town digging up the past."

May kept packing the archive box, keeping the phone wedged between her shoulder and ear. "What do you know about the necklace, Sue?"

"Why are you even asking me when I wasn't living with Diana then?"

"Because I thought *maybe* you might be able to help me. Give a shit about someone other than yourself for once in your life."

Sue took a big chug of whatever she was drinking. "Great chat, May. Gotta go."

The line went dead in her ear, and May threw the phone down on the desk.

What did she expect? It wasn't like her family knew anything anyway.

Except.

What had Sue said?

"I wasn't living with Diana then."

No, Sue hadn't. But May knew who *had* been.

Chapter Twenty

The lights were on at Sharon's place when May pulled up in a taxi.

Her mother's roommate lived in a one-story brick house that had no front yard. Just one single tree surrounded by cement. The address had been easy to find. Only one Sharon Hook in all of Bretford.

May had left the archive box in the basement and planned on telling Sam where she was heading, but he'd been in a meeting when she left the station. She'd text him later.

A curtain shifted in one of the rooms; then the front door opened as May walked up to it.

Sharon blew a puff of cigarette smoke near May's head. "Hello, June. To what do I owe the pleasure?"

"We both know I'm not June. Or Sam's niece. I have questions. Mind if I come in?" May held up a bottle of red wine. "Just in case you were thinking of saying no."

Sharon grabbed the wine bottle as an answer. May brushed past her and walked straight into the living room as Sharon closed the door and locked it.

"If I'd known we were going to have a party, I'd have worn something a little more fancy." Sharon looked down at her matching peach tracksuit set. "I'll get us some glasses."

May took in the living room as Sharon went behind a wall to another room. The space would have been cozy if it weren't filled with oversize, old furniture and the yellowing of smoke on the walls. The

TV was surrounded by shelving cluttered with knickknacks and framed photos. May picked one up.

Sharon was sitting in front of a birthday cake with a tall guy smirking behind her.

"Snooping already?" Sharon came up behind her and took the photo out of May's hand. "My sixteenth birthday. Look at how young I am there. My brother too. Hell, I'd give anything to have skin like that again."

"Smoking isn't the best skin care," May mumbled.

Sharon laughed as she stubbed out her cigarette. "Got some sass to you, hey? Just like your mom. Always giving me attitude."

"I'm sure she did." May hadn't known her mom to give anyone attitude.

Sharon sighed and placed the photo frame back down on the shelves. "Happier times, huh? When my family was still together and not dead and buried."

May knew the feeling.

Sharon brought the two glasses filled with wine in from the kitchen and placed the rest of the bottle on the antique mirrored coffee table. She sat in the faded floral armchair, which was clearly her spot. It faced the TV and had a crossword puzzle book and her reading glasses on the armrest.

"Sit down. Make yourself at home." Sharon was already sipping her wine.

May sank into the middle of the three-seater couch and dropped her bag beside her. "I guess I'll get to the point. I'm sure you know why I'm here."

"Well, if it's to sell me a set of encyclopedias, you're too late." Sharon tilted her chin toward the bookcase on the wall near the kitchen.

May pulled a folded-up piece of paper from her bag. "I wanted to ask you about the necklace. The one Mom always wore. Why isn't it on this list?"

Sharon's eye's widened as she read the official police document May passed her. "Where did you get this? Don't tell me you stole it." Her eyes glistened with what looked like excitement.

"I borrowed it. So tell me, where did the necklace go?"

A smile appeared on Sharon's face. "You're asking the wrong person."

May leaned forward. "Who is the *right* person?"

"I believe you're staying at his house right now." Sharon's smile didn't leave, even as she continued to sip her wine.

May let that sit for a moment. Conscious that she didn't want to give away her surprise. "What makes you say that?"

"Just a hunch." Sharon shrugged and pulled a cigarette from the box near her chair. "Mind if I smoke?"

"I do, actually." May didn't add that her pa had died of lung cancer even though he'd never smoked a day in his life. "Tell me about the necklace. I heard my mom never took it off."

Sharon kept her unlit cigarette in between her fingers. "That's right. She had it on the day I met her—orientation day—and kept that garish thing on even when she showered. Even talked to it sometimes."

"Talked to it. What do you mean?" May asked.

"I dunno. Put it to her mouth and whispered things to it. Mainly at night when she didn't know I could see her."

"What did she say?" May moved closer to Sharon.

"Never really heard. If it was a cross, I'd say she was talking to God. But it was a horseshoe, so not sure what religion that is." Sharon chuckled and swapped her smoke for her wine.

May stared at her own wineglass in front of her, knowing she was not going to drink any. Wine tasted like vinegar. "So when Mom disappeared, it was left behind in your dorm room. Are you positive of that?"

The wine slopped in her glass as Sharon nodded. "Abso-fucking-lutely. That's the *one* thing I am sure of. That necklace was sitting right by her bed, and I knew then that something was wrong."

"Yet you didn't call the police?" May bit her lip, trying to steady her voice.

"Listen here. It wasn't as simple as you're making out. I didn't know D. was missing for a few days, because I had my own life. There were plenty of nights when she was never in her bed. It wasn't until your grandparents called that I realized something was up. That was when I saw the necklace near her books. That's when we got the police involved."

May needed to get it all right in her head. "So the necklace was there when the police arrived, but then it never made it into evidence. How do you explain that?"

"I can't. Like I said, ask *your* new roomie. Sam was there the day they searched our dorm room."

May didn't trust Sharon—it was like she was hiding something behind her smile. "Do you know anything about my sister? June. She's missing."

"I heard. Sorry about that. And, no, I know nothing about your sister. She came to the bookstore one day. Asked me a bunch of questions. Looked bored the whole time and left." Sharon stood. "Look, if this is going to be some kind of interrogation, then I need to smoke. Let's go out back."

Sharon was up, grabbing the wine and both their glasses before May could say anything. They went out on the covered veranda, where fairy lights twinkled, making everything look enchanting. Yep, even Sharon.

She'd already lit a cigarette and was sucking on it like she'd been deprived for days. "Go on then. Give me your best shot before I turn into a pumpkin."

May glanced at her phone in her hand. She'd put it on silent. *How had it gotten so late? And crap. The detective had called three times already.* She'd have to wrap this up.

"Did you and Mom ever hang out socially? Outside of the dorm."

Sharon seemed surprised by the question. "Not really. Only once. When we first started school, we went to a party together."

"So you weren't friends then?"

"D. and I got along okay, but apart from being roommates, we weren't much else. Didn't have much in common. I also thought her boyfriend was a bit of a jerk. D. would come back late at night, or not at all." Sharon poured another full glass of wine.

May had her own glass on the barbecue grill beside her. "So where did she go? She was a good student, yeah? I didn't think Mom missed class or studying."

Sharon chuckled. "I never said she missed class or didn't study. She fit that in just fine—although how, I'm not sure. It was the coming and going that was annoying."

May kept firing questions, not wanting to lose momentum. "So, I heard you thought Mom's things had been moved and that's why you didn't report her missing. Is that true?"

Sharon leaned toward May, her words slightly slurred. "I know for a *fact* someone had been in our room and moved D.'s things after she disappeared. Even smelled her perfume, like she'd just been there. At the time, I thought it was just her, of course, but, well . . . it was creepy."

"Did anyone have a key?"

"Not that I know of. Only D. and me, and they were those keys that couldn't be copied. If you lost it, you had to get permission for another one." Sharon poured more wine, the bottle now empty.

"Maybe someone stole Mom's key?" May took the empty bottle before Sharon dropped it.

"It's possible." Sharon picked something from her tongue. "Imagine, though, being in that room all alone and knowing someone might grab me too. I had my older brother, Tony, come and stay with me for a couple of days after she went missing, which made it better. Although, it still scared me, so I had to get them to change the locks—which they did after two months. Can you believe it took so long?"

May shrugged. "Mom was back by then, though?"

"Yes, she'd been found, but she didn't come back to school. She moved to your folks' place, I think. I never saw your mom again, if you can believe it. Not that I cared by then—I had my own shit to deal with."

"What do you mean?" May pulled her knees to her chest in the chair.

"My brother, Tony, died a few weeks after your mom was found." Sharon stared into her wineglass.

"I'm so sorry."

"It was a long time ago . . . I mean, I loved him, but to be honest, he was a bit of a shit." Sharon forced a smile.

May nodded. "My mom's sister, Sue, is a bit of a shit too."

Sharon swirled the wine in her glass. "My brother changed as he got older. Like my dad when he got on the drink, Tony had a bit of a mean streak—although never with me. Then he thought he was 'all that,' making a bunch of coin from selling stolen cars. He would stay with me when he needed the heat off him. Not that he didn't know how to get around undetected. He acted dim witted but was far from it."

May found she was warming to Sharon. "What happened to him?"

"Not sure. I got a call from a cop in the city one day saying Tony was dead, and that was that. He wanted to know what to do with my brother's body." Sharon shook her head. "He's in the living room in an empty whiskey bottle. Reckon he would've liked that."

"Um . . ." May didn't want to ask.

"His ashes. His ashes are in the whiskey bottle." Sharon gave her a look like that was an obvious place to store her dead brother. "I didn't know what to do with his damn body or how to get him here. So I got him cremated so they could pop him in the mail. Easy, cheaper too."

May didn't know where to look. That wine near her head was suddenly very appealing.

Sharon didn't stop. "Who knows what happened. The cop told me he was found lying in his own blood and vomit. Probably drunk or rubbed someone up the wrong way. He wasn't good at making friends."

I know that feeling.

Sharon finished her wine and glanced at May's glass. "Not drinking tonight?"

"Help yourself." May pushed her glass toward Sharon.

"That'll change when you're older. Trust me. Soon drinking will be the only thing getting you through the day."

May hoped not.

"You reckon I'm in a sad state, huh? D. used to give me the same look sometimes." Sharon poured May's wine into her own glass, spilling some on the cement. It looked like a bloodstain.

May focused back on Sharon. "I don't think you're in a sad state. Having a bookstore is cool."

Sharon grinned, her teeth a pale shade of red. "It is kind of cool, isn't it?"

"So, you've been married two times? Never changed your last name?"

Sharon chuckled, but there was only sadness in her eyes. "The only thing I'll say about that is marry a man for his money. Being a wife is a full-time job—you may as well get something out of it. And *always* keep your name."

Sharon was definitely growing on May.

"Oh well, water under the bridge now, as they say." Sharon sighed. "Not all of us are as lucky as your mom to find a nice guy and have beautiful girls."

May didn't want to talk about that. "Hey, can you tell me about this mystery guy Mom was supposedly seeing? The one you mentioned to the police."

"I was wondering if you were going to ask me about that." Sharon sat up and put a cushion behind her back, lowering her voice. "D. was definitely hiding something. It always seemed weird that your mom had this secret, goes missing, and then turns up weeks later with no memory of anything. The whole thing is just bizarre, you know?"

Bizarre was one word for it. "Do you have any idea who Mom was seeing?"

Sharon thought about it. "I only had suspicions."

"Tell me."

"I reckon she was seeing someone important, like a professor or something. Someone she shouldn't. It had that feeling about it. She was so secretive about everything. Always whispering on the phone. He'd hang up when it was me who answered."

"Did you ever talk to Brad about it?"

"Only after she was found. We weren't exactly close. I guess the police told him about my suspicions, and he confronted me. He made out like I was making it up," Sharon snarled. "Of course, he did. No guy likes to think their girl is cheating on them, you know? Hey, I'm sorry to hear about D. Never easy losing your mom."

Sharon's face softened. Or maybe it was the twinkling lights.

"Yeah, thanks. It wasn't easy."

"Heard she slipped at the pool. Cracked her skull open." Sharon slapped her neck. "Damn mosquitos."

Nope, May wasn't doing this. "I should go."

"Sorry. Didn't mean to make you feel like shit. Just bringing it up because I never heard if they thought her death was suspicious or not."

"Why . . ." May sucked in a breath. "Why would it be suspicious?"

Sharon shrugged. "Makes you wonder if someone from D.'s past pushed her to her grave, that's all."

DIANA

That little shit was at the pool again.

Of course she was. June always came here when she ran away. The pool was where adults felt sorry for a five-year-old with an oversize backpack and fake tears. Where ice creams were handed out while I was being called to come and collect her.

June. The bane of my existence.

May squeezed my hand and stared up at me with those big brown eyes of hers. Ever reliable May. I doubt she'd ever run away.

"Hey, Diana." One of the young lifeguards greeted me at the pool gate. "Third time this month. She must really hate living with you."

Gee, thanks for the reminder. I should laugh. Pretend I didn't care. But I did care. I cared that my daughter seemingly wanted nothing to do with me. Look at her. Sitting on that sun chair like she's on a tropical vacation.

"Sorry if she's been a bother. I promise it won't happen again." Yeah, right.

I kept a hold of May's hand as we were let into the outdoor pool. I'd only been here a few hours before for my morning swim. That's why June came here. I'd told her once it was my happy place. So now she runs away here when she's upset, thinking it will make her happy too.

Fuckity fuck.

Being a mother was just a long line of putting out spot fires you didn't light.

"Hey, June. You ready to go home?"

She squinted up at me, those blue eyes piercing into my soul as usual. "No, Mama. I live here now."

"We don't live here, silly. We live at our house." May laughed.

June didn't know if she should laugh too. I could see it on her cute little face; she's confused. Her sister did that to her when they didn't agree.

"I don't like it there," June finally got out.

Like I didn't know that already.

I pulled a sun chair closer to the one June was propped up on and swung May onto my lap as I sat down. I needed to get to the heart of why this kid kept running away. "Why don't you like it at home, baby?"

June pouted her lips, considered it. "You think I'm yucky."

May gulped down a big breath, and I'm pretty sure I did too. "Baby girl, why would you think that?"

Damn. Had I been putting out some of my own shit on my daughter that I hadn't even been aware of? I always was a bad liar.

June tucked her legs under her and pulled her summer dress over her knees. Her lips trembling. "You always give May breakfast first. That's how come I know you don't like me."

Big fat tears fell down her face, and her cheeks were now a blotchy pink. I should've brought her hat and sunscreen. Bad mother.

"Oh, honey. I serve May first because she's always at the table before you. If you get to the table on time tomorrow, then I promise you can have breakfast on your plate first. We can even have smiley face pancakes if you like."

June's tears were gone in an instant. "Truth, Mama?"

"Truth, baby girl."

I adjusted May on my lap. She's quiet, as usual. Just laser focused on her sister. I would love to get in her head. She's a mystery to me. Not like June, who wore her heart and every other emotion like a T-shirt.

"Now, we need to talk about you running away every time you're upset."

Great. June's lips were trembling again.

Say the right thing here, Diana. For once. "It's okay to be upset, but it's not okay to run away from home. Do you know why?"

June blinked her tear-filled eyes at me.

May answered instead. "There are monsters, and they can eat you."

June's eyes went so wide I thought they were about to fall out of her head. "Truth, Mama?"

I was about to say no, but May's tiny hand squeezed my arm. I understood. "Yes, it is true. If you leave the house by yourself, the monsters will know. And do you know what they love most of all?"

Now both girls looked at me, wide eyed.

"Little girls all alone by the swimming pool."

June cried all over again, and May was a little unsure now, too, biting her bottom lip.

Nailed it, Diana. Nailed it.

I shouldn't make my kids cry, but fuck's sake, I've had enough of this running-away nonsense. One day June might walk out the door and never come back.

Know anything about that, Diana?

Shut the fuck up.

I pulled them both into me. Their apple shampoo going up my nose and filling me with a dread I hadn't felt in a while. The fear of something bad happening to them.

Focus. Be present. Be a good mom. You've got this.

"It's okay. Mama will have a talk with the monster and tell him that when you are with me, he is not allowed to eat you. I see him sometimes when I'm swimming in the morning, and he won't mess with me if I have a quick little chat."

Who knows if June was buying my bullshit. Next week she'd probably have a new phase she'd be going through anyway. Jumping out of trees or some nonsense.

"How about I get us all an ice cream and we can eat it on the way home."

Both the girls clapped. May wiggled in my lap and I sat her next to her sister. The sun glowed through June's flyaway blonde hair, currently in pigtails. May's darker hair hung thick and straight to her shoulders, tucked behind her ears. They both blinked up at me. Reminding me of when they were just babies.

I still had no idea what I was doing.

They were growing up so fast. I wished I could stop it. Stop time so I never had to tell them where they came from. Why they were born. How I was doing such a bad job of being their mother.

Fuckity fuck.

"I want chocolate."

"I want chocolate too."

I stood. My legs a little shaky. "Sounds like it's chocolate for everyone."

They clapped again.

Soon we'd all forget June's latest running-away episode. Thanks to May. How did she know how to do that? Scare her sister with the monster story so June wouldn't leave the house alone again. It's like the twins had special powers I didn't understand.

They'd need it. For what was coming. For when the monster really did come.

I grabbed my purse, leaving the girls behind me. I was in the wrong shoes for the pool and trod carefully. It's easy to slip over here. I'd done it before.

One day someone could crack their head open.

Chapter
Twenty-One

May and Sam sat at a quiet corner table, eating their meals.

The lights were dimmed in the restaurant, where the decor was stereotypically Italian. Red-and-white striped tablecloths. Breadsticks instead of flowers. Empty Chianti bottles used as candleholders with lavalike wax down the side.

It was their first chance to connect since May had been to Sharon's and the detective had finished his shift earlier that morning. It was a night off for him, and they'd decided to go out for dinner.

May returned to their previous conversation, still not able to get what Sharon had brought up out of her mind since the previous night. "So, do you think Mom's death may not have been an accident?" She watched Sam carefully.

"I'm not sure where she gets off putting these things into your mind." Sam swigged his beer, his mood sour. "Same with the necklace and implying I know something. Like I said, she loves drama."

May caught the detective looking at her barely eaten bowl of pasta. "But what if she's right and we missed it? That someone has been watching us all these years and did something to Mom. That June was a sitting duck the second she went out alone."

Sam wiped his plate with his garlic bread. "I'll do some digging. See if I can get the coroner's report."

"You'd do that?" May pushed her plate away; eating was impossible with the way her stomach churned.

"Of course I'd do that. I said I'd help you, and I will. We made a deal, remember?" His eyes smiled even if his mouth didn't.

"I'm glad I came here. I'm not sure how June did all that digging by herself." May glanced at his beer.

"Want something? I'm going to get another one." Sam was already waving the waiter over.

The young male waiter brought over the detective's beer and placed it in front of him. Sam nodded at May.

"I'll just have a black coffee."

"Sure thing." Picking up the detective's empty plate, the waiter left.

"You going to eat that?" The detective pointed to May's full plate of pasta. "I hate watching you waste good food."

"No, I'm done."

Sam sprinkled parmesan on top of the lukewarm pasta, twirled a big forkful, and then let the fork hang in the air as he took a swig of his beer first. "Feels good to have a couple of these tonight. Not on call—which doesn't happen very often."

"Do you like being a detective?" May leaned back in the small booth.

"I do. I've never wanted to be anything else."

"Why's that?"

"Had a family tragedy when I was a boy. My little brother died."

"He drowned," May said to herself.

"That's right. Phillip, or Phil, was what we called him. Thing is, he could swim like a fish, that kid." Sam picked at the label on his beer bottle. "They *say* he drowned, but I don't believe that for a minute. He had swum in that dam since he had diapers on. He knew it better than all of us. I reckon it was another kid in town. Alex. He didn't much like me because I snitched on him for taking another kid's bike."

"He killed your brother because you snitched?" May's mouth fell open.

"I could never prove it, but I reckon that's what happened. I could see it in his eyes. Alex had eyes like the devil. Nothing in them but rage." Sam dropped his fork back on his plate. "No one would believe a kid could do such a thing, but kids can be as cruel as adults. Problem was there wasn't any evidence, just my gut and a few things Alex said around town. I didn't know much about evidence back then. I was only twelve. But over those coming years, it was all I could think about. Find the evidence and put that fucker in jail—sorry for my language, May."

"Don't be sorry. I would've wanted to get the fucker too." May smiled. "So did they ever catch him?"

"No. I blamed myself. I should've been with Phil instead of hanging out with my mates. I knew Alex had it in for me, but I never imagined he could do something like that. Maybe I got it wrong, but I don't think so." The detective shifted in his seat. "I'd still like to nail the bastard."

"I'm sorry, Sam." May reached across but didn't touch the detective's hand.

"Me too. Would love to still have had my brother around."

May pulled her hand back. "Yeah, I know what you mean."

Sam looked around for May's coffee. The silence that had fallen on the table suddenly awkward.

"Gabriele," Sam called out to an old man behind the bar. "Sorry to bother you, but one of our drinks seems to have gone missing." The restaurant wasn't exactly busy.

The short man with a head of white hair came over. He acknowledged Sam, his Italian accent thick. "Ciao, Detective, good to see you again."

"How's business?"

"Can't complain. My wife does enough of that for both of us."

Sam said to May, "This is Gabriele. He's the owner."

Gabriele sighted the waiter and gave him a signal that he'd forgotten the drink.

"Sorry about him. He's new. Those university kids may be smart with big words but not so much with waiting tables. My daughter normally works nights, but she's under the weather." He flipped his dish towel from one shoulder to the other.

"How is Lorena?" Sam asked.

"She's running the restaurant now. I only come in if she's sick or I'm dragged here. Prefer my cards and wine."

The coffee was brought, and Gabriele placed it on the table himself, shooing the waiter away.

"I will leave you to it, my friends. The drinks are on me."

"Thanks, Gabriele. No need, but I know better than to argue with you." Sam held his beer up as a cheers.

"Gabriele, before you go," May said. "I was just wondering how long you've had this restaurant for?"

"It has been in my family for over thirty years now. Why do you ask, bella?"

"Do you know about Diana Wells? The girl who went missing about twenty years ago?"

Gabriele furrowed his heavy brows, looking to Sam for clarity.

"It's okay. I'm sure this is going somewhere," Sam said.

"Well, yes, everyone from that time remembers Diana Wells. Biggest news we had around this town. She used to come in here with that boyfriend of hers. Sweet girl. Beautiful. Shame my daughter isn't here—she would know more than me."

"Do you think your daughter would want to talk to me?" May asked.

Gabriele looked to the detective. "Sam, I think you might have to explain what's going on here."

"Diana Wells is her mother. This is May."

Gabriele put his aged hand to his mouth. "Forgive me. Of course you can talk to Lorena. I'll give her a call."

Sam nodded his thanks.

May did, too, as Gabriele walked away. A smile lit up her face. "Is that what you call a breakthrough or a new lead, Detective?"

Sam laughed. "Neither. I've already spoken to Lorena. But, hey, if you want to talk to her again, be my guest."

Chapter Twenty-Two

Lorena opened the door in her pajamas, blowing her nose loudly.

"Allo. Oh my god, I'm so stuffy!"

May smiled politely, trying not to stare at Lorena's short hair, which had become matted on top of her head like a bird's nest. They'd arranged to meet after Gabriele had given his daughter a call the night before.

"Come in."

May stepped inside and took in Lorena's apartment, which wasn't far from the police station. The open studio space had a loft bed above the living room. The walls were exposed brick, and all the wooden flooring gleamed from the sun beating through the large windows. May wished she lived in something half as beautiful and not the tiny room she rented.

"It's nice, isn't it?" Lorena said. "Had it renovated a year ago. None of the other apartments up here are anything like this. You're thinking it could be straight from a magazine, right? That's because it is."

Lorena directed May to a series of framed photos from a magazine that did, in fact, appear exactly like the apartment they were now standing in.

"This one is in New York. See, even the stairs going up to the loft have the same wiring across the frame. Makes the space more open like that." Lorena talked rapidly in her stuffy voice.

She sure is comfortable with strangers.

"It's amazing, Lorena. Um, I brought you soup. Where did you want it?" May held up the bag of food.

"Oh, look at me chattering away and not offering you anything. Here, give me that. I'll open it in the kitchen. Very kind of you. How did you know I was sick?"

"Your father mentioned it when we were at the restaurant."

Lorena nodded, taking the heavy-duty brown paper bag and placing it on her black granite kitchen counter. She grabbed two bowls and spoons.

Lorena opened the bag. "Which one is yours?"

"I didn't know what you liked or if you were vegetarian or not. One is chicken noodle, and the other is pumpkin."

Lorena's red swollen nose creased. "Vegetarian? My family would kill me if I was vegetarian."

"I guess the chicken noodle is yours."

The pumpkin soup wafted under May's nose, making her tummy rumble. They both took their soup over to the living room. Lorena cleared dirty tissues from the couch and coffee table before she placed her bowl and bread roll down.

"I'm sorry. I should've cleaned before you got here. I know I said to come over now, but I took that as 'Italian now'—which usually means an hour or so later."

"I can sit over here." May moved a pile of magazines from the armchair, which matched the grey woolen couch.

"Best not to be too close to me anyway." Lorena fell onto the couch and positioned her bowl on her knees. "So tell me about yourself, May. You living here now? What do you do? Dad said your mom is Diana Wells. She was pretty famous around here back in the day. And you've been hanging with Sam. He's a looker, isn't he? Probably a bit old for you, but still."

"Wow, you said more just then than I have all year." May smiled as she sipped the hot soup from her spoon.

"Ha! Yes. I do that. Starved for company, my mom says. That's what living alone does to you. I pounce on guests." Lorena chuckled. "So, what's the deal? With your mom? Did they find out who took her?"

May didn't mind the directness. She'd be here all day, otherwise. "No, that mystery never got solved."

"I don't want you to think I'm a bitch or anything, but I reckon your mom made it up. She always gave the impression she was high maintenance and looking for attention."

May's soup didn't go down quite as easily. "Why do you say that?"

Lorena put her bowl down and nibbled on her bread roll. "I served your mom in our restaurant quite a lot. She liked our food, or maybe her boyfriend did. They came in a bit. I should've been going to university, too, like your mom, but Dad insisted I take over the restaurant. So I did a business course online while I worked. Now I manage it. I'm doing okay, I guess."

May's head spun at trying to keep up with Lorena.

"Your mom was pretty. Like really pretty. Bet she's still pretty, huh? Not like me. Look at all the grey hair coming through my roots. Have to dye it every few weeks." She pulled her hair apart as if to prove it.

May didn't see any grey hairs and suddenly needed a nap. "My mom is still beautiful, yes."

"I bet she has a wonderful life. I never saw her after she disappeared. Is she happy?"

May had no hesitation in saying in the present tense, "Yes, she is very happy."

"I'm glad." Lorena's eyes glazed over as she stared at her uneaten soup.

"You okay?"

Lorena snapped her eyes to May's.

"Of course. Just sick of being sick."

May's phone vibrated in her back pocket. It was probably her dad. She knew she owed him a call. "Sorry, I won't keep you long. Gabriele said you might have something to share about my mom."

"Why don't you just ask *her*?"

May rearranged a cushion behind her back. "It's for an assignment for school, just have to get some fresh angles."

"Oh, fun. But first, I want to get this straight." Lorena plucked out a tissue and wiped her nose. "I didn't know your mom—she wasn't like a friend or anything. She just came into the restaurant sometimes, usually with Brad, um, her boyfriend. Or sometimes alone, studying. She was friendly enough, and I remembered her because she was so pretty. Okay, I was jealous of her. She looked like a movie star for Christ's sake." Lorena bit her lip. "Can I be honest with you, May?"

"Sure." May put her half-empty bowl on the table. Ready for anything.

"I had a little fling with your mom's boyfriend, with Brad. Now, before you ask, it was after she left town."

May had expected something worse. "Um, okay. So you dated Brad."

"Only for a couple of weeks. He knew I liked him—I wasn't exactly subtle about it when they came in. He missed her. Diana. Maybe he was a little in shock too. It all seemed so suspicious to me."

"What seemed suspicious?"

"Something felt off. I don't know. I can't explain it."

"With what?"

"With Brad. With Diana's disappearance. It was just a hunch. Nothing I can explain. Brad was charming, at first, but most of the time he was pining for Diana. Wasn't exactly flattering to a girl. My family wasn't too happy either—he wasn't Italian." Lorena blew her nose.

"So what happened? Why did you break up?"

"He met someone else. It was over before it began. Not that he was anything special, but there was something cool about going out with Diana Wells's boyfriend."

May waited for Lorena to catch her eye. "Did he hurt you?"

Lorena recoiled into the couch. "What? Did Brad hurt me? Why would you say that? Of course, he didn't hurt me. Well, not physically.

Sure, I was a little hurt when he broke up with me. Then he brought a new girl into the restaurant and expected me to serve them like he hadn't fucked me only a few nights before."

May didn't know how to respond.

Lorena's eyes narrowed. "You think Brad took her, don't you? Is that it? I can say for a fact he didn't. A girl would know these things."

May wasn't sure how true that was.

"You want some tea? I'm going to make tea."

"No, I'm okay."

Lorena pulled up her striped pajama bottoms as she walked into the kitchen. "Last time I ever saw Brad he was with his brother. Bit of a looker, like Brad, from what I could tell."

"Brad has a brother?" May turned to face the kitchen.

"Yes, although it wasn't Brad who told me. I asked Brad straight out if he had siblings, and he said no." Lorena filled up the kettle.

"That's weird." May leaned on her hand.

"I know, right? I happened to catch them one day behind the bar and grill, which shares the same alley space as my restaurant. We use the same trash bins most of the time. Annoying because they have more trash than us, but we've learned to live with them."

"So what happened with Brad and his brother?"

Lorena yelled over the boiling kettle. "Well, I was hiding behind some crates near the trash one night—smoking, which my dad hated—don't anymore, thank god. These crates never got moved, and I set up a good hidey-hole where I could check who was coming but they couldn't see me. If Dad smelled cigarette in the kitchen, I would blame the chef, who was a renowned chain smoker and always stank to high heaven. He's gone now."

May prompted. "So, you were having a smoke . . ."

"Yes. I was having a smoke, and all of a sudden Brad and some guy came out of the back of the bar. Which was weird because it's for staff only. Who knows why they were coming out there."

"Maybe the other guy worked at the bar?"

"Okay, smarty pants, you don't think I wouldn't know if he did? I know everyone who works at that bar, and I had never seen this guy before."

"Just a suggestion."

Lorena softened. "This guy definitely didn't work there. They both looked a little heated up. I put my cigarette out so they couldn't see me. It was pretty dark back there. Brad was asking what he was doing in town. The other guy said he needed money and Brad owed him. Brad said something about already paying him back and that he owed this guy nothing. Then this guy said clear as day, 'I'm your brother—you will always owe me.' The whole thing seemed suspicious."

"Maybe he meant *brother* in a different sense. Like bros? Friends?"

"Well, they sure looked alike if they weren't brothers."

"How could you see them if it was so dark?"

Lorena scratched the back of her head where her hair was sticking up. "There were lights when they exited the bar. I saw enough to know he looked just like the guy who had recently dumped me."

"Did you tell the police?"

Lorena shook her head. "Tell the cops what? That Brad has a brother, and he owes him money? Why?"

May's face went slack. "Because it may have been connected to my mom's case."

Lorena paused. "Guess that could be true, but by then your mom wasn't even on my radar. I was angry Brad broke up with me." Lorena poured the hot water over a tea bag.

She casually added, "Besides, I never believed Diana. I told you that."

"You seem so sure my mom lied about her disappearance." May itched to tell Lorena about her and June.

"I just know."

May picked up her bowl and brought it to the kitchen. "So, did you get his name? Brad's brother?"

"Not sure." Lorena thought about it. "They left the alleyway after that, and I never saw Brad or that guy again."

May asked, "Did you ever talk to a blonde girl about a year ago? Eighteen. Her name's June."

Lorena snapped her fingers. "Wes! The brother's name is Wes."

~~Days Mom's been dead: Um . . . why is this still a thing?~~

Friday, September 2 (better)

Hi Mom,

If you are reading this, I am dead. Ha ha.

Just kidding! Don't get all weird. Jeez.

Okay, so I just did a drive-by of the house at the end of Old Cemetery Road!!

And when I say "drive-by," I mean I drove up super slowly on the one-way dirt road that my car hated because of all the potholes and rocks, landed smack in front of said creepy house, had nowhere to go so had to do a fifty-million-point turn, and then hauled ass out of there.

The house was EXACTLY how you described in your ghost story. Wooden with flaky paint. A big barn out back (and no, I DIDN'T go and look if there were shovels inside!).

So this is when my life starts turning into a horror movie. Pay attention, Mom. No covering your eyes and being a chicken, okay?

Get this . . . I'm doing my fifty-million-point turn to get out of there, knowing I was trapped on this horrible one-way road, and then . . . (scary music) someone came out of the bogeyman house!

I know, right?! I almost DIED, I was soooo scared. He came out on his falling down porch (no swing) and just stared at me. He got a good look at me too. Shit, shit, shit.

What have I done?

BUT, you know what? I got a good look at him too! I'm not going to lie, he looks a LOT like Brad. Which might make him Wes, his brother. I read something about him in the police file.

Is this who took you, Mom?

Then how is Brad our dad? I'm so confused and a little bit (lot) scared. I'm just at a rest stop writing this while it's fresh (I also needed to pee!), and then I'm going to go back to Harold. I should be back before anyone noticed I left this morning.

My plan is to tell Dad and May (finally!). I'm going to tell them everything. Yep, EVERYTHING! Then I'm going to call that detective guy and see if he can check this place out. I mean, did he even look here the first time? Hard yikes!

Anyway, next letter will be how they bust this lowlife and put him in jail for good.

I don't care if he's our father or not. Or if Brad is our father. Or who our real father is. Jeez, it's all very dramatic isn't it?!

Is my dad a killer? GASP! A kidnapper? GASP! A leader of the Galactic Empire? DOUBLE GASP! Luke . . . I am your daddy (heavy breathing). Use the Force, Luke.

Ha ha. Sorry, Mom. Got distracted.

Well, now it's time to get my life together and go to the city with May. Finally start our lives like we should've already.

Even if she doesn't want me there. I can always change her mind. LOL.

You wait! I'm going to be famous, Mom. You'll be so proud of me!

Anyway, better go. Someone just pulled up next to me, and I want to get home before it gets dark.

Love ya, Mom!

Always, June x

Chapter Twenty-Three

May called Sam as soon as she escaped Lorena's house, but the detective already knew about Brad's brother.

"His name's Wes. The only reason we flagged him is he had priors for assault and selling drugs. He was in police custody when your mom went missing, May. A bar brawl. I thought I told you this?"

"No, you didn't, and I didn't see anything in the police files. Are you sure his story checks out?"

"Trust me, he was accounted for." The detective's words came out rushed, like he was busy. Understandable. He was back at the station today.

She talked quickly, wanting to make something stick. Anything. So she knew where to look for June next. "Maybe Brad had an accomplice?"

"No, it wasn't Brad either. We went over this."

"But he could've taken Mom with him, organized it with his brother or something?"

"Brad and his brother haven't lived together since they were kids. They're on opposite sides of the state. We checked all of this, May." He sighed. "Hey, I have to go."

May's initial excitement at another potential suspect had well and truly gone. "Of course. I was just sure I had something."

"Be right there," he whispered to someone. "Sorry, I really have to go. I'll call you when I'm done."

"Wait!"

"What is it? You okay?" He didn't sound annoyed, just concerned.

May rushed to get her next thought out. "Do you know if June ever went there? To Wes's house?"

The detective told someone to hang on. "I'm not sure. I didn't handle your sister's disappearance."

The town square of Bretford was now a bunch of colored shapes in front of May's eyes. "Can you check?"

"I'll make some calls."

"Can I come by the station? Look at the files some more?" She knew she sounded desperate.

"Of course. Just wait in the reception area for me."

They hung up. The soup curdled in her stomach at the thought of June knocking on the wrong door.

June, where are you?

May could see the police station from where she stood, so she took her time getting there. Knowing Sam was busy right now. A heaviness sat deep in her gut as she ambled through the center of town, marked by walking paths and green grass.

She couldn't shake the feeling she was getting everything wrong. That she'd followed the clues to the wrong place. That she'd missed a clue back at home. Maybe she should go back to Harold? Start again. Ransack the house if she had to.

Any plans for heading back to the city were long gone. She'd lose her job. That was okay. She hated it anyway. If she stopped paying rent on the small room she stayed in, then she'd lose that too.

None of it mattered now. All she cared about was finding June. Now that she knew her twin was out there and waiting for May to find her, she couldn't stop.

May entered the air-conditioned reception area of the police station and sat in the same waiting room she had met the detective in only three days before. It may as well have been months. This was the first time she'd come in here during the day, though.

A different police officer manned the front desk. He smiled at May when he caught her looking at him. The smile she responded with came easily; she was getting better at seeming like a "normal" person.

The door behind her opened, and Sam came out holding two mugs of coffee.

"Perfect timing, May. Let's sit outside and enjoy these, courtesy of the station."

May took her coffee and followed the detective out to the front of the brick building, where they sat on a metal bench. Trees shaded them from the harshness of the midday sun. A small breeze sent a cluster of dirt into a spin. May sighed heavily.

"Penny for your thoughts?" Sam asked.

"Ha! You sound just like Sharon. She said the same thing to me the first time we met."

"That's someone I never thought I'd be compared to," Sam grumbled. "How about just telling me what's on your mind then?"

May stared into her coffee cup. How to explain everything she was thinking? "You know, the world can be so beautiful sometimes. Yet most of the time, all I see is the darkness. Like I'm in a room that has no way out. Have you ever felt like that?"

Sam sighed. "You're too hard on yourself, May. The last year—the last few years—have been rough on you. You're allowed to feel like this . . . and don't forget Diana and June would've wanted you to be happy."

May stepped her boot down into the swirling dirt. "Maybe. I just feel like I'm a waste of space. Like I don't mean much anymore without June."

"Is that why you seem to struggle with eating anything?"

"In a way." It surprised her that a lie hadn't come out of her mouth. That she was about to tell the truth. "Maybe I've always had a thing with food. I was the overweight twin, and June was the skinny one.

So cliché, isn't it? While she hung out with her friends, I'd be at home bingeing on chocolate or chips hidden in my room."

His voice low, Sam said, "You must've had a reason to be doing that."

"I was never going to be as perfect as everyone thought June was, so why even try? When I felt as if I wasn't enough—which was all the time—I would turn to food. It made me feel good, even if it was just for a moment." May's eyes followed a mother and toddler walking hand in hand into the police station.

Sam placed his mug beside him on the bench. "So why the shift?"

"Something June said before she disappeared, when we were fighting. She could be nasty sometimes."

"And what was that?"

"That I disgusted her, and she couldn't stand looking at me." May flicked out a bug that had fallen in her coffee. "And she only wanted to be around me again when I stopped taking up so much space."

Sam groaned. "Siblings can be cruel. I don't want to even think about the things I said to my sister growing up. You know June didn't mean it like that, don't you?"

May nodded. "I mean, I wasn't exactly an angel myself. At the time, her words didn't really have much of an impact and I certainly didn't take them literally. The thing that stung was that June said she didn't want to be around me."

"So, you thought if you took up less space, she would come back?"

"Must have, even if I wasn't really conscious of it. It's bad enough that June consumes me emotionally, but now I guess she consumes me physically as well. She always did have so much control over me."

"Well, we have to change that, or you won't be around if June does come back."

"I appreciate you saying June will come back." May regarded him. "Look, I know what I'm doing isn't healthy and I miss how I used to look, if I'm going to be honest. It's like I've lost control over everything, but this one thing feels in my control. I don't know if that makes sense."

"It does makes sense. You've been through a lot." He turned to her. "Should we go back inside? I set up an area for you in the conference room to look at the files. No one will bother you."

"Thanks. That dungeon of boxes is all kinds of creepy."

"Why do you think no one goes down there?" Sam laughed as he stood with his mug.

"I have a confession to make . . ." May took out the evidence list from her bag and handed it to him. "I was just borrowing this, I promise."

She knew she had to tell him, or Sharon would do it for her.

"Thanks for fessing up." The detective studied it. "It's been a while since I looked at this list. Brings back some memories."

He handed it to May. "Put it back where it belongs, hey? And if you want to remove anything else, just ask me first."

"Sorry." May blushed and folded the list, placing it into her back pocket.

The detective acknowledged a woman in a police uniform walking out of the station. "Better get back to it. Nice to be on day shifts again for a while."

May put her bag over her shoulder. She emptied her unfinished coffee near a tree and followed him through the doors.

He stopped.

She slammed into his back. "What the—"

He spun back around. "Give me a look at that list again."

May's heart skipped as she put her bag and mug onto the chairs in the reception area and pulled the list back out. Had she done something wrong?

Sam grabbed it from her, unfolding it quickly. His eyes scanned the page. "There. Do you see that?"

He pointed to the final entry. May leaned in, her heart now nearly bursting out of her chest.

There was no date for when the item had been checked in, and the writing was tiny and hard to read: *Key to locker at bus station.*

She frowned. "I don't get it. What am I looking at?"

"That final entry. It's new"—Sam's eyes latched onto May's—"and I've never seen it before."

They both said at once:

"June."

Chapter Twenty-Four

The bus station was quiet. A midafternoon lull.

Not that May's mind was quiet. There had been constant chatter ever since she had found the small key loose in her mother's archive box. It had been easy to miss at the bottom of all the files.

May held the key in her fingers now. It had a red plastic cap cover with the number *517* on it. The lockers were coin operated, so June must have bought a locker and kept the key.

"Should I open it?" May whispered. "What if I don't like what's inside." She didn't know who she was talking to. No one was with her. Not even Sam, who was back at work.

She'd promised she would report back to him as soon as she had June's next clue. Or call him *immediately* if she thought anything was suspicious or warranted a forensic team.

There was that chatter again. What if you find something horrible? What if it's something you don't want to know? What if you're too late? You're too late, too late, too late. Shut up.

Her fingers trembled as she slotted the key into locker 517 and twisted it to the side. It clicked into place, and the medium-size door swung open easily.

May squinted. Only wanting to take in bits at a time. Just in case. Nothing wild. Just a plain shoebox. Nothing written or marked on the outside.

May lifted it out and examined the inside of the locker for anything else. Nope. Just the shoebox. Carrying it like it was a fragile artifact, May moved over to the nearby bench.

She was both desperate to open it and afraid of what she would find all at the same time. She was tempted to just put it straight back in the locker but knew it would haunt her dreams—like that beating heart from a creepy story she once read.

She had to open it. She owed it to June.

To her mother.

Not now. May rubbed the bridge of her nose, said a silent prayer, and lifted the lid.

Sitting on top was an envelope with her name on it. The writing her mother's. *Weird.* Why was there something from her mother? Tears pricked her eyes, but she willed them away, picking up the letter and putting it aside. Underneath, the box was filled with newspaper clippings and photos.

The photos were of her mother. Her younger mother. They had faded in color and curled up at the edges.

May picked through the images.

In one photo, Diana stood in front of a white Volvo with her hands stretched to the sky. May flipped the photo over, and written on the back was: *Road trip to University.* May didn't recognize the car.

The next photo was of a group of girls, dressed up and obviously going out somewhere. They stood in a dorm hallway, varying their heights so they were all visible. Diana squatted in the middle.

She stroked her mom's young, fresh face and long dark-brown hair. May scanned the photo and almost missed Sharon, who looked so different from when she had just seen her. In the picture, Sharon smiled brightly, with a blunt fringe and her hair twisted up with tons of bobby pins. No indication that many years later, her face would be a map of lines from a life that had not been kind.

May turned the photo over and her mom had written: *First party on campus!*

May went to the next photo, one of Diana with Brad. May recognized him immediately—his bright-blue eyes a dead giveaway from the photos she'd found online. They were at a park, with Brad sitting on top of a picnic table and her mom on the bench seat below. Brad had his arms wrapped around her neck, and she had her hand clasped around his wrist. They both showed a lot of teeth as they smiled.

What had happened before and after this photo? Had they been fighting? Had Brad told Mom he loved her? Photos were so deceptive, a snapshot in time. A forever fragment of supposed happiness.

Diana had written: *Day out with Brad.*

May shuffled through the rest of the photos. Most were of her mom and Brad. There was only one more of Sharon, sitting on her dorm bed with an oversize guy who looked out of place. Nothing on the back to say who the guy was. Probably her dead brother.

Then another one after it of her mom on her dorm bed alone, her hand held up to the camera like she wasn't happy with having her photo taken. Nothing was written on the back of that photo either.

An announcement rang out through the bus station. May's heart skipped a beat at the loud male voice barking out that there had been a delay on one of the buses.

She suddenly felt exposed. Like someone was watching her. *Bullshit.* Chatter, chatter, chatter was back. *Shut up.*

May shook her head and took a deep breath. *Focus.* She went back to looking at the photos. There were about forty in all. May couldn't understand why they had been hidden in this box, as none seemed like they needed to be kept a secret.

She stopped at a photo containing the mysterious necklace. Her mom sat with her hands under her chin and her fingers fanned over her cheeks. The delicate horseshoe necklace that her mom had lied about hung from her neck.

Diana looked straight down the lens of the camera, and she had a smile May hadn't seen on her mom before. Part cheeky and part seductive. It troubled May for some reason.

Who took this photo, Mom?

May shuffled through the rest of the box and opened up the articles written on her mother's disappearance. Some while she had been missing and most after she had been found.

May skimmed them for any new clues, and the name that continued to stick out was *Detective Davis.* He had taken over as the lead investigator, one of his first cases since starting at the police station only the year before. Reading his name filled May with pride. She knew this man now. He wasn't just a name on a page anymore.

None of the articles talked about Diana being pregnant or of the twins. If this had happened to her mom today, her secret wouldn't have stayed private for long. Social media would've changed that.

Her mom had been lucky.

Under all the newspaper articles, May found a dried purple flower but had no idea what its significance was. She'd been through the box, and now she had no choice but to open her mom's letter.

The speaker crackled loudly above her.

May shivered.

DIANA

Fuckity fuck.

I still had blood on my fingernails. Damn. How was that possible when I was sure I'd washed all of it off?

The pen trembled as I stared at it in my hand. I had to write this letter. It was time. No, it was long overdue. What happened just now at the movie theater . . . ugh. I couldn't even think about it without wanting to barf.

A quiet day with my girls for their fifteenth birthday. Yeah, sure. There had been nothing quiet about today.

I dropped the pen and rubbed the dried blood like I was Lady fucking Macbeth.

Out, damned spot. Way too polite.

Get the fuck off. Much better.

What on earth had happened back there? Driving thirty minutes to Kerrindale to see a movie. A nice, fun rom-com with my girls. First lunch. Then movie. Then ice cream or the bookstore. Or both. Drive home. Perfect day.

Perfect my ass.

First lunch. Tears, so many tears, as June didn't like how her burger was cooked. May sulking because she'd forgotten to bring . . . what? Something. Lunch = disaster.

Second the movie theater. May wanted to sit near the back. June wanted to sit in the middle. I just wanted to sit in a bucket of wine.

My girls. Fifteen and acting like two-year-olds. When did they turn into complete psychopaths who had a hundred emotions a minute?

Was I like this? Probably. Poor Mom.

I got them to compromise by suggesting we sit in between the back and halfway. Are we there yet?

Movie trailers started. Great. Two hours of quiet bliss watching someone else get their happily ever after.

Man started laughing loudly and talking at the screen. He's a big guy. Right in front of June. June told him to shut up. I told her to shut up. May shrank in her chair.

Where the hell was that bucket of wine?

Man kept going. Movie had started. This was going to be a problem. How much of a problem, I had no idea.

June had now gotten out of her seat. Tapped man on shoulder. I asked May to go and get an attendant—who would probably also be fifteen years old.

Wine, please. All the wine.

The man had turned around. His hand on the back of his chair. June yelled at him to be quiet. The other patrons yelled at June to be quiet.

It all happened so quickly.

I didn't see June get her sparkly metal nail file out of her purse.

I did see her stab the back of the man's hand with such force I heard the cracking of bone.

The attendant's timing impeccable as he shone his flashlight at us. At the blood. June's glitter nail file sticking out of the man's hand. It's all illuminated by the light.

Wonderful.

The man had gone white. Silent. Shocked. I looked over at my daughter who had sat back in her chair, watching the movie. Eating her fucking popcorn.

May was in the aisle, looked like she may vomit. The attendant did vomit.

Wonderful.

I grabbed the scarf from my neck. Wrapped the man's hand. Applied pressure. Told him I was sorry. Thought about how June would survive jail.

Turned out I didn't need to worry. June told the police the man had tried to hit her. Self-defense. The man wasn't pressing charges. I was so confused. Did I miss something? Did I miss the moment the man struck at my daughter? Maybe when I was telling May to get the attendant?

We're all home now. The girls in their rooms. Me in mine. Gary watching football. Knowing that all my nightmares had come true. That the bad blood I was so worried about would be running in her veins.

I needed to get this out. Give it to her soon. Warn her.

It's time.

Dearest May,

If you're reading this it's because I've told you my darkest secret or because I'm no longer with you—either way, I hope you know that I never meant to hurt you. Everything I've done is because of you and June. You both fill me with so much joy and were a gift I never knew I wanted, until you arrived.

From the moment you were both put in my arms, I knew my life had no meaning until that day. You are both my everything, and I love you more than any words I could write on this page.

I know you're wondering why this letter is only for you. I also trust you are reading it alone. If not, then please do so now. It is important.

I need to tell you a story. One you may already know.

I was nineteen and still so young and naive. I thought horrible things happened to people on the news or in books—I never imagined they would happen to me.

When I was at university, I was abducted. And, as you probably know, it was because of this that you girls came to be.

Firstly, I don't want you to think any differently of Gary—he will always be your father.

Secondly, the man who took me is dead. He can never hurt you or June, and you have no reason to go looking for him. As far as I'm concerned, his name died with him. I will never speak it, nor will I write it here.

Thirdly, and this is the most important part, his blood binds us in ways that I cannot change. For years, I worried that the blood of a monster would run stronger than mine.

Now I know this to be true. In one of you, anyway. You know what I'm talking about. You have seen glimpses. And today at the movie theater it slapped us in the face.

Or maybe I look for evil too much. This has become my burden. My curse.

I'm telling you this now because you have to watch your sister. You need to help her suppress any urge she has to be cruel like him.

That is all I ask. Watch and suppress. Only you can help her, May. Only you can calm her if his blood takes over. I've seen you do it before.

You're different. Trust me when I say that. I know it makes no sense, but you are.

Do not tell your sister about this letter. I know June, she will never forgive me for my words.

Please, May. For once, listen to your mother.

Take care of your dad for me. He is a good man. One I am lucky to call my husband. He does not need to know of this letter, or what I've told you.

I trust you, my darling daughter. All you need to do is watch and suppress.

I love you, May. Now and forever.

Always,

Mom xx

Chapter Twenty-Five

What the hell?

The letter didn't make any sense.

Why hadn't her mom told May who took her? And if he was dead, where was June?

Her mom had called him a monster.

Did she really think June was a monster too? Someone May had to "watch and suppress"? She had no idea what these glimpses of bad blood were that her mom was talking about. Sure, June had stabbed that guy in the movie theater, but he deserved it for trying to hit her. *Had* he attacked June? That day was such a blur.

It was like her mother had seen a completely different June to the one she'd known all her life. It made no sense; June was the "perfect" one. If anyone was cruel or had bad blood, it was May. Not her twin.

The bus station was filling up with people now, yet May couldn't move from the bench. Her body had seized up. Frozen in a state of shock. Her mind whirled with so many strands of information, secrets, lies, and questions that nausea had set in.

Where had June found the box of her mom's things? And why was the letter only addressed to May?

She grabbed her phone from her lap and dialed her father. He answered on the first ring.

"May, finally. I was getting worried."

"Sorry. Lots going on." She heard him typing. "Catch you at a bad time?"

"It's okay. I'm all yours now." The typing had stopped. "I heard you went to Bretford." There was a sadness in his voice.

"Yep." May closed her eyes. Rubbed them. She was definitely getting a headache. "I had to, D-Dad."

"And work?" Exhausted voice now.

"Work is giving me some time off. It's fine. I'm fine. I'm safe, I promise." Was she safe? "Look, I had to ask you something. Did you ever see a shoebox that Mom kept filled with old photos and articles from when she went missing?" No way was she mentioning the letter.

"Um . . . that's not ringing a bell." Gary cleared his throat. "Why? What's going on up there?"

Should she tell him about June's clues? No way.

"Nothing. I'm just trying to piece together some things. I thought I remembered Mom having a shoebox of old stuff. Guess I was wrong."

"If you want me to look around, I'm happy to do so. Whatever you need to help with all of this, I'm here for you."

"Thanks, Dad." Was it always going to feel weird to call him that now?

"May . . . I . . . I don't like how we left things. That you are dealing with this all by yourself. Why don't you come back here to Harold? I was thinking of going to see your grandparents at the farm over the weekend. Why don't you come with me?"

May hadn't thought about her other grandparents in all this. "Do they know? About Mom?"

He sighed. "Some. Not everything." The loudspeaker announced a bus was about to leave. "Where are you?"

"The bus station in Bretford. Just borrowing the free Wi-Fi." She didn't know why she was lying. "Hey, I should go. I promise I'll head back to Harold soon. Say hi to Gran and Pop for me."

"Okay, love." Sadness again. "Just be safe, okay?"

"Okay."

May hung up before it got any more awkward. She should have told him she was staying with the detective, but somehow, she thought that might make him worry more. Then he would know she was really investigating her mother's and June's disappearances.

May tucked the shoebox into her side as someone sat near her. So her dad didn't know anything about it or its contents, which meant her mom must have kept it hidden. So how did June find it? And when? Unless . . . unless her mom had given it to June.

Then why was there a letter only to May?

Ugh! Too many moving parts to keep track of. May rubbed her temples. The headache building. Or maybe it was all the questions making her brain explode.

May picked up the shoebox and stood.

She knew what she had to do.

Chapter Twenty-Six

"I'm building a murder board."

May needed to explain herself as soon as Sam came into his apartment. His living room was covered in handwritten notes, string, Sharpies, and paper. Plus a large corkboard she sat in front of on the floor.

"Well hello to you too." He locked the door behind him and put the archive box of her mother's cold case on the coffee table near May's head. "Guess that's why you needed this."

May nodded. "I need to pull everything we know together and put it into one place. I want it gone from my brain and onto this corkboard."

"Sounds like I've got a detective in the making. Soda?" He dumped his keys and phone onto the kitchen counter and opened the fridge.

"Sure. I've ordered us pizza. Should be here soon." May placed a thumbtack in her mouth.

Sam handed her an open soda and twisted the top off his own beer. "So we're making a night of this, are we?"

"You don't have plans, do you? Date with Sharon, maybe?"

"Ha ha. Nope, all yours." Sam studied some of the notes lying on the floor. "Nice work. You're establishing a timeline."

"Whatever you say. I'm not really sure what I'm doing. But you said June had mentioned murder boards, and it sounded like a good idea. Plus I have a real-life detective to help me, so how hard can it be?"

"You sounded cocky like your sister just then." Sam laughed, sitting on the couch. "Alright, what have you got?"

May rubbed her neck. "Lots of questions and no answers."

"Welcome. You're officially a detective." Sam swigged his beer. "Mind if I have a look through that?"

"Knock yourself out." May picked up the shoebox. "I couldn't find anything useful. Just Mom's letter to me. You think he's really dead?"

Sam was going through the box and mumbled something noncommittal.

May kept talking while the detective read her mother's letter. "I mean, if he's dead, then where the hell is June? Do you think something else happened to her? Maybe she ran into another psycho. The world is filled with them."

He finished and put the letter back into the envelope. "You think your mother was right? That June had something going on with her?"

"I'm not sure. Maybe? June can be manipulative, but she's not violent or anything. Well, apart from that time at the movies, of course."

"What happened at the movies?" Sam sat back into the couch.

"She stabbed a guy with her nail file because he was making too much noise."

"Ouch." Sam winced.

"It wasn't pretty. It's just weird, though. Why did Mom only say that stuff about June? And not me? I mean, wouldn't I have this bad blood too?"

The detective scratched his head. "It's a good question. I wonder why June left this here, in Bretford? She never said anything about it to me."

May considered this. "I don't know. This is why I'm doing this board. I feel like there are too many things to keep track of and I'm completely lost."

"It can get like that when there's a buildup of information but no clear leads." Sam shuffled forward on the couch. "Where did you want to start?"

They went through the archive box, Diana's shoebox, and the clues June had left. Carefully joining dates, timelines, and any connections between the two cases with the red string May had purchased. The pizza came.

Soon enough everything in May's head was in front of her. Even if they were still just questions on the corkboard. It suddenly felt like a weight lifting from her, and her mind was finally clear, her headache gone.

A murder board had sounded ominous.

But this was exactly the catharsis she needed.

Two days missing.

Mom,
I'm scared.

Chapter
Twenty-Seven

May woke to a text from her dad.

Morning sweetheart. I had a look for that box of Diana's you mentioned and couldn't find anything. Sorry. I did spot this when I was cleaning your room though. Thought you may have dropped it.

She waited for him to send the next message.
It was a photo of text handwritten on a scrap piece of paper:

Look up high,
But never low.
It's into the wardrobe,
I have to go.
I don't know who,
And I don't know where.
But time will tell,
If you even care.

June's handwriting.

May texted back thanks and to have a good time at his parents' farm. Then read the message again. It meant nothing to her.

How had it gotten in her room? She thought about texting her dad and asking him exactly where he'd found it but didn't want to bring attention to the riddle. What was June playing at?

The detective had already left for the day, so she couldn't show it to him.

Something felt off. Like either she'd missed a whole series of clues back at home or June was trying to lead her astray. Or someone else astray.

May folded her sheets and made coffee. Caffeine first. Then thinking.

Carrying her mug back with her, she stood in front of the murder board. What was she missing?

It had been a year since June vanished. Said goodbye to her dad and Sue, saying she would be back later. She had on a fitted Princess Leia T-shirt and jeans. Took her backpack with her.

June didn't arrive back for dinner. Still wasn't back by midnight. Her phone was off. That's when May got the call. Her dad asking if June had driven to the city and was there. May had no idea where she was.

Friends were called. The nearest hospital. Then finally the police, who said she would probably turn up the next day. Teens often went out, ran out of phone battery, and forgot to tell their parents they were staying at a friend's place. Only June never showed up.

Then her backpack, with her phone and bloodied clothes she'd had on that morning, had been found at a rest stop a month later. Her car was still yet to be discovered. Same with a body.

May didn't focus on that part.

It was all there. All on the murder board. May's eyes skimmed over the times and dates and notes. Lots of question marks. Mainly about June's clues. When had she planned them? Had she known she was in danger that day and wanted to let May know? Why hadn't she just told May?

Nothing made sense. Just like the latest message. *It's into the wardrobe, I have to go.* Why would June have to go into a wardrobe? For safety? A hiding spot, maybe?

May sipped her coffee.

A stab pierced her stomach. She winced. June had left her clues. *Just* in case something went wrong. Then something *had* gone wrong, but May hadn't been quick enough. It'd been a year. Could her sister still be alive after a year?

It hit her like a rock to the head. May staggered to the couch. Placing the trembling mug on the coffee table in front of her.

She was too late.

June had thought it had been a game. A childish game like they played as kids. When had she realized her mistake? That her clues hadn't worked and her twin wasn't coming to save her?

Had June felt safe after reading her mom's letter to May? Saying that the monster was dead?

May nodded to herself. That was it. June had gone on a wild-goose chase and found something she shouldn't have. She'd woken someone. And if it wasn't the monster, then it had to be someone connected to him.

May would find her sister. No matter what. The heaviness blanketed her, knowing June was probably dead.

A stray tear fell down her cheek. She let it do its thing.

The murder board was a blur of colors and shapes. Either the answer was right in front of her face or it was still yet to be discovered. It didn't matter if June was dead. May still had to find her. Bring her back. Bury her for real.

May knew what she needed to do now. And it required her mother's car.

As she picked up the phone, three words repeated over and over in her head.

I'm coming, June.

I'm coming, June.

I'm coming, June.

I'm coming, June.

Chapter Twenty-Eight

Sue sat in the kitchen of Pat's house eating toast. She flipped through the job classifieds in the local paper while waiting for her mother to get up.

She hated to admit it, but moving in with Pat wasn't so bad. Gary didn't want her around him—that much was clear—and things were heating up with her new boyfriend, so maybe she wouldn't be here for much longer.

She'd have to introduce him to the family soon. He'd even asked to meet them, which most guys shied away from. This one was different. He'd asked so many questions. Seemed to care about her and her life. Maybe she'd finally get her happy ending, like Diana did with Gary.

For now, though, living with Pat would do. Her mom was easy to live with—all she did was drink scotch and take naps. They even played cards and had a few laughs, which was nice. It was easy now that Sue was the only child left, no longer having to demand her mother's attention away from Diana.

She looked around at the kitchen that hadn't changed since she was a child. Like time had stood still, but her aging body hadn't gotten the memo.

She missed her father, who gave the best hugs and always told her she could be anything she wanted—even when she got things so wrong all the time. She wished the kitchen were filled with dancing and laughter and hope like it had been when they were kids. When Diana was just her boring sister. Before everything became about her.

Sue walked to the sink and poured herself a glass of water. She stared through the window at the warming day. It was lovely out, and yet she felt dark inside.

She couldn't believe May had called wanting to get Diana's car back. Now what was she supposed to do?

May wouldn't even use it anyway. *Those girls have only ever thought of themselves.*

If it weren't for the twins, her life would be very different. They had changed everything—and not in a good way.

Sue glanced back at the kitchen table, where the newspaper sat open.

She had an idea.

DIANA

If Sue didn't get out of my face, I was going to punch her.

Why did she have to be so annoying?

Sue stood with her hands on her hips, lifting up the hem of her school uniform. "Think you're so smart? Wait till I tell Dad you stole ten bucks from his wallet."

"That was *you*! I saw you take it out with my own eyes." I'd be late for high school if we kept this up. Which Sue would. All day if I let her.

"Like Dad would care if you stole from him. I could tell him you murdered someone, and he would still think you were the best person in all the world."

Ouch. But also true.

"Whatever. I'm heading off. And don't follow me." Impossible. Sue followed me everywhere.

I grabbed my schoolbag and packed lunch Mom had left on the kitchen counter.

Sue was already out the front door. Her lunch was still there. Ha! Like I was going to tell her that. Like she would tell me. Screw her.

"Your booooooyfriend is out here again."

Jeez, did she have to tell the whole neighborhood?

"He's not my boyfriend." Grumble, grumble.

It's too early for this.

I pulled the door shut but didn't lock it or Mom would have a conniption when she got home from helping with the blood drive down at the scout hall.

"Hey, Willy."

"Hey, Diana."

He was in his usual spot. On the tire swing. Looking like he fit there perfectly because he was so much shorter than me and still looked like a young kid and not an eighteen-year-old.

Sue ran ahead. Annoying me no longer part of her master plan for world domination.

"I bought you some flowers." Willy held them out. They were the roses from our front yard.

"I told you to stop bringing me stuff. It's kind of getting creepy."

He shuffled his feet in the dirt, not knowing what to do with the roses.

"Give 'em here." I grabbed them from him before he cried or something. "Ouch!"

Thorns.

"You okay?" He was by my side, his face bright red. His complexion always giving him away. "Sorry, I didn't have time to remove them."

"That's because you literally got them from our garden." I threw them onto the porch for later. "Come on, we'll be late for school."

Willy's mouth hung open. "You're gonna walk with me?"

"Sure, why not?" I was in a better mood now that Sue had gone.

"Gee, thanks, Diana." His face was ablaze now like he'd been badly sunburned. "We can separate when we get closer to school if you like. I won't be offended."

I shrugged. Willy was growing on me. Especially now that I knew why he'd been such a creeper for ages. I mean, I got it—this town was all kinds of backward, and it's hard to know who to trust around here. Especially with secrets as big as ours.

But still. No need to be in my face like that.

"Today's the last day you can come to my house. We had a deal, remember." It wasn't a question. Of course he remembered.

I couldn't hear his answer because he always followed two steps behind me as we walked toward school. The cracked pavement was like an obstacle course, so we both kept our eyes down.

"Anyway," I began, knowing this would be our last conversation. "You all good now? Know what you need to do?"

"Yep. I can take it from here." His voice was soft behind me.

I stopped so he could catch up. In another world we could've been friends. But Harold wasn't that world.

"You going to be okay?" I could hear him properly now that he was right beside me.

"Thanks to you. Yep."

I owed him big time for not snitching on me for stealing that chemistry test.

Big time.

All I'd had to do in return was show him how to apply makeup and sew. Something about playing Dungeons & Dragons and going to Comic-Con. I didn't understand it, but I didn't need to. If that's what he needed as a trade to not rat me out for cheating, then easy peasy. I was also more than happy to keep his secret. Wearing makeup around here could get a guy killed.

"Don't move." He stopped and put his arm in front of me to do the same.

I lifted my head up.

Shit. A brown snake. The fucker was lying across the footpath sunning itself. Bold move out in the open like that. Normally you never knew a snake was lurking nearby.

"Hang on." Willy pulled his school tie off from around his neck and flicked it in the snake's direction.

It didn't move.

"I think it's dead." Willy let out a massive breath.

I totally did the same. "You sure?"

"Looks like a bird dropped it from up high." He leaned closer. "See how its guts are open like that?"

"Gross!" I swatted him on the arm. Not hard or he might bruise.

"Fuckity fuck. That scared the shit out of me. I hate snakes." Willy kept on walking, steering clear of the dead snake.

Fuckity fuck, huh? I hadn't heard that before.

Thanks, Willy. I'll be stealing that.

Chapter Twenty-Nine

May leaned against the wall of the bus station she'd arrived at less than a week ago.

"There you are. You said to meet at the ticket office." Sam was breathless as he came up to her.

"I did, but I wanted to wait at the gate. Didn't you get my text?"

"Text?" Sam looked down at his phone like he had heard the word for the first time. "I hate texts. Never look at them. Pick up the phone if you need me, okay?"

"I forget you're like a million years old." May chuckled.

"Ha ha. Pick on the old guy. Now, you all checked in? Can I get you anything for the trip? Snacks or magazines or anything?"

He sounded like he did when she first arrived. "No, I'm okay. My plan is to go back over everything again. I've got lots of photos of that murder board, don't worry. A parting gift from me."

"Well, thanks." He smiled. "Let me know if you work out anything new."

"I'm sure I'm missing something. *So* many things." May glanced at the moving queue for the bus. "That's why I have to go back to Harold. You get that, right?"

"I understand."

Why was this so hard? Maybe she should stay.

Sam slapped his thigh. "Hey, I wanted to let you know I heard back from the coroner in Kerrindale . . . about your mom."

May held her breath. This was it. She'd been dreading this moment.

He cleared his throat. "She said it was an accident. A skull fracture from slipping on the concrete."

May nodded. Let out her breath slowly. "That's . . . that's good. Well . . . it's not good, but you know what I mean."

"I do." Sam acknowledged the bus with his chin. "Well, I guess that's you."

"Guess so."

Sam checked his phone.

"You have to go?"

"No, I'm waiting on a call."

The bus driver yelled out for the final passengers to board the bus. May and the detective looked anywhere but at each other.

May grabbed her bag. "I better go."

"Yep. This is it, kiddo. Do you mind if I give you a hug?"

May nodded. It surprised her that the intimacy wasn't uncomfortable when Sam's arms engulfed her. Something had definitely shifted in her since she arrived in Bretford, something she hoped would stick around once she left.

"Be safe, May. Please call me—no texting—when you get in. You're welcome back here anytime. I mean that."

"I'll come for a visit again. I appreciate everything you've done for me while I've been here." May shifted the bag on her shoulder.

"Got used to having you around." Sam glanced at his phone again, then up at May. "Well, bye then." He shuffled his feet and flicked his eyes around the station.

May couldn't help him with all the awkwardness of their goodbye. She had no clue what she was doing either.

Sam nodded once and strode off.

If he looks back at me, I'll see him again. She bargained with the detective's back. *Look back. Look back.*

Look back.

He never looked back.

Chapter Thirty

May was back home again.

Bloody Harold and all its bullshit.

She checked the mailbox before she headed inside the house. Her dad wouldn't be there, as he was already at the farm. This suited her just fine. She had too many of her own questions to add any more to the list.

Mrs. Slattery, from two doors down, spotted her and came over to say hello. Great, just what she needed.

The sun beat down on May's head, and her black jeans stuck to her skin. "I'm sorry, Mrs. Slattery, I just got into town again. I should probably head in."

Mrs. Slattery nodded. Her chin wobbled a little as she did so. "Dear, before you go. I wanted to say how sorry I was that you found out about your mom's past. Your dad told me, and I can't imagine how you're feeling."

May blinked into the kind eyes of her neighbor. "You knew? About my mom, I mean?"

She smiled warmly, holding May's arm for support. "Diana told me one day after I asked about a visitor she had. I think it was all a little much for her and she needed to unburden herself."

"What visitor?" May put her bag on the ground.

Mrs. Slattery looked up the quiet street, thinking. "She never did say. A tall man, with a cap on. I'd never seen him before. I was supposed to look after you girls, but she sent me away, and I saw him as he was leaving."

"Did he have blue eyes?"

"I couldn't say, dear. It was a long time ago. She'd just moved in with your father. You girls were only tiny."

"What did Mom say?"

"She seemed a little spooked when I came over to check on her soon after he left. Then the past gushed out of her like innards cut from a whale."

Wow. Not the best reference.

"What exactly did my mom say about her past?"

Mrs. Slattery looked confused. "Well, you already know. She was taken and that you girls were a result of that. That whoever took her died—thank goodness for that. No offense, dear. She never did name him, though."

"Okay, so she really *did* tell you everything." It was May's turn to be confused. How did Mrs. Slattery seem to know more than anyone else?

As if reading her mind, Mrs. Slattery said, "Your mom needed someone to confide in. And I was grateful to be that person for her. I never told a soul about you girls, and I never will. Your family has been through enough."

May patted the old neighbor's hand, which was soft under all the raised veins. "So Mom never said who the guy was that visited that day? Maybe it was whoever took her?"

"If it was, she never said." Mrs. Slattery clicked her tongue against her teeth. "But he must have brought some shocking news because your mom wasn't the same after that day. Terrible thing she had to live with."

"Oh." Another dead end. "Thanks for telling me . . . and for keeping Mom's secret. I'm happy she had you to talk to."

"I was grateful for the company."

May released Mrs. Slattery's hand from her arm, the familiar scent of roses and bleach reaching her nose. "I really have to get inside. I'm sorry I can't invite you in."

"Never mind. Another time." Mrs. Slattery shuffled home; her blue cotton dress danced as she walked. May studied the street for anyone watching them, but it was sleepy Harold as usual.

Mrs. Slattery stopped and turned around, shading her eyes from the sun. She called back, "I don't remember his eyes, dear, because he had sunglasses on. Those mirrored ones."

Mirrored glasses? Why did that ring a bell?

"Okay, thanks!" May waved goodbye.

May raced inside and pulled out her mom's shoebox. She flipped through the photos. Stopping at one of her mom and Brad sitting on the grass, with the university behind them.

Brad had on mirrored sunglasses.

Had Brad come and visited her mother after they'd been born? Why?

Wait. That meant he knew about the twins. But he'd had an alibi, and his paternity test was negative. Even if Brad visited that day, he wasn't their father. Was he? Could the paternity test be wrong?

May rubbed her eyes. She'd barely slept on the bus. Her brain was doing that thing again where it stopped working.

She was hungry. That was it. May helped herself to some toast and tea as she considered her next move.

Sue would be here any moment with the car. Then May would drive to see Brad. Then Wes. Or Wes. Then Brad. It didn't matter. Maybe Bill the baker one more time before she left Harold. No. He didn't know anything.

She'd have to avoid Pat or there would be no getting away from Harold.

And Sam? What should she tell him?

May nibbled on her toast. She would worry about that later.

A car pulled into the driveway. Sue used her key and walked in without knocking. She ignored May at the table, going straight into the kitchen.

May looked up. "Well, hello to you, too, Aunty Sue. Thanks for bringing the car."

Sue tossed the car keys on the kitchen counter and helped herself to a glass of wine from a bottle in the cupboard. "What do you even need it for?" Her words came out like a cobra spitting venom. "You won't drive it in the city. I know you, May. You're too scared to drive there. You're only taking it to spite me."

"Little early for wine, isn't it?"

Sue ignored her, gulping it down in one go. "So, are you going back to the city now? Had enough of playing detective in Bretford?"

May turned away from her aunt.

"Oh, don't act so shocked. I knew as soon as you found out about Diana's past where you were going. Bet you didn't find anything, did you?"

May stepped away from her aunt. "As if you care."

Sue poured another glass of wine, her voice softer now. "How did your investigation go? You find your father?"

"Like I would tell you if I did." May was officially exhausted and wanted Sue to leave.

"I'll find out, you know. Have my ways. I'm not as clueless as everyone thinks."

May's blood went cold. What did Sue know?

"Find out about that Brad character, did you?"

May didn't know where this was going. She met Sue's eyes. Impossible to gauge what was behind them.

"Don't you want to know what I think happened?" Sue broke her gaze and rustled around in her handbag.

"I'm sure you're going to tell me anyway."

"Don't get smart." Sue pulled out a packet of cigarettes and opened the patio sliding door halfway.

"You're smoking now?"

"Why not? Did it when I was your age and wanted to feel young again." Sue aimed the smoke outside. May was amazed she was being so courteous.

"So, this is what happened. Very simple." Sue blew smoke rings as she spoke. "Diana got pregnant by Brad—who she clearly didn't love. Then faked her own abduction to make it appear like it was another guy. Simple."

May strode up to Sue, who flinched as May grabbed her aunt's cigarette. She took a long drag and handed it back.

Sue stared at it like it contained poison. "I didn't know you smoked."

"I don't." May sat at the kitchen table. "Sue, that theory makes no sense. Why would Mom go to all that trouble? Why wouldn't she just terminate the pregnancy and break up with him?"

Plus May knew Brad wasn't their father, but as if she was going to tell Sue that. Let her talk herself in circles.

"Diana would've never gotten rid of you girls. No way. Plus, she had Mom and Dad to support her. It was the easy way out."

"Doesn't sound very easy to me." May shook her head. "Besides, Mom raised us practically alone until Dad came along."

"Yes, her knight in shining armor. Convenient, don't you think? My always-lucky sister. Things seemed to fall in her lap on command."

"It doesn't explain why she would fake an abduction. Why not come back here to Harold? She could've dropped out of school, broken up with Brad, and still had us. People have babies all the time."

"Oh, May, you're so naive." Sue flicked her cigarette butt outside and slid the door shut. "Diana loved drama too much. If reality TV had been a big thing then, she would've had her own show."

June was like that too. Maybe Sue was onto something. Although, it was all too elaborate a plan to be real.

"It doesn't add up. If Mom coveted the spotlight so much, she wouldn't have gone into hiding when we were born. She would've made a big deal out of it."

Sue flopped into a chair. "But she couldn't, because of Brad."

This again.

"Why? What is it about Brad?" May was happy to play along.

"He was violent with her."

May took a breath. "Mom told you that?"

"I heard her and Mom talking about it one time. She was scared of him and his temper. I guess that's why she doesn't want him anywhere near you girls."

May put her head in her hands. "It doesn't explain why she would go to all that effort to leave him. I just can't imagine Mom doing something like that for attention. There were so many other things she could've done if Brad was violent."

"Goddamn." Sue pushed her chair back, letting it hit the wall. "Why did I think you would listen to me? No one else ever has. I may as well be invisible in this family."

May knew that story well.

Sue grabbed her handbag and keys, which she flung on the table next to May. "Take the horrible car. And my pointless life while you're at it. Take it all."

May knew better than to say anything. She was relieved Sue was going.

As she got to the door, Sue spun around. "I'm so sick of no one listening to me. I have a story to tell, too, you know? This time it's my voice everyone is going to hear." She slammed the door as she went out.

A feeling of dread ran through May. What did Sue mean by *this time it's my voice everyone is going to hear*?

May had run out of shits to give.

Hi Mom, I don't have a lot of space to write, so I'll be quick. I'm in a dark shed, and I don't know who has taken me. It smells in here. Like your story when we were kids. Rust and chicken shit. My brain hurts. I think he hit me. I think he's drugging my food. I mark off the days on the dirt floor. It's been three weeks. You were found after three weeks. I don't think I'm going to be found, Mom. I'm not getting out of here. I know that. Maybe one day they'll find my body. May will find me. I know she will. I'm scared, but I'm also not. It's weird. It's okay, Mom. We'll be together soon. Lucky, hey? Fuck that. I don't want to die.

Chapter Thirty-One

May had pulled June's room apart but couldn't find anything else resembling a clue.

Now she was doing the same with her own room. The riddle her dad had texted her was on her bedside table. Written on the back of a Brake 'n' Bite receipt.

Look up high,
But never low.
It's into the wardrobe,
I have to go.
I don't know who,
And I don't know where.
But time will tell,
If you even care.

What the hell did that even mean? Was this about June's disappearance or from an old treasure hunt May had missed?

May's head swam, and even with the window open, it was hard to breathe. Her childhood room so much smaller than she ever remembered it.

It was time to make a plan.

The problem was, Where first? Wes's or Brad's? Both of them lived hours away from Harold *and* on opposite sides of the state.

Her gut was telling her to start at Wes's. Even though the police had checked out his place, maybe there was somewhere else he was hiding June.

But why would he need to take June? Why would Brad?

Mom had said the monster was dead.

Bullshit.

The word may as well have come from a loudspeaker in May's head.

BULLSHIT.

Her mom was lying. The monster was still out there, and she was going to find him.

Who? Wes or Brad. Brad or Wes.

May had both their addresses. Wes's from the police file and Brad was easy to find online. *Where did you go, June?*

May fell back on her bed. Her head swirling again.

Just make a decision.

Her phone buzzed in her pocket. May checked the screen for who was calling. She didn't know the number. It was probably the detective checking up on her. What had he said? Call. Don't text. She'd done neither.

She hit the green button. "Hello."

"Hello, is this May Simpson?"

"Um, yes. Who's this?" May sat up and leaned against her pillows.

"This is Jay Ferguson from the *Bretford Times*. Is now a good time?"

"Um, who? From where?"

"I'm from the *Bretford Times*. I wanted to talk to you about your mother, Diana Wells, and her abduction that led to the birth of you and your missing twin sister."

What the hell was going on?

"I . . . um. I don't know what you're talking about." Her voice was barely above a whisper. "I have to go."

"May, wait—before you hang up on me." Jay's deep voice filled her head. "I'm going to print this story in the next forty-eight hours whether you comment or not. I have a very reliable source who has come forward, but I would like to give you an opportunity to tell your side."

May shook her head. This wasn't happening. "I don't have anything to comment on."

"You have until the close of business today to change your mind. Call me—"

May cut in. "Wait, who's your source?"

Jay paused. "I'm not at liberty to say."

"Then my only comment is 'Go fuck yourself.'" May's finger had to press the red disconnect button a few times before she finally hung up on him. She was shaking.

She already knew who the source was.

Aunty Sue. This was what she had been talking about when she said her voice would finally be heard.

Great. Just fucking great.

So now the world would know about her and June. About their father not being Gary. How could Sue do this?

If the article came out in the next two days, then she needed to leave. *Now.* She'd officially run out of time.

May picked up the receipt from her dresser and read over the puzzle one more time. Still no help. She flipped it over. Veggie burger with triple cheese and no mayo, with a chocolate shake. Definitely June's purchase.

She'd already checked the date, but it was impossible to read. This could have been from years ago. Except . . .

Except that there was definitely no Brake 'n' Bite in Harold and the closest one was on the highway, forty-five minutes away. May checked the location on the receipt. Jade Town.

Jade Town? That was even farther away, and no one in her family had been over that way as far as she knew. Plus it was nowhere near Brad's or Wes's places.

What was near Jade Town?

May brought up the photos of the murder board on her phone. She and Sam had put a map of the state up and pinned all the main locations. Harold. Bretford. Wes's house. Brad's parents' house, where he was at the party, and the town where he lived now. Old Cemetery Road, where Diana had been found.

Shit!

That was it. The Jade Town Brake 'n' Bite was only fifteen minutes from Old Cemetery Road.

Shit shit shit.

June had gone back to where her mother had been found walking alone and in distress after having been missing for three weeks.

Problem was it was three hours away and it would be dark by the time she got there.

Too bad.

This had to be it. This had to be where she would find June.

Chapter Thirty-Two

"You did what?" Pat squawked.

Sue sat on the steps of the veranda, enjoying the sun as it made its way over the front of Pat's house. Pat had a battery-operated fan blowing on her neck and a wide-brimmed hat covering her face. She sat on a bench overflowing with cushions, her gin and tonic within reach on a planter box.

Pat continued. "Are you out of your bloody mind? Why would you want to destroy this family any further? We've all been through enough."

"It's just a half-baked story." Sue fanned her fingernails, now painted cherry red. "Look on the bright side. I'm getting paid for something that no one will ever read."

"You have no right to sell your sister's story. She'll be rolling over in her grave. Do you know how dangerous this could be for those girls? For Gary? Us?" Pat groaned. "You don't think, do you?"

Sue waved her hands to dry her nails. "No, I don't think. I'm a fool who can never do anything right. No one seems to mind that Diana had twins under dubious—"

"I'll not have you speaking ill about Diana. Your sister did a brave thing having those babies, which I may not have always agreed with, but I'm thankful she didn't listen to me. We did everything we could to protect her and those girls. Now you've gone and messed it all up."

Sue took a sip of her beer. "Well, it's too late now. I've already done my exclusive interview and told the reporter everything."

Pat brought her cane down on the veranda floorboards. "Whatever happens next, you will be entirely responsible for."

"Get over yourself, Mom. It's not that big of a deal. Nothing's going to happen, trust me."

"Trust you? Give you a swift kick up your rear end, more like! This is what I get for having you girls so late. If I was a young, spritely thing, you wouldn't know what hit you."

Sue placed her large sunglasses back over her eyes so her mom couldn't see her rolling them. How was this still her life? Listening to her mom complain and reminding her how she was never going to be as good as Diana. "No wonder this family is so damn dramatic. It's the only way to get attention."

Pat took a long sip of her drink. "What did you tell him—this journalist guy? Must've been a doozy for him to give you money. He's going to want it back when he finds out you don't actually know anything."

"I didn't get paid much, so don't go thinking I'm rolling in it now." Sue painted the second coat of polish on her nails. "I know plenty. You'll find out soon enough when you read the article. It'll have everyone guessing if she made the whole thing up."

Pat brought down her empty glass on the side table. "Don't be ridiculous, child! Why would Diana make up a story as grand as that one?" Pat adjusted her cushion. "You've no idea what she went through, and now you're digging up old wounds again."

"I know you think I'm clueless, Mom, but what I'm doing is actually genius." Sue didn't need a pageant smile; this one was real.

"Think about it," Sue continued. "First Diana goes missing. Then, June goes missing after she starts looking for her blood daddy."

Pat nodded, waiting.

"So, who's next?"

Pat's face paled. "May."

"That's right. Now she's on some wild-goose chase in my car, and soon enough she's going to end up just like June."

Pat wasn't much for tears, but Sue saw them looming. "We don't know what happened to Junie—she could still be alive."

"Since when do you believe that, Mom? You were the one harping on about having that funeral for her." Sue scoffed. "Trust me on this. If Diana told the truth, I'm drawing that monster out. Then we can face him once and for all. If she didn't, then something else happened to June."

Pat stared at her empty glass. "But how on earth will we protect May when she's not here?"

"I already thought of that." Sue chuckled. "I told that journalist she lives here with us, in Harold. I dare this guy to come and find us."

"Sweet baby Jesus. What have you done? I'm too old for booby traps and camouflage. This isn't a game, Sue."

"I know it isn't. But I have a feeling you won't be needing any camouflage, Mom."

"Why's that? You have grenades I can blow out my ass, instead?"

Sue laughed despite herself. "You won't be needing anything because no one's going to show. Finally, I can prove that Diana isn't the innocent one in all this."

"You've said your piece. Now, keep pouring me drinks so if anyone does show up, I'll be too drunk to care."

Sue blew on her nails. "When these are dry."

Pat sighed. "I always said you'd be the death of me."

Chapter Thirty-Three

It was raining as May drove onto Old Cemetery Road.

The dirt was slush underneath the wheels, and she turned on the high beams. There was only room for one car, so she kept to the middle of the road, away from the ditch on either side. She hunched herself closer to the wheel, straining to see anything through the rain. Potholes were everywhere, and all she could do was go over them slowly, praying she wouldn't get stuck in one.

The night was pitch dark, no streetlights, no full moon. Nothing.

May could only just make out the trees lining the fenced paddocks that surrounded the remote road. No house lights, no sign of life. Nothing.

Her heart battered her chest so hard she thought it might crack open. There was fear, of course, but there was also anticipation. She was close; she could feel it.

I'm coming, June.

The car crept along the narrow road, getting farther and farther away from the highway.

There was no turning back now. May knew that. She would find June either alive or dead. She would find either a monster or nothing at all. Either way, she had a baseball bat sitting next to her. She'd knock someone's head clear out of the ballpark if she had to.

May wiped the windshield, which was misting up. Even with the defroster on, the car was struggling to keep up with the rain and her rapid breathing. She saw it then. The outline of a house.

This was it.

Turn around.

That wasn't going to happen. She'd texted Sam instead of calling him. She didn't need him trying to talk sense into her like her head was currently trying to do. At least she told him where she was going, but he hadn't responded yet. It would've been much nicer to have him next to her instead of the baseball bat, but there wasn't much she could do about it now.

Turn around.

"No." Her voice filled the car and gave her an instant chill. "I'm doing this. For June. For Mom."

Tears blurred her eyes. The road was a dead end, but the derelict house at the end of it was there just like in her mom's story. She had no choice but to pull into the nonexistent driveway. No turning back now.

The rain was coming down heavily and pounding onto the silent car. It was impossible to see more than a few feet in front of her. Anyone could be out there.

June could be out there.

May pulled the hood up on her sweatshirt, grabbed the baseball bat, and checked her phone one last time. Nothing back from Sam. Of course, he was busy.

She had this.

Yep, she had this.

With a final gasp of breath like she was about to plunge underwater, May opened the door and jumped out of the car.

It was instant. The rain soaking her to the bone. She pushed back her hood. What was the point? The baseball bat she pulled up, though, in both her hands, right in front of her face. She was ready. She would kill anyone who stood in her way.

The storm pelted her face and made it hard to see as she picked her way through the dirt and the sludge of the run-down yard. Not that it could be called a yard; it seemed like a barren wasteland of weeds and rusted bits and pieces. From what May could see anyway.

She wiped her eyes with the heel of her hand and gripped the baseball bat in the other. The house was dead in front of her now. Completely dark, silent, but like it was watching her every move. It was old, decaying. Its once-white paint peeling off in large chunks to reveal rotten weatherboards.

All of her wanted to call out her sister's name. Let her know she was here. Finally. That she was safe.

But that would be suicide if a monster was lurking.

May bypassed the house. Wanting to check the surroundings first and not be snared inside a death trap. Had June come here? Had she gone inside?

May shivered. And it wasn't from the rain.

Turn around.

With the bat firmly in two hands again and stuck out in front of her like a barrier, she trod slowly. Carefully. Passing the crumbling porch, coming around the side of the house. The wind whipped her face and threw her off balance.

Breathe, damn it. Breathe.

The barn at the back of the house was impossible to miss. It was a dark, ominous structure standing strong among the storm. One of its two doors flapped in the wind.

Thud. Thud. Thud.

Her heart was surely doing the same thing, but by now May had become numb to her own fear. Parts of her were on high alert instead. Like her brain had slowed to take in the enormity of what she was experiencing.

May stepped toward the barn. One foot, then another.

Thud. Thud. Thud.

The barn's double doors were in front of her.

Using the baseball bat, she nudged the entryway open.

Slowly. Carefully.

She held her breath. Her ears trained now for any sound that wasn't the storm. The darkness inside the barn was an abyss, impossible to adjust her eyes to. She would have to go in.

The smell struck her first. Like a slap. Stale chicken shit. And . . . what was that? A metallic smell like rust or . . . blood.

May covered her mouth. Ready for the vomit swelling in her belly. She had to get out of here. Come back when the detective was with her. Smart.

She swung around, the doors thudding again. No. That wasn't the doors. That was something else. A tapping sound coming from the back corner of the barn.

Her heart tapped, tapped, tapped along with it. The vomit was threatening to rise as the metallic smell increased. May's feet moved in the direction of the sound. She had to know. She was ready. Wasn't she?

The baseball bat now a small comfort. Seemingly tiny in the expanse of the empty barn. The tapping kept going. Calling her. Drawing her in.

She was close. To the far wall. To whatever the sound was.

Her eyes did their best to adjust. To see what was all over the wall. To see what a stray branch was tap, tap, tapping against.

May lowered the baseball bat as she understood what she was looking at.

A memory shot through her, so fierce she had to steady herself.

Not a memory. A story. One her mom had told.

About the man who dug graves.

With all the shovels he kept.

Just like those hanging on the wall.

Chapter Thirty-Four

Her mom had been here.

All those years ago. That hadn't been a ghost story to scare the twins but a warning of what was out there. Her mom was telling them where she'd been taken.

June had to have known. Come here as well.

"June!" May's voice echoed around the barn and mixed with the storm.

She didn't care who heard her now. Let them come. She was ready. Spinning on her heel, she ran back to the barn doors. June had to be somewhere, and she was going to find her.

The storm battered her as she dashed to the house. She heard herself screaming. Like a warrior about to do battle. It was like someone else had taken over her body. That suited her just fine.

The back steps buckled under her weight as May leaped to the back door. It swung open easily as she pushed on it. She took in the gutted space. The broken floorboards. Peeling wallpaper. Half-torn-down walls. No one had lived here in a long, long time.

Her eyes had adjusted to the dark now, which made missing the large gaps in the floors easier. The rain clattered on the roof and spilled in through holes. If anyone was nearby, it would be impossible to hear above the noise of the downpour.

Breathe. Just breathe.

"June," May whispered. "June, are you here?"

The baseball bat led the way down the hall. A bedroom. Empty. A bathroom. Gross. Also empty.

May stepped over a huge chunk of broken floorboard. Below was mud and dirt. There was only one more door at the end of the hall. She inched toward it. The bat now shaking in front of her eyes.

She scanned the room from the doorway. Nothing in here. Completely empty, apart from some torn curtains hanging from the windows, which hadn't held glass for who knows how long.

Wait. There was something behind the curtains. Was that a foot sticking out?

Oh, fuck. TURN AROUND.

May ran into the room and swung the bat at the curtains. They tumbled to the ground and sent up a damp dust right into her throat. She coughed, still swinging. At just air now. The curtains hadn't needed much to fall and were now a pile on the floor.

What had she seen?

May used the bat to pull the mound of rotten fabric toward her. Yep, there was definitely something under it all. She looked toward the bedroom door. Nobody out there, just the sounds of the storm. That was her story, and she was sticking to it.

Kneeling down, May pulled the curtains up. She dropped the baseball bat near her foot and grabbed her phone from her back pocket. Using the flashlight she lit up what had been hidden behind the curtains. A pile of folded papers, wrapped in a hair tie.

Her stomach growled and mixed all at the same time. She took a deep breath and pulled the tie off carefully and unfolded the first piece of paper.

Oh, shit. June's handwriting again.

Days Mom's been dead: 121.

Hi Mom!

Well, well, well. I figured I would only write one letter to you and the two of us would never have any
secrets to share ever again.
Turns out I WAS WRONG!

Letters to her mom? So June *had* written more of them!

May's numbing fingers opened each letter as quickly as she could. Her eyes skimming the pages. Taking it all in.

Brad *was* their father. What? But the police report . . . and June had gone to his house? Was she nuts? And she what? Saw Wes *here*? At this house. *Shit.*

May opened the last two. They took her seconds to read. There wasn't much there.

June was scared. She said someone had taken her. Drugged her. *Hit* her.

Shit shit shit. The last letter was almost a year ago and had ended:

It's okay, Mom. We'll be together soon. Lucky,
hey? Fuck that. I don't want to die.

May's insides burst. What little she had inside her stomach came up in a warm flood of liquid, covering the baseball bat.

She spit out what was left in her mouth and let the tears gush out of her as she threw the pages onto the floor.

I'm too late.

May will find me. I know she will.

But I didn't. I didn't find you.

The years of guilt, of grief, of pain spilled out of her. Her sobs so loud they challenged the storm for dominance.

She didn't care who heard. She didn't care if someone was here. She was ready. But not to fight. To die. May had nothing left now. Not without June.

All that hope she'd clung to over the past year was gone now.

She had been so sure June was alive, and all this time she'd been here. With a monster. Only . . . only that monster had a name. June had said it.

Wes.

She'd seen him here. At this very house. Then she'd disappeared from the rest stop. He must have brought her here because she hadn't stopped the car or come inside. She'd been too scared. He must have followed her.

So where was she now?

In the barn.

May knew in her heart that June was there. Buried somewhere. Her mom had gotten away, but June hadn't.

The tears kept coming, and maybe they would never stop now.

May had to find her sister. Put her to rest. Then she would find Wes, and she would kill him.

But . . .

June had said she'd done a paternity test on Brad, and it had come back positive. So Wes must have been an accomplice. *Bastards.* She would kill them both.

May picked up the letters and shoved them down the front of her soaked jeans. She left the baseball bat because she wouldn't need that now. She would claw Wes's eyes out when she saw him. Slowly. Let them pop against her thumbs.

Something inside of her stirred. A fire. An anger. Her tears had cleansed her, and now she was left with pure hate.

This man had ruined their lives. Now she would ruin his.

But first she had to find where he had buried her sister.

Then she would bury him.

She said it aloud. Liked how it tasted in her mouth.

The name of a dead man.

"Wes."

DIANA

People talked about finding the one all the time.

I'd heard it enough growing up in Harold, I thought my head would explode. Most afternoons, after school, a group of us would watch the boys practice basketball. The conversation would go a little like this: "John is the one. I can just feel it." "Barry let me on the back of his bike today, so I didn't have to walk. He must be the one." "The only reason I let Ian kiss me is because I know he's the one."

What a crock of shit. A theory designed to brainwash us into thinking life is a fairy tale where, at any moment, a prince would come riding in and save the day. Happy ending. Roll credits.

Roll my eyes.

Apparently, I would know he was the one the moment I saw him. That was the theory.

Total barf.

Funny thing was, when I did see him, I knew.

He. Was. The. One.

Not that he rode up on a horse, or saved the day, or anything, but fuckity fuck if I didn't know right away.

He was everything cliché about how a prince should look. Tall, dark hair, and handsome, sure, but boy did he have an edge to him. I needed to know more because I could never know enough.

Orientation day at university had finished, and I was walking to my dorm building. I was looking forward to setting up my room and getting to know my roommate better. There was talk of a party later that night.

I had also found a necklace that day. Just sitting on the grass, twinkling up at me. It was beautiful, and later, I would find out it was expensive. I called it my lucky charm because the moment I put it on, things clicked into place for me.

My "prince" was walking in the opposite direction. Dressed in jeans and a white T-shirt and wearing mirrored sunglasses. He had the beginnings of a beard and looked like he'd just stepped off an action movie or something.

I noticed him. (How could I not?) I couldn't see his eyes, but I was sure he noticed me too.

If it weren't for my new necklace, I never would've stopped. My story over before it began. Shit ending. Roll credits.

My lucky charm had other ideas.

I'd just passed him when he said, "Excuse me. You dropped this."

(If my necklace falls off and he picks it up, he must be the one.)

"Who, me?" I asked. Of course, he was talking to me. There was no one else around. I could feel myself turning a shade of pink as he stared at me.

"Is this yours?" He stepped closer, the necklace I had found only that day in his hand.

I touched my neck to make sure.

"Yes. Yes, it is. Th-thank you." He made me nervous, and god-damn, he smelled good. A hint of tobacco and . . . soap? Maybe. He was clean. Always a good sign.

"The clasp looks like it's broken. You need to get it fixed, or it'll keep falling off."

That would explain why I had found it in the grass.

"Oh, right. I'll do that." Robot me was making an appearance.

He smiled at me, lifting up his glasses. I smiled back, sure he could see our whole life play out in my eyes like I could in his. Corny to be sure, but I saw it. I saw it all.

If he had tried to kiss me, I would have let him. Tra-la-la!

He asked, "Do you go here?"

Only I was in a land far, far away where one doesn't need to make conversation to start a life together.

"Are you okay? I asked if you went to school here."

"Sorry! Yes, I do. Today was my first day." *Welcome back, Diana.* "Well, orientation, but I guess that counts. Do you go here too?"

"No, I work in town. I moved here a couple of weeks ago."

He didn't look much older than me (or was his permanent smile deceiving me?).

"Maybe we can have a look around town together sometime? Both being newbies." Those were *my* words spilling out of *my* mouth.

"Oh, well . . ."

Fuckity fuck.

"I can't believe I said that. You have a girlfriend . . . or a boyfriend." It wasn't a question. Of course, he had a partner. The guy was gorgeous.

"No, it's not that. I probably shouldn't fraternize with students, that's all."

"Why not? Are you a professor?"

"A professor? Gosh, no. I'm not that smart." He laughed. He was simply sublime. "You know what? There's no real reason I can't hang out with you."

Holy flipping cow. Our life together would start here.

Right.

Here.

"Sorry, I don't know your name."

"Diana." (Your soon-to-be wife.)

"Diana." He said my name like he was savoring a fine wine.

I would savor *him* like a fine wine.

"Do you have a number I can call you on?"

Shit. "I do, but I don't know what it is yet. I haven't written it down. Can I get yours, and I'll call you instead?"

"You won't forget me?"

His eyes twinkled like my necklace had.

"Of course not! I can call you later if you like?" (Too keen?)

"I only have a work number right now, but I'll be there tomorrow. Why don't you call me then?"

"Okay!" (Definitely too keen.)

I pulled one of my notebooks out of my bag, and he wrote his number on the inside cover. Just a number.

"Are you going to tell me your name, or do I have to guess?"

I already knew it. It was Prince Charming.

"How about you guess?" His teeth shone in the sunlight.

"Do I get a hint?"

He walked backward. His smile pointed firmly in my direction. "It has three letters, and one of them is the letter s."

He picked off a purple flower from one of the bushes growing along the path. He walked back and put it behind my ear.

"Call me tomorrow, Diana."

And just like that, I had met the one.

Chapter Thirty-Five

May was back in the barn.

The name of the soon-to-be-dead man fueling her with a hatred that she'd never known before.

Wes. Wes. Wes.

It was timed perfectly with the thud thud thud of the barn doors.

Her flashlight on, she was looking for any sign that June had been there. Or was still there.

Her phone lit up with a call.

Crap.

"Hi, Detective."

"It's still Sam. I just saw your messages. What did I tell you about not texting—where are you?"

"I'm—" May scanned the barn, her voice low. Her voice was like a beacon, even with the storm still pelting onto the questionable roof. "I told you where I was in my messages."

"I was hoping that was a joke." He sighed. "What are you doing out there?"

"I thought I found something in June's clues . . ." Should she tell him about June's letters? About Wes? No. He would stop her.

"I'm listening."

May kept her eyes on the barn doors; if anyone came in, she would be ready. "It was nothing. I got the clue wrong. There's nothing out here."

He hesitated.

She waited. Was he onto her?

"May . . . I-I don't like you out there by yourself. I thought you were going to keep me looped in."

"I did. I sent you those texts." Thunder clapped overhead.

"Sounds like you've got some weather out there. Do me a favor and get out of there, would you? I meant it when I said not to do this alone. Come back to Bretford."

Bretford sounded good about now.

"I can't. I have something to do first." May cleared her throat, vomit still coating it. She needed water.

"I don't like the sound of that. *What* do you need to do first?"

"I'm leaving now." May headed toward the barn doors. "I'll call you later. I'm about to go out into this storm and don't want to get my phone wet."

"Hang on." It was hard to hear him now that she was almost out of the barn. "I have to ask you about a call I got today."

"What call?" Rain lashed her face as she stepped outside.

"A journalist. Some tell-all article." His voice was louder, sensing it was hard for her to hear. "What are you playing at, May?"

"Me?" She yelled. "He called me too. I have no idea what's going on. I'm definitely not the tell-all part."

"This isn't good. I really think you should come back here. Lie low until we see what comes of it . . ."

May stopped listening. There was movement. Over by the trees near the back of the barn. She rubbed her eyes.

Was someone there?

No. It was just the wind. An animal sheltering from the storm maybe.

There it was again. Something was hiding behind the tree.

"May, are you listening to me?"

She was walking toward whatever it was before she could stop herself. No. There was nothing there. She was scaring herself now. Only. Wait.

What was that behind the barn?

"Um . . . Sam? I think . . . oh shit." May stopped dead.

"May? What is it? Are you okay?" His voice was loud yet so far away.

Her words came out slowly. "I . . . found . . . it."

"Found what?"

She didn't even bother wiping the rain blurring her eyes. She knew what she was seeing.

"May, whatever you've found, just get out of there. I'll send someone right now."

"The car . . . it's here."

"What did you say? The car? What—May don't touch anything. I'll have someone out there soon. Do you hear me?"

How could she hear him when June's car was right there? In front of her. Hidden behind the back of the barn.

"May, say something. Tell me you're okay. Get out of there, May. Stay on the phone with me. May, are you there?"

The detective's words were somewhere far away now because she was frozen. Frozen in fear as a head appeared from behind the tree.

Then a leg.

Then a whole person walking toward her.

He was all in black, his face covered. Almost a mirage in the storm. Was this real?

"May, the police are on the way. I need you to find somewhere safe or get out of there. May?"

She lifted her arm up to stop the blow.

She should have brought the baseball bat.

She wasn't ready.

Nope, not at all.

Chapter Thirty-Six

"What, you think I was going to hit you?"

May put her arm down. Not quite believing what was in front of her. No. *Who.*

"June?"

"You look like you've seen a ghost." June laughed. "Don't worry, I'm real."

"June . . ." May couldn't talk. Or move, it seemed.

"What, no hug for your long-lost sister?"

May rushed at June, almost bowling her over. They hugged tightly. Both of them drenched.

"For fuck's sake, May. You're like a skeleton. What, you only eat when I'm around?" June pulled back. "Interesting way to get attention."

"Are you okay? How did you get here?" May stepped away from her sister, inspecting June all over. She scanned the trees. "Holy shit, June. How did you get away?" She looked around again, panicking. "Is he following you? We have to call the police."

May looked at her hand where her phone should have been.

"You already called the police. They're on their way. I took your phone before you almost fainted." June waved her hand in front of May's face. "You okay? I mean, lucky I wasn't a killer. You just stood there waiting to be stabbed or something."

"Oh." Nothing felt real right now. Was she dreaming?

June grabbed May's arms and shook her. "Snap out of it. We need to get out of here. I don't know how long we have."

"Who is it? Wes? Brad? Where are they? Why were you hiding behind that tree? June, what the hell is going on?"

June shook her again. "You need to stay calm."

"Calm? Stay . . . calm!" May slapped her sister.

"Ow! Not exactly the welcome I was expecting." June rubbed her cheek. "What was that for?"

"You left me." May stared at her hand like it belonged to someone else. "You left me those silly clues . . ." May's voice faded like she had run out of batteries.

"I know, and I'll explain everything. Let's just get in Mom's car and get out of here. We can talk on the way."

"Way to where?"

June rubbed her forehead. "Get a grip, and stop asking questions. You'll understand everything when I tell you."

"You want. Me. To. Get. A. Grip?"

"Don't be so dramatic." June grabbed May's arm and dragged her back toward the run-down house.

"Give me my phone back. I need to call Sam," May yelled above the wind.

June ignored her and stalked ahead, never letting go of May's arm. May gave in and let her; she could barely even keep up with what was happening. It was nice to not be in charge for a while.

"Here, give me the keys," June said as they got to the car.

"It's open. They're under the front seat."

June rolled her eyes. "Seriously? Your only means of escape and you leave it open?"

"I didn't want to take any chances. If I got caught, they would've taken the keys, and then I would've been screwed." May couldn't believe this was what they were talking about after all this time.

"Get in. I'm driving." June hunted for the keys and sat in the driver's seat.

May didn't argue, hopping in the passenger seat.

June stuck the keys into the ignition, but May grabbed her arm. "Stop. Look at me. I need to make sure it's really you."

"Make it quick." June glanced at the house. "This is not the time for confessions of your undying love for me."

The twins shuffled around until they faced each other. May took all of her in. June looked the same . . . but different. Her hair was shorter and darker, plastered wet against her face. Her cheeks were fuller. Her eyes still clear and blue.

Your eyes give away all your secrets.

That's what June had always said, but May couldn't see what secrets June was hiding behind her eyes. Nothing new there.

"Did they hurt you?" May whispered.

June put her hand on May's face; her lips trembled. "Don't you worry about that. I have you now, and that's all that matters."

Tears fell and joined the raindrops on May's cheeks. "I let you down. I should've been here earlier. It's all my fault."

June pulled May's face closer to hers. "Listen to me. You didn't let me down. And it's not your fault."

"Truth?"

"Truth." June looked away. "Let's get out of here."

May didn't argue. She would never argue with June again. Hell, she would never leave June's side ever again.

June turned the car around in the mud and drove down the dirt road back to the highway. The rain thundered down on them and covered the silence now hanging heavy in the car.

May grabbed a tissue from the glove compartment and wiped her face. They were on the highway now. They were safe.

"Do you have money?" June sat forward in the seat, focusing on the road.

"A bit. Why?"

"I'm starving. There's a Brake 'n' Bite up ahead."

How could her sister think about food right now?

June side-eyed her. "You have to eat too. Honestly, you don't look well."

"Of course I'm not well. I mean . . . this is all a head fuck, to be frank." May paused. "You called me fat. Do you remember that?"

June scoffed. "I did no such thing! Don't be such a drama queen."

"You did. You said I was disgusting, and you couldn't be around me while I took up so much space. It was just before you disappeared." May sipped from the water bottle sitting in the cup holder, her hand still quivering.

"What, and you took me literally?" June tucked her dripping hair behind her ear. "Since when do you care what I say anyway? Doesn't matter now, does it? You're the skinny twin, and I'm the chunky one. That must make you happy."

May almost spit out her water. "You are not! You couldn't be the chunky one if you tried. You look amazing—as always. No one would know you've been missing for a year."

June went quiet. "Well I have . . ."

"I'm sorry." May reached out for her sister's hand. "I didn't mean to act like an insensitive asshole."

June grabbed her hand and squeezed it.

"You need to tell me what happened, June. You need to tell me everything." May squeezed back.

June put her head against the seat. "Okay. But remember, once you know everything, there's no going back."

May didn't need to think about it. "I only want to go forward. Tell me."

June took a breath and started.

Chapter Thirty-Seven

"It all started when I found the box Mom had hidden, the one with those bizarre letters she wrote to us."

"You got a letter too?" May gasped.

"Try not to interrupt, okay?"

May nodded, although she wasn't sure how possible that was.

"That shoebox is where I found the article I put in Magic." June stopped May from asking another question. "Just wait, okay? I'll tell you everything."

"Hurry up already." May picked at her fingernails.

"It was the best article to leave with you. It didn't say too much, and it summed up where it all started for Mom. I put it in Magic when you were at my funeral—which was just all kinds of wrong, by the way."

May's mouth hung open. "I don't understand."

"Well, I don't understand either. I mean, who has a funeral for someone who isn't even dead?"

"That's not what I meant. I don't understand why you would do that. Why didn't you just *give* me the article, instead of playing childish games?" May pulled off her wet sweatshirt; a chill had started in her bones. "Wow, you were there? June, you better start explaining."

"Let me tell you the whole story before you have a total meltdown." June reached for May's leg.

"Don't touch me. I'm so angry with you. I'm angry with Mom too. You're both liars."

June shook her head and pulled her hand back. "That's fair, but you'll understand. I promise."

"I better. I can't believe you were there that day and you didn't even say anything. Do you *know* what I've been through? What we've *all* been through?" May shivered as she turned up the heater, her wet clothes giving her a chill.

June sat forward again, her knuckles white on the steering wheel. Tears were welling up in her eyes.

"June, I'm sorry. That was shitty of me. I can't believe I said that after what you've been through. I read your letters." May pulled them from the front of her jeans. "They might be a bit wet."

"I don't care. Throw them away. I never want to see them again." June's lips shook as she spoke.

"I won't interrupt, okay? Tell me." May wanted them to stop so she could hug her sister again. Take her pain away.

"You know those letters Mom wrote to us about watching and suppressing?" June whispered. "They're exactly the same. Word for word, just switch out our names."

June flicked her eyes to May as she processed what that meant.

"Mom thought I was dangerous too?"

"I guess so." June shrugged. "I freaked out when I saw that as well. I read the letter before I even got to the other stuff. It was a lot to take in. Mom grabbed by some monster. Dad wasn't our dad. That both of us could be serial killers."

"That's not funny." May shook her head. "And that's not what Mom said."

"We could be, though, given our real father is a psycho. You never know, it could be my true calling." June did a creepy smile.

"This is serious, June."

"I know it's serious. I'm just trying to lighten the mood. I mean, I don't feel like a serial killer. Do you?"

May recoiled. "Of course not! Don't be ridiculous."

June hit the steering wheel. "What about that day at the movie theater, though? I was totally crazed that day, remember? Mom even said so."

"You freaked out because that guy deliberately provoked you. That doesn't make you a serial killer."

"But I stabbed him in the hand. It drew blood, May. Blood!" June did the stabbing motion with her hand over and over.

"Stop it!" May put her hand over June's and kept it there. "Hey, if you don't want to talk about this, then we don't have to. Let's wait until you're with Dad and Pat."

June sighed. "Did you see who our Dad is? I wrote it in my letter."

May sat back in her chair. This was happening. "I saw."

"He looks like me, May. He really looks like me. It's spooky, but kind of cool. I was always jealous of you looking like Mom, but now I have someone who looks like me too."

That was news to May.

"I told him, you know?"

"You told Brad he's our dad? Why?"

June did a bad impression of a smile. "Because I wanted him to tell me what he did to Mom. I thought he'd confess if he had nowhere to hide."

"This isn't some crime documentary," May mumbled. "So what did he say?"

"I video called him just so I could see his reaction. He denied it, of course, and he was angry. Really angry. He punched a wall."

May didn't know what to say.

"Then he threatened me. Said if I told anyone, he would kill me."

"June! When was this? Why didn't you tell me when it happened?"

"I wanted to, but I was scared." June sniffed. "I didn't want him finding out about you. I couldn't risk it."

"I can take care of myself." May flinched as a truck screamed past, sending up a spray of water onto their car. "You should have told me."

"Then I went to that spooky old house from Mom's story and saw his crappy brother. Wes. He must've followed me to that rest stop. Before I knew it I was in that stinky barn. At first I didn't know who'd taken me, but then he made a mistake. Showed his face." June stopped.

"That would've been so scary."

"That's when things got interesting."

"What, like they aren't interesting enough already?" May rubbed her eyes. They weren't far from the Brake 'n' Bite, and she needed coffee or sugar or a bottle of vodka.

"Pay attention, May." June glanced in the rearview mirror. "You haven't read all the letters I wrote to Mom. Some I've kept in a safe place. For later. If we need them."

"What are you talking about?"

"Listen up, May. Let me tell you a story."

Hi Mom!

Sorry I haven't written in a while. It's worth the wait, I promise!

You see, I have a brand-new development. A fresh lead. A new suspect in the "Who's Your Daddy?" competition. Is it a competition? Sure, sure it is. Because I'M making it one. Or did you make it one with all of those boyfriends you had? Questions, questions.

So you know how I did that paternity test on Brad? Of course you do, how could you forget?

Anyway, he denied being our father. Said he didn't have anything to do with your disappearance. Said you hadn't had sex in ages (um, gross—didn't need to know that!). Said he was with his family. At his stepfather's 50th birthday.

That all checked out. Apparently.

But it DID get me to thinking. Where was Wes that weekend if Brad was with "family"? Shouldn't Wes have been there too?

You know Wes, don't you, Mom? I'm soooo onto you. (Also, um, they were brothers. Ick.)

This is where it all gets interesting.

Because there was a lot the police file left out about Wes. Like a LOT! Remember how they said Wes was in custody during the time of your abduction? A police brawl or something? Well, that was true because of the police records, BUT they left a few things out of Wes's backstory. SUPER important things.

Pay attention, Mom! I'm telling you a story. Ready?

LOL. Like you have anything better to do.

Once upon a time, there was a guy called Wes who lived in a town built up around a fruit cannery. Wes's home had once been his old man's—who was long gone now, after he rolled his truck one night. Wes knew the booze had gotten his old man and would get him, too, one way or another.

Wes didn't remember having a mother OR a brother (dun, dun, dun). It was always just him and his old man. The first time his dad struck him, it was square in the mouth. He had left the hose on, wasting precious water. He has never wasted another drop since. (I'm embellishing for dramatic effect here, Mom, but I'm pretty sure this is what happened.)

On the morning of Wes's eighteenth birthday, he got a visit from the local police. Told him his dad was dead. "Didn't even brake," they had said. "Must've happened in the night." "Drunk as a skunk." "You're an adult now. Makes all this easier."

It was then that he found out about his past. His father's toxicology report flagging a hidden identity. A mother he thought had died. A brother he didn't even know he had.

His old man had changed his and Wes's names long ago. Once upon a time, he was Jarod. A kid who had a family. Back in those days, it was his mom who got the beatings. Tried to escape with her young children one day. Didn't get far. The old man did a number on her and took off. Grabbed Wes because he was closer and quieter. The other one, Brad, was a tantrum-having screamer (can confirm). Wes was easy pickings.

It was kidnapping, of course. Reason enough for new identities, including cutting a decent slice out of Wes's young face. The scar was a branding for a new life.

Wes didn't remember any of this as the police asked him about the kidnapping when he was a child. Not even a small nugget. It was like a magic trick. One minute he had a family, and then—poof—they were gone. Then years later—poof—they were back again. (I'm getting good at this story thing.)

Wes couldn't believe his luck. All his life he had asked to be like the other kids, with a ma, and a sibling to hang with. Now, he had it. Like he had rubbed off a scratch card and won the grand prize.

So then one day a beautiful, stunning, fabulous, charming, intelligent, GORGEOUS princess knocked on his door. (It's me, Mom. I'M the princess. LOL.)

The man called Wes had a faded scar that ran across the side of his face like someone had sliced him open a long time ago. The princess wanted to touch it because that's just how she was.

The princess said in her sweetest voice that she was Diana's daughter. But Wes did not react. Nope. Not at all.

The princess tried again. This time in her firm voice.

Asked him directly about ~~Mom~~ Queen Diana (you're welcome) and what happened in Bretford. Well, didn't that put a firecracker up his butt! (Not literally. Jeez.)

He mumbled about Bretford and that time. Something about a "bloody bastard." Saying Queen Diana's name in the strangest way—

The princess sure was confused because she didn't think that Queen Diana had ever met this man. (Looking at you, Mom.)

The more beer Wes drank, the more he loosened up and came to trust the effervescent princess. He spoke of all the beatings growing up. How he didn't remember ever having a mom till he was older. How his evil dad took him when he was only two. They started a new life, and he had no idea that in a faraway land he had a brother.

A (wicked) brother called Brad. Brad who got the much better deal, getting to stay with their mother and growing up with a rich stepfather who never once hit him.

Wes jumped for joy (internally, obvs) when he found out he had a family. He went and visited his brother in Bretford and expected a grand ball. All he got was . . . well, nothing.

Because wicked Brad did not remember him. He did not know he had a brother and thought their father had died when he was a boy.

Wes was so confused. Probably cried.

After all, Wes's mom had welcomed him back with open arms. Helped remind him of who he was. When he was Jarod. How her evil husband had changed Wes's name when he took her son. Named him Wesley after a school he always wanted to go to when he was a boy.

How he didn't just change Wes's name or give him a mark that scarred his face but changed his birthday too. Making him a year older than he was.

Which meant . . . yep, yep, yeppers!

That poor Wes and wicked Brad weren't just brothers . . .

But twins.

And they all lived unhappily ever after.

Love, Princess June xx

Chapter Thirty-Eight

"Wait. They were twins?"

May took a bite out of her breakfast sandwich. They were now sitting in the Brake 'n' Bite parking lot; the rain had finally stopped.

June sipped her shake. "Yes. And get this, Brad didn't even know they were twins. Even though they're identical."

"That doesn't even make any sense." May felt better now that she had food in her stomach. And June by her side.

"His mom never said a word to Brad." June shook her head. "Sound familiar?"

May ignored that comment. She had to keep June on track now that she was finally talking. "But how could he not know if Wes was identical?"

"Brad said Wes didn't look anything like him. Wes has a bigger build. His hair darker . . . oh, and that scar makes it impossible to tell."

"So they both didn't know they had a brother or that they were twins. Shit, that's a lot." May felt for them. She knew that sensation of having the past come and strike you silently like a snake.

"Fuck 'em. They deserve all the bad things." June grabbed one of May's fries.

"Why didn't their mom say anything?" May asked.

June swallowed loudly. "Maybe to protect Brad? Somehow losing a twin brother seems worse than just losing a brother. I don't know. Don't care either."

May nodded. "So, we should—"

June cut in. "They don't even have a relationship now anyway. Wes said that the last time he saw Brad was when he visited Bretford that one time."

Her sister was stalling for some reason. There had to be a point to all this. "When was that? Before or after Mom went missing?"

"Good question. Apparently it was both. The week after Wes showed up, Brad met Mom. Not that he dated her right away. It was weeks before she would go on a date with him, he told me."

"So Wes could have had something to do with it? Even though he was in custody then?"

"Wes had everything to do with it. I know how him and Mom met," June murmured.

"What? Oh shit . . ." May paled. "You don't think that's who Mom was secretly dating? Is that why he was talking that way about her when you were there? Maybe they were in love?"

"Ding, ding, ding." June rang an imaginary bell. "After I went and saw Wes, things got weird. I knew I was being followed. I just couldn't tell if it was him or Brad. They both had secrets and something to hide."

"So that's why he followed you to the rest stop? To stop you from talking. Wes, I mean."

"I guess so. He'd been kidnapped as a kid, so maybe it wasn't so extreme he'd do it with Mom and then with me." June picked at her burger. "It's weird, though. I had a lot of time in that barn alone, and things weren't making sense. If Wes loved Mom, then why did he take her? And why did Brad threaten to kill me if I told anyone about him being our dad?" June waved a pickle at May. "They were either in it together or one found out about the other being with Mom. Maybe it was payback, jealousy. Maybe Mom was already pregnant, and Brad found out?"

May's head was starting to spin again. "The police file says that Brad wasn't our father, but you're saying that the paternity test you did says he is."

June looked up at her sister, her eyes sparkling. "I told you this was where it gets interesting."

"Well, get on with it already."

"Think about it. If they are identical twins, what does that mean?" June waited, studying May's face.

May wasn't sure she understood. Then it came to her. "They have the same DNA."

"Ding, ding, ding. Gold star for May."

"That's it. I'm calling the detective. Give me my phone back."

June wiped her mouth with a napkin. "No."

"What do you mean no? Like hell I'm not calling him." May put out her hand. "I trust him. He'll help us."

June wound down her window and sucked in some air. "What, like he helped Mom? Yeah, right. I did more in one year than he's ever done in twenty years."

"That's not fair," May whispered.

"It *is* fair, and you're not in charge here, May. I am. Which is why I've organized a surprise." June grinned.

May stared out the window at the cars getting back on the highway. Which was exactly what they should be doing. "Why do I have the feeling it's less of a good surprise and more of a bad one?"

June laughed. "Because you know me so well, that's why. I missed you, more than anything."

"You really mean that?" Something was off with her sister, but if May came out and asked, June would clam up—she never had liked anyone spoiling her dramatic buildups.

"Of course I mean it. Now do you want to know what my surprise is?"

May wasn't sure she knew what she wanted anymore. June was back, and that's all that mattered. Why did this not feel like it should? What was she missing?

"Can I just have my phone back? Let's call Dad and Pat at the very least." May's eyelids were heavy. When was the last time she'd slept?

"Okay, fine. I'll tell you." June wiggled in her seat like an excited kid. "We're meeting Brad."

May grabbed her sister's arm. "We're what? Why would we do *that*? Have you completely lost your mind?"

"Brad has a lot to answer for, and we need to know the truth."

May opened the car door. "I don't need to know anything. I'm not going anywhere. I'll call the detective from someone else's phone."

"May, wait. You're being a drama queen again." June picked up her burger. "Besides, Brad's meeting us here. So get back in the car."

Chapter Thirty-Nine

Brad was at a loss as to why June wanted to see him again.

His threat had been clear. Hadn't it? Why was she coming back now?

Money. She wanted money.

That ridiculous paternity test.

He didn't understand how he could be the kid's father. He hadn't had sex with Diana for months before the abduction. She was always too tired or busy. Not that he minded—he had other women if he wanted them.

Since June had surprised him with the test results, he'd given Diana a great deal of thought. One night from his past niggled away at him, burrowing into his brain. It was the night everything had changed with Diana.

Friday evenings at university usually played out the same way. Partying. Drinking. Waking up with a fuzzy head, and no memories to hang on to. Diana rarely came with him, and that suited Brad. But this one Friday night was different. He woke up in Diana's bed alone, no memory of how he'd gotten there. She ignored him for days afterward.

Her flinch every time he touched her, after that night, told him everything he needed to know—that his temper had gotten the better of him, again. That maybe he'd done something he shouldn't have. Had he? When she went missing a week later, he'd almost been relieved.

That night was the only explanation for being June's biological father. He wished he could remember, but he didn't. Diana had been his girlfriend then, for Christ's sake; it wasn't like he needed permission. Sure, he'd been rough before, but she'd never said no. If she'd said no, he would've remembered.

If only Diana had told him about being a father. He would've been there for her. He would've done the right thing. Marriage, the whole lot. If she'd wanted it.

But that was the past, and now he had another life. If his wife found out he had an adult child, she would never forgive him. She'd already excused him twice for affairs she found out about, but a child? No, she would leave him and take the kids with her.

Brad shut down his computer. That blackmailing troublemaker expected him, and he would align his thoughts on the drive. It was better he met her far away from his home or his office. The last thing he needed was for her to call him here again. There was enough chatter from the last time. He'd lost his temper. Of course he had. How could he not? He hadn't expected to become a father to a kid he didn't know anything about.

Today they would meet again, somewhere neutral. No one he knew would sight them out there. He would sort this out once and for all. There was no way she was going to ruin his life.

Brad grabbed his jacket from behind his chair and picked up his computer bag.

His assistant, Angelica, stuck her head in his office doorway. "I know you're heading off for the day, but there is a call for you. A journalist from Bretford. You went to school there, didn't you?"

Brad ignored the pry into his private life. "What does he want?"

"I don't know. He said it was urgent."

"Take his number, and tell him I'll call him back. Don't tell him I'm gone for the day. If he calls again, say I'm in a meeting."

"No problem. Anything else?"

"Yes, don't call me on the cell. I am not available. Got that? *Not* available."

"And your wife? If she calls, what do you want me to say?" Angelica had been his gatekeeper before.

"Same thing. I'm in meetings all day. I might be late home."

"Got it." Angelica tapped her nail on the doorframe. "Well, have a good afternoon."

"Will do. I've had this golf session booked for ages. Looking forward to it."

Brad knew his lie stank. It didn't matter. Angelica no doubt thought he was seeing a new girl. Which wasn't untrue.

Only this one would get what was coming to her.

Chapter Forty

May woke to the stench of fast food. Her sister sat beside her, dipping fries into her thick shake.

"Afternoon, sleepyhead. Here." June passed May a paper bag from the back seat. "Don't worry, it's a small size. Nothing too wild. Your shake is in front of you."

May rubbed her eyes. "When did I fall asleep?"

"Ages ago. That's why I went and got some more food."

May opened her bag. "Thanks. I'm actually hungry."

"Might be cold by now. Didn't want to wake you." June spoke with her mouth full.

The sisters sat in the car with the windows open. The dark clouds were still overhead. June must have moved the car because they were now parked away from the Brake 'n' Bite parking lot, in front of a block of toilets and wooden picnic tables.

"Is this where we're meeting Brad?" May asked, opening up her burger.

"Yep, he should be here soon. Eat quickly before he shows up. Might need some extra energy."

"I don't even want to know what that means." May took a sip of her shake. "You okay? This must be hard, seeing him again."

"I'm good. You're here, so I'm not too worried." June used her straw as a spoon for her thick shake.

"Yeah, because I suddenly developed ninja skills in the last year." Neither of them laughed.

They ate in silence.

June glanced behind her. "That might be his car coming now. Come on, let's go outside."

May's stomach dropped as she put the burger back in the bag. This was it. She was about to meet her real father. Or was that Wes? Time to find out once and for all.

Both girls took their drinks with them and met the expensive car, which parked alongside theirs.

"You sure you're okay?" May grabbed her sister's hand.

June squeezed May's hand in reply.

Brad swung open his door and stepped out. May's insides might as well have been skipping rope. She shouldn't have eaten any of the burger.

Brad was tall, with sandy-blond hair and, when he lifted his sunglasses onto his head, the bluest eyes she had ever seen.

Is this really my father? My uncle?

Brad's eyes narrowed at May. "Who's this? I thought we were meeting alone."

"I wanted you to meet my sister. May, this is Brad—he used to date Mom."

May shot her sister a look that meant, What are you doing?

"Nice to meet you, May. I didn't realize you were coming or that Diana had more children." Brad glared at June. "You never said."

"I have a habit of doing that." June shrugged. "Nothing personal."

"Should we sit down?" May said, already walking toward the tables. There were people scattered about, so she didn't feel like they were in any danger.

"No need to sit. Here, I brought you this." Brad handed June a large padded envelope.

"What is it?" June didn't take it.

Brad lifted his bare wrist up like he was looking at a watch. "It's ten thousand cash. Just take it and then leave me the hell alone."

June laughed, and May couldn't stop her mouth falling open. A payoff? Really?

"She doesn't want your money. Neither of us do. We just want answers." May sounded bolder than she felt.

June punched May's arm and whispered, "Are you sure? I mean, there's no harm in taking it. He owes us."

"Us?" Brad stepped back. "What's going on here?"

June walked backward toward one of the free tables. "Surprise, fucker. There's two of us."

"June!" May gasped.

"What?" Brad and June said at the same time.

"I'm outta here." Brad opened his car back up and threw the money in the front seat.

"Brad, wait. You're here now. Can't we just talk?" May said in her best pleading voice. "We just want to know about our mom, that's all."

He looked at his invisible watch again. "Five minutes and then I'm out of here."

May joined June, who was already sitting at the table, glaring at Brad. He checked his phone screen before putting it face down but didn't sit.

"*Five* minutes."

June slurped the last drops of her shake, then said, "May is my twin sister. Guess you have two children you didn't know about."

"Nice try. Like hell you're twins." Brad stared at May. "You don't look anything like me . . . or her."

"We're fraternal, dumbass."

May touched June's arm. "Don't be rude. Give him time to catch up."

What was her sister playing at? Did she deliberately want to poke the beast?

"How do I even know you're telling the truth?" Brad shook his head. "This is unbelievable. Diana sure has some explaining to do."

May didn't disagree with him. "Our mom was only protecting us, Brad. You can understand that. Now, we just need to know what she was protecting us from."

"I have no idea why she was protecting you both. Or why she kept this from me. If you're insinuating I hurt your mother, then you have the wrong guy."

Brad certainly didn't give the appearance he would hurt them, but didn't they say that about Ted Bundy?

May pressed her sister's leg under the table so she didn't run her mouth again. "So how do you explain the match on the paternity test, then? We are not saying you're the one who assaulted Mom—"

Brad slammed his fist on the table, making the girls jump. "I did not assault Diana! I wouldn't do something like that."

"Told you he was a psycho!" June clenched her fists on top of the table. "Just try it. I'm not afraid of you anymore."

"Afraid of me? What the hell are you on about?" Brad genuinely looked confused. "I'm out of here. Call my attorney. I don't need this shit."

People were beginning to stare.

Crap.

"Hey, everyone calm down. Brad, don't go. I promise June will keep her mouth shut while I just ask some questions. Please, we deserve that, don't we?" May's words stuck in her throat as she quickly glanced at June. As usual she couldn't read her.

Brad wiped his hands on his pants. "Fine. But any more accusations like that and I'm calling my lawyer."

"We just want to know what happened when my mom went missing." May rubbed her temples. Great, her headache was coming back.

He paced in front of the table. "I've told this story a million times already. Even had a journalist harassing me about it just today—"

"What?" June cut in.

"I'll tell you later," May whispered.

"I'm only going to say this once: I had nothing to do with Diana's disappearance."

"Then how do you explain—"

"June, please. I've got this." May took a breath to steady her voice. "You know we have to tell the police about the paternity test. Don't you?"

"Fine. Whatever. I wouldn't mind seeing it myself while you're at it." Brad stopped and looked directly at June.

"Wait. You haven't seen it?" May asked Brad but spoke to June.

June shrugged. "Like I was going to send it to him. Jeez."

May closed her eyes. *Keep it together.* "We'll get you a copy. Same with Wes."

Brad stepped closer to the table. "Did you say Wes? My brother, Wes?"

"Check out the brains on Brad," June said with obvious sarcasm.

"Seriously? You're quoting from *Pulp Fiction* right now?" Brad rolled his eyes. "Like I haven't heard that one before."

"What?" June laughed. "It's a classic."

"And you got the quote wrong, for the record."

May didn't quite know what was happening right now. "Are you two alright?"

"Perfectly," said June.

"Peachy," said Brad.

"So, anyway . . ." May wanted to bang her head against the table. This was not how she had imagined this playing out. "Should we talk about Wes?"

"May, let's go." June crossed her arms. "He's not going to tell us anything."

May turned to her sister. "What are you even talking about? You're the one who wanted to meet him, and now he's here. He threatened you, and I want to know why."

June punched May's leg under the table.

"Ow! That hurt." May glared at her sister and rubbed her leg.

"Jeez, May. Did you have to bring that up?" June said, her arms still crossed.

"It's why we're here. Well, it's one of the reasons we're here." May swiveled back to Brad. There were people around. She had to know. "Why did you threaten my sister that you were going to kill her if she ever told anyone about the paternity test?"

"What?" Brad leaned in closer. "What did you just say? I did no such thing."

June mumbled, looking at May. "You're such a jerk."

"What did you tell your sister, June? That I threatened to kill you? I did no such thing. The only threat I made was that you were never to visit my house unannounced again, or there would be trouble. Trouble. Not. Death." Brad rubbed the bridge of his nose. "Hell, I just didn't want my wife knowing about you."

May whispered, "Is that true, June?"

June shot her palms up in the air. "You got me."

Brad stood, grabbing his phone. "I don't know what this is all about, but I've had enough." He looked down at June. "I was kind to you, even when you told me about that senseless test. Look, I know I'm not perfect, but I don't deserve this kind of slander." Brad came over to May. "Go to the police. I have nothing to hide."

Tears fell down June's face. "I'm sorry I lied. Brad was nice to me. He didn't threaten me like I said. I don't even think he knew I'd gone missing."

May put her arm around June's shoulder even though she wanted to slap her again.

"What's she talking about, May?" Brad asked.

May was officially in a real-life soap opera. "June has been missing for the last year. Your brother kidnapped her."

"Wes? But that's impossible—"

June clambered over the table. Brad took a few steps away from them, his palms up. May pulled her sister back, not sure what was happening.

Then June screamed and screamed and screamed.

DIANA

The knife sliced into the flesh, and the spray hit my face.

Just great.

Bloody sports day.

I was on orange duty. Again. My third year running. Who knew I was such an expert at cutting oranges into quarters?

"Want one, honey?"

May looked up from reading one of those Secret Seven books she and June loved so much. "Cool, thanks."

She took the slice I handed her. Her rosy cheeks so adorable on her chubby face as she gave me a massive grin. Her teeth were all over the place, and the dentist said she would probably need braces, but gosh, she was so cute it almost hurt to look at her.

When did my girls get to be ten already?

May was hiding; of course she was. She hated sports day. With a passion. Maybe that's why I always volunteered for orange duty. So May had somewhere she could escape to.

Her sister, on the other hand. Who knows where she was?

June had already won four gold medals and was probably off winning another one. It was hard to keep up with all the events going on around us. High jump, long jump, shot put, hurdles. Screaming kids. Whistles. Starting pistols. Screaming kids.

The sun didn't help either.

I had already applied sunscreen on May fifty times, and she was still pink. Which meant June would be sunburned by the time we got home because . . . well, because you're a bad mother. That's why. I'd only applied sunscreen on June once.

"Mom! Mom! Mom!" June's voice carried all the way across the oval.

I felt May tense. Or maybe that was me tensing.

"Hi, baby girl," I called out.

June's face was bright red, and she had on her green shorts and green tank top. Green was her team color. May's was blue.

"Did you see? Did you see?" She was puffing as she ran to the front of the trestle table.

Oops. I didn't see.

"Of course I did. Well done!" June always won. It was a safe bet.

Her face told me I'd made a mistake. Reading June was like that book May had in her hand. Easy.

She crossed her arms. Also burned. "You didn't watch, did you? The most important event of today and you missed it."

Think quick.

No, quicker than that.

I had nothing. June would be onto me no matter what I said. I always was a bad liar.

"I'm sorry, baby. You don't have to win all the time." I would be paying for this bad parenting all week now.

June pulled a gold medal from behind her back and put it around her neck. "I actually did win, but I just wanted to see that you watched."

May tucked herself closer to the table. Hiding. I should do the same.

"I'm sorry, baby girl. I've been so busy with the oranges."

"Whatever." June picked up a slice and leaned over the table to her sister. "Why are you here? You're going to get in trouble. Everyone has to compete."

Not untrue.

The orange slurped as June bit into it. "I have one more event. Are you coming, Mommy?"

May stared up at me with her wide eyes. If I was going, then so was she.

"Of course, baby girl. I wouldn't miss it." I put my hand down to May. "Come on, darling. Let's go and watch your sister win. Again."

May squeezed my hand as she pulled herself up from the box of oranges she was sitting on. "Will I get in trouble, Mom?"

I wiped a fleck of orange off her face and pulled her heavy blue sweatshirt down. "No, honey. It'll be okay."

June stood watching us.

Okay. Big smile, Diana.

Here we go into the masses. "Where are we off to? You lead the way—"

June stomped her foot like she was five and having a tantrum. "Don't call me baby or baby girl. I hate it! Why can't you call me darling or honey like May? I'm not a baby anymore, you know?"

Fuckity fuck.

Always getting it wrong.

"I'm older than you by a whole month." May stuck out her tongue.

Great. That old chestnut. Here we go.

I took June's hand and kept May's in my other before World War III started.

June grabbed my waist as we walked. May let go of my hand.

Ten years I'd been doing this.

Would it ever get easier?

Chapter Forty-One

A crowd had gathered, and June was still sobbing uncontrollably.

The sun had faded fast, and lights near the toilet block had already come on. Brad was making a phone call, murmuring something about a restraining order.

May dabbed a wet towel that someone had handed her on June's face. She didn't know what to do. She couldn't get through to her sister. June had become hysterical, and now she wouldn't stop crying.

Understandable after everything she'd been through. May needed to get her to a hospital, but June wouldn't budge.

High beams swept across their faces at the picnic table.

May recognized the car pulling up on the other side of her mom's. How did he know she was here?

Sam stepped out of his car and walked over to the table. A gush of relief rushed over May, making her want to cry.

The detective would fix everything.

"Hello, folks." He held up his badge to the crowd. "I've got it from here. Thank you very much."

Inquisitive families, couples, and lone travelers disbanded but didn't really go anywhere. Watching by their vehicles. Some had their phones up. Waiting for something interesting to happen.

"Fancy meeting you all here. Little late for a picnic, isn't it?" Sam undid his jacket and put his badge away.

Brad did a double take, ending his call. "Oh shit, what are you doing here?"

"I could ask you the same thing, mate." Sam said the word *mate* like Brad was anything but. Then he surveyed the scene, landing on June in May's arms. "Do I need to call an ambulance?"

"June?" May said in her ear. "The detective from Bretford is here."

June whimpered, tucking herself in closer to her sister.

"She was fine one minute, and then she just lost it. Understandable . . . after everything." May gave him a concerned look. "We should definitely take her to a hospital. Get her examined, too . . . you know."

"For the record, I had nothing to do with this." Brad held up his hands.

"I'll deal with you later. Don't go anywhere." Sam pointed to the seat in front of him, and Brad immediately sat.

"How did you find us?" May glanced down at June, but she was still sobbing.

Sam gave an exhausted sigh. "I came as soon as you called me. Have had the police on the phone the whole way. They found June's car. Forensics are there now."

May narrowed her eyes. "Yes, but how did you find me here?"

"I'm a detective," Sam said. "It's what I do."

Brad snorted.

"Let's see who's laughing soon, huh?" Sam gave May an awkward smile.

Brad quickly shut up. "I didn't do anything. These two have lost the plot—"

"Do I have to read you your rights?"

Brad did a zip sign over his mouth and pulled out his phone.

May smiled at the detective. Everything was going to be okay now. It had to be.

May sat in the waiting room of the closest hospital with the detective.

He was on a call. June was being examined. May wished she were in there with her, but June had asked her to wait outside. Brad had been taken into custody for questioning while forensics finished up with June's car and the abandoned house.

Neither she nor Sam had spoken for a while. May had done her best to fill him in on everything, but as usual, she still didn't understand the half of it.

All she knew was that her sister was broken. And something terrible had happened. May just didn't know what or with whom or how she'd escaped or . . . May was done with questions. She'd had enough. June was back, and that was all that mattered.

Sam finished his call and came and sat next to her. They'd finished their coffees long ago. She should get them another one.

May sensed a shift in the detective. "What? What did you find out?"

"I honestly don't know where to start." Sam suddenly looked a hundred years old. "There's been some developments."

Shit shit shit. "Just tell me."

The detective chose his words carefully. "June definitely said that Wes had taken her, held her at the barn out on Old Cemetery Road, where her car was found. Is that correct?"

"Yes? Why?" May could barely speak. "Did they find him?"

"They did." Sam paused.

May waited, her mind racing.

He cleared his throat. "Wes has been in prison for the last two years, May. I just spoke to the general manager there, and he confirmed it. Wes hasn't been allowed parole in that time."

"But . . ." Her throat closed up.

"It looks like your sister started correspondence with him a while ago, but that has since ceased."

"I . . . don't. What?"

Sam grabbed a fresh bottle of water near his chair leg. "Here, drink some of this. Focus on something else for a second."

May ignored the water he handed her. "So was Wes a twin? Had he been kidnapped?"

"All of that is true." Sam took a moment. "May, there's something else."

May grabbed the water, opened it, and chugged it down.

Sam waited until she was done. "Your sister's car. It looks like it has been driven recently."

May sighed with relief. "Well, anyone could have driven it. That doesn't mean anything."

"We'll do some more tests." Sam nodded. "I just thought you should know that her car hasn't been hidden behind that barn for a year like she had you believe."

"June will be able to tell us. I know she will."

Sam hadn't stopped nodding. "I'm sure she will. I just wanted you to know."

"And Brad? If it wasn't Wes, then it must be Brad. June did a paternity test. It came back positive."

"I'll look into that. Don't worry, we'll get to the heart of this. I promise you."

An elderly couple came in and sat in the chairs opposite them. They both looked like they'd been crying.

May stood. She needed fresh air. No, she needed the bathroom. No, she needed to not be here anymore.

Who the fuck knows what I need.

"I need to pee." May handed him back the water and picked up her bag. "I'll be right back."

"Are you okay?"

"Of course. June's back. That's all that matters, right?"

She left before he could read her face.

Know that she was lying.

Chapter Forty-Two

May sat on the cold tiled floor of the bathroom stall, her bag beside her.

It was gross, but she was beyond that now.

She wanted to get up, storm into the examination room, and demand June tell the truth. Only her body wouldn't budge. She was frozen to the floor. She'd become good at that lately.

She had her phone back, and on it was a message from Marcus. Her ex. How long had it been since he'd suddenly stopped texting? She'd never taken him for the ghosting type, but people always surprised you. Now he was asking if they could talk? Weird. Her life in the city felt like a million years ago. She couldn't think about that now.

The tiles were sending a chill through her jeans right into her skin. May tugged her legs to her body to get warm. If only her mom were here. She would know what to do. Know how to get the truth out of June.

She could explain what her letter meant. "Watch and suppress." What had her mom figured out? How could she know June better than she did? Because her mom knew something May didn't. Something that she'd seen well before May had, which meant she'd been looking for it.

She'd been looking for it in both her daughters if she'd written them each a letter.

May pulled the Secret Seven book out of her bag. Her mother's letter was in between the pages, along with the article. She tugged them out, and the receipt with June's riddle fell onto the floor.

She'd forgotten to ask June what it had meant. Would June have told her anyway? Or just spouted more lies?

She already knew the paternity test would come back negative. Because Brad had already been tested. She'd seen it with her own eyes in the police file.

And Wes had been in jail when both June and her mother had gone missing.

Who was her sister protecting by lying about Brad and Wes? And where had she been all this time?

May had had enough of all the crap. All she had wanted was for June to be found, and now that she was, it all came flooding back to her.

Their fight. Why she had left to go to the city. It was like June's disappearance had erased all that and made her into some kind of saint. Only her sister had never been a saint.

May picked up the receipt from the floor. She read the riddle again, with fresh eyes this time. Looking for the lies. The bullshit.

Look up high,
But never low.
It's into the wardrobe,
I have to go.
I don't know who,
And I don't know where.
But time will tell,
If you even care.

No doubt that she cared. May had given up her whole life for June. One word stood out.

Wardrobe.

Why? An itch scratched at her brain. A memory. What was it?

It's into the wardrobe, I have to go.

Wardrobe wardrobe wardrobe wardrobe. Into the wardrobe I have—

Narnia.

The wardrobe from Narnia.

They had always looked for Narnia in the wardrobe.

Pat's wardrobe.

In her attic.

Just like in the Secret Seven book that they'd loved as kids, now sitting on top of her bag. About the girl who everyone thought had gone missing but had hidden in plain sight.

The girl who had slept in her grandmother's attic.

June wasn't held in a barn.

She'd been in Pat's attic.

Hidden in plain sight.

Hi Mom!

Me again. Did you miss me? Everyone else is missing me, which means...

It's almost time. I can feel it. Did you feel it too? When you decided to fake your own disappearance?

I bet you did because you and I are so much alike, aren't we, Mom? And this feeling is better than anything I've ever felt.

I'm about to show myself. I've set up all the clues, followed May around. She's close. Soon she'll find me out at that creepy house you told us about. It will be a wonderful reveal. Better than yours even, Mom.

You see, this is what you did wrong. You kept it all a secret. Went into hiding after you were found. Not me. I plan to use my disappearance to get the fame and fortune I deserve.

I set it up like a legend. Going missing on the same day as you was a stroke of genius, don't you think? Added that bit of mystery that will play out so well when the miniseries comes out. I'm going to play myself, naturally. I'll have it in my contract.

Anyway. I just wish you were still here so I could make you feel like I did growing up. That I would make you feel like I did EVERY day. Like a big pile of shit. Yep, that's right. You made me feel like shit.

I'm not dense. I could see you hugged May differently than how you hugged me. Don't deny it. How you would whisper and share stories with her. Like I was invisible. No matter what I did for attention, I was ALWAYS invisible.

Well, I showed everyone just how invisible I could be.

I showed May that if she wanted to leave me, then I would leave her. How dare she try and live her life without me. I went to the city a couple of times, you know? Would follow her around. She seemed so happy. She even had this guy she was seeing. Marcus. It didn't take me long to break them up. I stole May's phone and texted him. Told him she'd found someone else. Then deleted the messages so she'd never know.

I'm not a bitch, Mom. It was for her own good. He would've broken her heart eventually.

The shitty thing was it took her so long to care that I was gone. She didn't even come looking for me. None of them did.

It was me who planted the idea of having my memorial after a year. I couldn't wait any longer, Mom. I was getting BORED! People were forgetting me.

So every night I would go down and whisper in Pat's ear that I was dead, that they should bury me on the date I disappeared. Move on. Closure. Blah, blah, blah. I heard about that working. Osmosis or some crap.

Sent Dad a bunch of links about funerals for closure from a fake missing person's support group email.

Jeez, people are easy to manipulate. Pat and Dad discussed it like it was THEIR idea. I knew May would have to come back. That's when I set off the biggest and best treasure hunt I have EVER pulled off.

My masterpiece.

I wish you were here to tell me how proud you were of me. Of everything I have done.

Now I'm going to be famous. You wait. I have it all planned. It'll be just like when you died and Mr. Milham gave me the best piece of therapy advice ever. My trauma will do the "talking." (Know anything about that, Mom?) No one will question me or my lies. Everyone will think I'm protecting myself with my "trauma." Then I'll have them believing I'm protecting someone else. I'm a genius.

So, I know why I did all of this. But why did you, Mom? Maybe you did like mysteries after all. Where did YOU go? What bullshit did you spin from all your "trauma"?

And why did you say I have bad blood in me?

Speaking of! I have a bone to pick with you. What is this "watch and suppress" crap? Why didn't you ever write ME a letter like you wrote to

May? I'll tell her I got the same one, but I didn't get ANY letter like that from you. I would like to think I'll find mine one day. I didn't much like the one you wrote to May. It was a little unfair and totally NOT true.

I don't have bad blood. I only lie like you do, Mom. That's my only fault.

Not like May, she's perfect. Isn't she? Don't deny it, you always loved her best. The way you looked at May was never the same as the way you looked at me, like you hated me sometimes or something.

Maybe one day I'll work out why.

Just between you and me, I never did find out who our father is. I said it was Brad, but we both know that's a lie. The paternity test I said I did wasn't real.

So the question is, Who is our real dad?

Anyway, I hope May and I didn't ruin your life.

Love, June xx

PS Next letter will be what I've REALLY been doing for the last year. You're going to LOVE it! :)

Chapter
Forty-Three

Pat's attic was tinier than May remembered.

She had driven her mom's car from the hospital, while the detective and June were in his—much to June's disgust. May had beaten them to Harold, so no one knew she was up here in Pat's attic.

May wasn't ready for company just yet.

June's examination had turned up nothing. Not even dehydration. Very curious indeed.

It just supported May's theory of where June had been staying all this time. Plus all the discarded food wrappers and water bottles that were strewn about the small room were a dead giveaway. Photos from Pat's fridge, that May thought Pat had thrown out, sat in a pile beside June's makeshift bed.

In all these photos, May was smiling (not squinting), and she may have been bigger then, but at least she had been happy. She'd forgotten what that even felt like.

May lay her head on the musty pillow, imagining her sister holed up in the confined space over so much time. It didn't seem like something June would do, but May didn't know what her sister was capable of anymore.

She willed tears to come. Relief from a family she no longer knew and a life that was now a lie—but like the packet of saltine crackers near her head, she was dry. Maybe she actually understood June's need for hiding. Right now, May wanted her own escape from reality.

She gazed up at the dark sky through a small skylight, the attic heavy with heat.

May's eyelids drooped. Sleep might be the only escape she would get today, as the conversations from below filled the room. June could hear everything up here. No wonder it was such a great spot. Eavesdropping on her family all this time. The familiar voices downstairs sounded like they were coming from another world.

June was delivering her next act. With a captive audience, no doubt. June was probably wondering where she was.

The detective hadn't said a word yet, but May knew he was there. Returning to a family from his past that brought nothing but trouble.

He was her only small comfort.

May wanted no part of what was happening below her. She'd had enough of listening to June's stories. Lies. Everyone justifying her memory due to the trauma she'd suffered. What trauma? May wasn't sure there had been any. It was possible she didn't care. Not right now anyway. She would leave the puzzle of her sister for others to solve.

Her days of investigation were over.

June's sobs floated into the room, taunting May. Yet now she felt nothing. It was like her twin was a stranger to her.

June's not a terrible person.

June's not a terrible person.

June's not a terrible person.

June's a terrible person.

It was like counting sheep.

May slept.

Chapter Forty-Four

Sharon was doing an early inventory at the bookstore when the morning papers were delivered.

A familiar image jumped out at her from the front page. Diana's eyes, from her student-ID photo, stared back at her. A chill ran up Sharon's spine.

TWIN TWIST IN UNIVERSITY MYSTERY read the headline.

Sharon skimmed the article.

Why didn't they contact me? She hated feeling irrelevant.

Too many secrets, D. I should've known those girls were sniffing around for a reason. Trying to find their daddy, hey?

Her laugh filled the empty bookstore. She enjoyed the echo of it.

"Timed your death just right, didn't you? Always were a lucky bitch," she said under her breath. Dead means secrets stayed buried.

Sharon reread the article, but she already knew the rest. No new leads. Abductor unknown. Exclusive quotes from Diana's sister. Blah, blah.

She read the final paragraph. A last-minute addition: *June was alive. More to come.*

Like your mom. Alive and well.

Strange coincidence or dumb luck? *Neither.*

Memories of Diana and their dorm room played in her mind. Something had always bugged her.

She never took that garish necklace off.

Sharon was certain it had to be a clue. Not for her, but for the person who would eventually find it.

She had always known who'd taken it, but no one had ever thought to ask her—not directly anyway.

Sharon's fingers tingled with excitement as she dialed his number.

DIANA

I'd been sitting in the blackened dorm room for longer than I cared to admit.

I couldn't make up my mind. I was drawing a blank everywhere I turned.

If I called my mom, she would sort it out for me. She would make it better. I wanted so badly to tell her everything, but I knew I wouldn't. Not this time.

I needed more time to think. I needed everyone to disappear.

No. I needed to disappear.

The first flutter of an idea came to me then. I rolled it around in a space that hadn't been much help before but had now sparked to life. I was sure I would find a fault.

I didn't.

I switched on my bedside lamp. The room filled with light like how my brain now filled with ideas.

It was good to feel something. A little control could go a long way.

I hadn't been in control for months. Not knowing if he still loved me. If he would ever love me. I had tried to protect our relationship, which he wanted to stay hidden, by dating Brad, but that had been no better than putting a Band-Aid on an arterial spurt.

Not even my secret held comfort. Once, I had thought it would bring us together. Now, I knew better.

I touched my stomach. Still so flat.

When would I show? It was still so early.

I instinctively rubbed my necklace. My lucky charm. It didn't feel so lucky anymore. I undid the clasp and placed it on my desk. It would be symbolic. He read signs for a living, after all. This one would be like leaving it in large letters: YOU ARE FREE.

Time moved swiftly after that; it always did when a plan became a reality.

With what cash I had, and the clothes on my back, I closed the door to my dorm room, knowing I would never return. University would eventually become a temporary blip in my past, because I was going to be a mother instead.

If I had just told the truth, everything would've been different.

Instead, I became the girl from Bretford who disappeared.

Chapter Forty-Five

The detective apologized to the room as his phone went off. He stepped outside Pat's place, into the dark, and accepted the call.

"Davis here."

"Sam?"

"Sharon. It's early." He recognized the raspy voice instantly. "Now's not a good time."

"I won't take much of it, but it's important. I know you'll want to hear this."

She had his attention. "Go on."

"Did you see the article yet? In the *Bretford Times*?" Her voice had a quiver, which made him nervous.

"I'm not in Bretford right now. I'm dealing with another matter."

"You found June."

"Yes." Sam paused. "How did you know?"

"The paper mentioned it. Seems Diana's family finally wanted to spill their guts on those two girls." Sharon sounded smug.

If the newspaper already knew, it wouldn't be long until the TV crews showed up. The detective ran a hand through his hair, scanning the quiet suburb. The streetlights created ominous shadows on the road.

"You still there?"

"Yes, I'm here. Hey, thanks for letting me know about the article. You actually helped me out."

Shame someone from the station hadn't shown him the same courtesy.

"Sam, I didn't call about the article. I called because I know something that could be useful . . . or harmful. Whichever way you want to look at it." He was sure she was smiling as she talked.

"Get on with it, Sharon."

She cleared her throat. "I know you took it, Sam."

The detective stood still, waiting for more.

"I know you took Diana's necklace. The only question is why."

Sam sat on the porch steps. He glanced around even though he knew he was alone. The air took on a chill he hadn't noticed before.

His voice wouldn't betray him. He'd had practice over the years. "What are you on about, Sharon?"

She sighed heavily in his ear. "I kept your secret. Now I deserve the truth."

"The truth is the necklace was collected for evidence. Where it ended up after that is anyone's guess."

"You're lying. I know it never made it into evidence, because you took it. Don't deny it. I finally saw that evidence list. I know I'm right."

"Like how certain you were that Diana had come back to the dorm?"

A bird called out above the detective's head, its shriek shattering right through him.

Sharon whispered like someone was listening next to her. "I was outside when you did a search of our room. When I left, the necklace was on her desk. When I came back in, it was gone. Don't deny it."

"I'm not denying anything. The necklace went into an evidence bag like everything else that was important. That's why it wasn't in the room when you returned." He rubbed the bridge of his nose. "I was doing my job, Sharon."

Neither of them spoke.

Sam checked the door behind him, which was still closed. "You know, something has always bugged me about you saying Diana had come back to the dorm."

Sharon hesitated. "Yes?"

"You said items were missing from your room or had been moved around after Diana had disappeared. You smelled her freshly sprayed perfume."

"That's right. I wasn't lying. I was scared. I figured someone was breaking in or was trying to tell me something."

"So you thought it was Diana?"

"That's what I wanted to believe, but Diana had been gone for a couple of weeks by then. I freaked myself out not knowing who had come into my room. I had my brother, Tony, stay with me for a few nights because I was so scared."

"That's understandable. So he never noticed anything while he was there? I didn't realize he was around during that time, or I would have interviewed him."

"It was only for two or three nights. Then he took off like he always did, without saying goodbye. I never spoke to him after that, and nor could you have. He died, remember?"

"I don't recall knowing that. I'm sorry." Something niggled behind the detective's eyes, but he passed it off as tiredness. "That perfume thing had always bothered me."

He knew why. He'd only just smelled the same scent. In the kitchen. *Must be Sue wearing her sister's perfume.*

Movement in the house behind him made him lower his voice. "Hey, thanks again for the heads up on the article, Sharon. I have to go. I'll come into the café for coffee when I'm back."

"Sam . . . before you go."

"Make it quick, Sharon." He sighed.

"I think you knew her . . . you know, before."

Sam didn't say anything, listening only to the throbbing of his head in his ears.

"You did, didn't you? Was it you I spoke to on the phone when you called our room?"

"Sharon, that article has made you question the past, and now you're grasping to make something stick. I understand. I get tunnel vision too. If I find anything out, I'll tell you."

"Yes, but what about—"

"I have to go."

Sam hung up.

That bloody necklace.

Chapter Forty-Six

May woke with a start, sure someone had called her name. The attic was still dark, and it took her a moment to get her bearings. She felt for her phone, checking the time. She had been out for hours.

Her whole body ached as she stretched and pushed her feet against the wall. Her toes pressed against something. Using the flashlight on her phone, she pulled out a stack of envelopes wrapped in a ribbon.

May flipped through them. They were letters addressed to Wes in prison.

Across all of them was: *Return to Sender*.

None of the letters had been opened.

May shuffled through them. They were all the same. All unopened and returned to sender. Except for a couple at the end that were open.

May's heart raced as she glanced around her, using the phone to fill the black corners with light. The small, dark room suddenly gave her the creeps.

She picked up one of the letters and shone the light down onto the page.

It didn't take her long to read what was written. Her eyes flying over the words. Another letter to her mom. This one confessing it all. Her whole psychotic plan. The fake paternity test. Her manipulation of May. Wow, even Marcus. She'd always wondered why he'd ghosted her.

Well, now it was official at least.

Her twin was a sociopath.

Awesome.

So her mom *had* been onto something.

May pulled herself up and headed downstairs.

"There you are, child. When did you get here?" Pat said as May shuffled into the kitchen.

Everyone was sitting around the table. Including some guy she'd never seen before. He was bald, with a mean scar on his head, and striking blue eyes that drilled into her. His muscular frame swallowed Pat's wooden chair. May thought he looked familiar but couldn't place him. This must be the guy from the slaughterhouse Sue had told her about.

Sue sprang up behind him. "This is my boyfriend, Ant."

Hilarious. He was the furthest thing from an ant.

Ant put up a hand.

May put up a hand back. If he wasn't going to say anything, then neither was she. She didn't need any of Sue's crap right now, including her new boyfriend and his creepy stare. Why was he even here?

"What took you so long?" June asked, sitting cross-legged on one of the chairs in Pat's dressing gown.

May ignored her. "Where's the detective? He didn't leave, did he?"

"I'm right here, May." She swung around to where Sam stood next to the doorway. She almost considered running into his arms but figured that would be weird. "I was just out front making some calls."

May sensed someone behind her. Her father. "Hey, Dad, what time did you get here?" May rested in his arms instead.

"An hour ago. I drove straight here from the farm." He broke away from May and went over to June. "I had to make sure this one was really back."

June tried to catch her eye, but May ignored her and went to the cupboard. "Who wants a drink?"

"Oh, child, you read my mind. About time we celebrated Junie's return." Pat's voice lowered. "Where have you been?"

Escaping. "Taking a nap." May pulled out glasses for everyone.

"Typical, leave us with all the mess while you have a relaxing sleep." Sue looked around to see if anyone would back her up. Ant didn't say anything, just stared at May pouring the drinks. *What was his problem?*

"I wouldn't call this a mess." Gary squeezed June's shoulders.

Sam added, "There's still a lot to sort out here. The police don't take lightly to time wasters."

May placed glasses of straight scotch on the table for everyone. Ant grabbed his with both hands, one of which was missing a thumb, and chugged it down—putting even Pat to shame.

May handed Sam a glass last.

"Not for me. I need to head back."

"Oh." May returned to the sink, unsure of why she so desperately wanted him to stay.

Pat tapped her cane on an empty chair. "I won't hear any more nonsense come out of your mouth. Have a drink and get some rest. You can't possibly drive the two hours back to Bretford now. The station can do without you, I'm sure."

Sam didn't move. "I would love to, Pat, but I must get back. There are some fires to put out in Bretford, with that article coming out and digging up the past."

May didn't join everyone's glares at Sue; instead she rubbed her eyes.

Sue sighed. "Here we go. You'll all thank me soon enough. Been getting calls all day about that article. We could make some real coin now that June's risen from the dead."

Ant smirked, his face moving for the first time. Something fired in May's brain.

Where do I know him from?

Sam got the first word. "Did you have to let them know about June being back, Sue? Couldn't you have given the family a few days' reprieve?"

"Wait, I didn't tell them about—"

"It was me. I called the reporter from the hospital." May scanned the faces of her shocked family.

"Why did you do that?" June went to stand.

"Sit down, June. Don't come near me. You too, Dad." Gary and June stayed where they were.

"Love, you okay? You look paler than usual. Come and sit next to me." Pat put out her hand.

"I'm fine, Pat. In fact, I've never felt better." May sat on the edge of the sink. "I wanted people to know June was back. I've had enough of her calling the shots."

Sue laughed.

"Good one, May." June got to her feet. "Now the media is going to start hounding us. What am I supposed to say to them? I'm not ready for talk shows yet with my hair looking like this."

"Why don't you tell them the truth?" May shook her head. "Oh wait, you can't. Can you? Because you don't know what the truth is."

May could feel the detective's eyes on her from the door, maybe judging her. She wished she didn't care.

Gary spoke softly, "May, it's been a long night. Why don't we talk about this after we all get some sleep?"

"No, Dad. I'm so sick of this family and all its secrets. How about we tell the truth for a change?"

May walked around the table, tapping everyone's head as she went. She stopped at June. "Remind you of anything, June? Duck, duck, goose, perhaps? Reckon you know who the goose is this time?"

June swiveled around, gaping at her sister. "Hey, don't be so upset. Once you know everything, you'll understand."

"Truth, June?"

June smiled. "Truth."

"Bullshit."

"No, not bullshit. Everything I told you was true." June darted her eyes around at her family. "I was totally honest when the police were here. I promise."

"Your promise means shit." May pulled the letter June had written out of her back pocket and slammed it on the table in front of June.

June's eyes met May's. Suddenly understanding.

"Try explaining your way out of this, dear sister."

DIANA

I made two mistakes when I disappeared. The first was dropping my purse the day I left, and the second was coming back.

I'd been gone for three weeks when I woke up with blood on my underwear.

With no baby in my belly, I could go back to Bretford.

And I did.

I had planned on staying at university now that I wasn't going to be a mother. I honestly had. Even took a shower in the dorms when I returned.

There was still fingerprint dust all over my things. Sharon had only been bothered to clean her side of the room (no surprises there). My necklace was gone, but I didn't expect it to be there. And someone had definitely been sleeping in my bed.

On any other day, the dorms would be packed with students, and I would've been spotted—but the dorms were quiet. In fact, the whole campus was quiet. Did I know I was coming back when there was a big football game? Sure. I'm a planner.

Disappearing in the first place was supposed to be easy. Except, I dropped my purse somewhere and suddenly had no money. Fuckity fuck. So I made a phone call, and he was there. My old school friend Willy. Only, he was Bill now.

So, when I called Willy—Bill—early Friday morning and told him I needed to get the hell out of Dodge (Bretford), he came and got me. He was living above his parents' bakery in Harold by then, where he worked as a baker, and I took to living there too. Only until I could figure out what to do with my baby, I promised myself.

Bill had a wedding cake to bake for the weekend I was "technically" missing, and that kept him busy. I only knew how to do two things anyway: sleep and cry.

I was never afraid of anyone finding me because Bill had his room sealed up like a safe—still afraid his secret of having a room filled with costumes being discovered.

He cried with me when I lost the baby. He was as invested as me by then. Emotionally and criminally.

He drove me back to Bretford because I asked him to. Not asking what my next step was. I'm not sure I even knew what that was.

Maybe I was hoping my Prince Charming had missed me so much he would want to get back together, make our relationship public finally.

What I hadn't planned on was the monster who had a key to my room and took advantage of a girl in a towel. What I hadn't planned on was Sharon's brother, Anthony.

Tony.

It was in his sapphire eyes and his creepy smirk as soon as I came back from the showers. I had seen it many times before, but this was the first time we'd been alone.

Life-changing moments can come down to something as simple as: wrong place, wrong time.

I don't remember much after that. Sometimes you can do that. Forget.

Liar.

He must have hit me because when I woke up, I was in the back of a car. Dressed in clothes from my closet. I smelled like I'd been drenched in my perfume. I figured he was taking me somewhere to kill me, and part of me welcomed it.

When the car stopped, he grabbed me by the hair and threw me onto a dirt road near an abandoned house. Told me if I ever said anything about what he'd done to me, he'd kill me. I had no trouble believing him.

Then he was gone.

I'm not sure how long it took me to move. Minutes? Hours? All I knew was, it was now dark, and I was cold.

Then a young girl's voice sounded as if she was right there beside me. *He's coming back. HIDE!*

So I did. I rolled myself into a ditch on the side of the road and covered myself with dead leaves. I knew it was his car because of the exhaust. A rattly, beastly sound. I don't know how many times he went up and down that road with his high beams on, but I didn't move an inch.

It wouldn't be until later that I found out he'd dropped me at Old Cemetery Road. Maybe it meant something, or maybe it was nothing at all. I don't like to think about it.

Tony "died" a few weeks later. It was easy enough to find him and follow him in my car after he'd been drinking. I ran him off the road, not minding if I joined him in whatever hell we went to. Only, he survived. So did I.

It was weird. I could have killed him as he was pinned right there in his car, with all that blood coming from his head. But I didn't. I'm not a murderer.

He thought he was so tough. Yet he sat there crying like a baby. Begging for his life.

I didn't kill him. I warned him instead.

Said he needed to stay dead. If he didn't, I would kill him. I meant it. He knew I did after I smashed his thumb in the door when he tried to get out of the car.

Or maybe because he looked me in the eye as I did it and saw I had evil in me like he did. Maybe I *was* a murderer.

I read the obituary that Sharon put in the paper, so I knew he'd followed through on his promise.

Good. He deserved no legacy.

And my girls are most definitely not his legacy.

It wouldn't be until years later that I recognized the girl's voice that saved me that night on the dirt road. She would stare at me with her big brown eyes and say "Come on, Mommy. June will finish counting soon. We have to *hide*."

Chapter Forty-Seven

May left the kitchen and everything it held behind.

The detective was already out front. He put up his hand, signaling May to wait while he was on the phone.

She had all the time in the world. No longer having a job and doubting if she would return to the city. She didn't care what her life looked like now. All May knew was that being alone, she was stronger than she could've ever imagined.

June had taught her that. May's life had cracked in two when her sister disappeared and shattered all over again now that she was back. May couldn't think of a time when her sister wasn't controlling her life in some way.

I let her.

Sam put his phone away and sat beside her on the steps.

"Sorry, just fielding calls all over the place. This is a mess, isn't it?" He looked as shit as May felt.

May stared down at her black boots. "Would you believe me if I told you I didn't care?"

Sam chuckled. "No, but good on you for trying."

"I really don't think I do. Our true father is in that kitchen—that's all I need to know."

The detective got up from the steps. He ran his fingers through his hair.

"You do that when you're stressed. Have you noticed that?"

"Do what?"

"Put your hand through your hair. Guess this family stresses you out a lot, huh?"

"It's been a rough week for all of us. It's hard playing catch-up with your sister."

May scoffed. "Tell me about it. Try being a twin competing with that."

Sam stared off into the sky. He ran his hand through his hair again, then stopped himself.

"You want to tell me what's bothering you?" May asked.

Sam glanced up at the empty kitchen window.

"Detective? It's okay. I feel like I let her down too."

Sam's eyes met hers. "Who? Your sister?"

"No. Mom. You wish you could've done more. I feel the same way. I let her down, too, in the worst possible way."

Tears formed in the brown eyes that matched hers.

"Oh, May. It's not your mom I let down. It's you."

DIANA

The knock at the door was thirty minutes early. She shouldn't be here yet.

I had just put the girls down for their afternoon nap, hoping they would sleep while my new neighbor Mrs. Slattery came to look after them. At three years old, the twins were becoming quite the handful.

I pulled off my rubber gloves, even though I hadn't started cleaning the breakfast dishes, and went to the door.

"Hi, Mrs.—" Blood rushed through my body like a tidal wave. I never thought I was going to see him again. "What . . . what are you doing here?" I glanced down the sunny street, half expecting Mrs. Slattery to be walking in my direction. Lucky for me, the footpath was bare.

"Hi, Diana. It's good to see you."

I instinctively looked upstairs, thinking of the girls. How could I not?

"I'm sorry I didn't call. I didn't want to do this over the phone."

When was the last time I saw him? At the hospital? I had done my best to forget him, and now here he was.

"Quickly, come in."

I ushered him inside before anyone could see him. Harold would have a field day with a mystery man on my doorstep.

"You look well."

"Thanks, but you don't have to say that. The girls keep me busy, so I forget about brushing my hair, or showers, or sleep. Eating sometimes too." I was rambling.

"Well, I think you look great." He smiled, and my stomach flipped. It was like the first day he grinned at me on orientation day; he even had the same mirrored sunglasses on his head.

I needed to keep busy. "Coffee?"

"Sure, if you're having some."

"Of course."

We were talking like everything was normal.

I prepared the coffee, not wanting to look at him. I didn't trust myself. He stood at the counter, his eyes seeing through me like they always did.

"How's Gary?"

That wasn't the question I was expecting. "Really? You came here to ask about Gary?"

He ran his hand through his hair. Thank goodness. He was as nervous as me.

"I'm sorry. I was trying to be polite. I should get to the point."

"Maybe that's wise. My neighbor will be around shortly, and I don't know how to explain you being here."

What if I didn't want him to leave?

I finished making the coffees, and we sat across from each other at the kitchen table. It was an old table from Pat's house, because we couldn't afford new furniture. I hadn't even wiped it down from breakfast; there were bits of food and spilled milk everywhere. I should clean it up.

"Leave it. It can wait."

Damn him for always knowing what I was thinking.

My hand shook as I picked up my coffee cup.

He noticed, of course, and lightly put his hand over mine that was on the table. I let out a breath that had been trapped inside me for years. His touch brought back so many memories, ones I thought I'd archived forever.

I pulled my hand away.

"Sam, you can't be here. I'm married now. I'm a mother now."

He put his hands in his pockets. Good. Bad. Hold my hand again.

I decided then and there—if he wanted me back, I would say yes. It was as simple as that.

Fuckity fuck.

He stared at his coffee cup. "I debated whether I should come or not—trust me when I say that. I couldn't not have this conversation. You know it's been a long time coming . . ."

Here it was. He was going to say he still loved me too.

"I hope you'll understand."

"I do too." Oh, crap. He didn't say it.

He frowned. "I do too, what? You can't possibly know why I'm here."

"Yes, I do too understand . . . um, will understand when you tell me." What was he going to tell me?

"It's about the twins."

My face fell; this couldn't be good. "What about the twins?"

His hand was back out of his pocket, taunting me. He was playing with his hair again.

"There has been an update on their paternity."

I had never told a soul. That was the promise I made the day Tony disappeared. The day I "killed" him.

So now everyone would know the truth.

"Did you hear me, Diana? We know who one of the girls' fathers is."

"Yes, I suppose you do . . . hang on, did you just say *fathers*, as in plural?"

"Yes, I did."

Why wasn't he looking at me? What was going on?

"I asked the hospital to take some blood work from the twins when they were born, and we did a paternity test on Brad then. Do you remember? He was the only suspect at that stage."

"Yes, I remember. It wasn't a match. I already told you that. I knew it wasn't Brad."

I didn't like where this was going.

"That's right. At the time, Brad was eliminated. Only something didn't sit right with me, and I'm sure you know why it didn't."

"Come off it, Sam. I'm not a criminal in your interview room. So stop treating me like one." I sipped my coffee, which tasted like dirt. "Of course you had to check if you were the father, but I knew you weren't. Don't you think I would've told you?"

I could tell he was doing his best to hide his frustration. "How on earth would you know if I'm the father or not?" He put his hand back in his pocket. "Hell, no one even knew about us . . . did they?"

Bastard.

"No. No one knew about you. I've never told a soul. How dare you say—"

There was a knock at the door. Mrs. Slattery.

Fuckity fuck.

"I'll get rid of her."

I did. Telling her I wasn't feeling well.

I returned to the kitchen, sat at the table, and tried to read what was behind his eyes. The eyes always give it away. I would teach my girls that one day.

Was it possible to want someone to stay forever and leave at the same time?

He'd left me before. He would do it again.

"Sam, I want to get something straight. Once and for all. I loved you. I wanted to be with you, but you needed to keep me a secret. Like your job would've cared that we were together."

"Diana—"

"Let me finish. When I disappeared, I *was* pregnant. You never knew that—don't interrupt—and I know I should've told you." I was about to break his heart like he broke mine. "Turns out I didn't need to. I lost it. I lost our baby."

Annoying tears started then. That's what happens when you bottle things up for too long. He went to hug me, but I stopped him. A lifetime of hugging Sam was over the minute I saw the blood in my underwear.

"Diana . . . I'm not sure exactly what you think happened, but you didn't lose my baby."

But I saw the blood. "Say that again."

"You didn't lose my baby."

He was talking, but I heard nothing. My head spun, and I was sure I was going to faint.

Prince Charming would catch me, no doubt.

I loved this man, from the first day we met. A love I had never experienced again, nor did I deserve. I couldn't go back there. My life was different now. I had Gary. He was a great father. Kind, stable, uncomplicated. Nothing like my relationship with Sam had been. Gary was too good for me. I may not have been wearing a "lucky" necklace the day we met, but Gary was my *true* Prince Charming.

"Diana? Are you okay?"

Debatable. "You just told me I didn't lose our baby, or did I dream that?"

"You didn't dream it." He rubbed his lip. "Diana, let me talk. Okay? I have to get this out."

I didn't disagree.

"Like I said, something always bugged me about Brad's test being negative. I couldn't put my finger on it until I saw the paternity document. I realized they had only tested May's blood, not June's."

I held my breath.

"May wasn't a match with Brad. So I tested myself, and well . . . you know where I'm going with this, don't you?"

"But I lost the baby, Sam. I know I did. There was so much blood, and our little baby was gone."

"Except, she wasn't. She was growing inside you when you must've had sex with someone else . . ." His voice betrayed him, which didn't happen often.

I realized what he was saying. He didn't know. He didn't know about Tony.

"It was no one special. Just a foolish mistake to get back at you. I'm sorry." I didn't know which part I was apologizing for. I would never tell him, or Tony would be dead for real. Maybe—

"It's okay. It's my own damn fault for always pushing you away. Thinking my job was bigger than the both of us."

"You were always hoping I would find someone else, weren't you? So you could live your life being some hotshot detective—without some student holding you back." He couldn't deny it. It was true.

"Diana, I'm so sorry. I was a jackass. If I handled things better, none of this would have happened."

Neither of us were blameless. Although, it was me who had made a mess of everything. If only I had told him the truth instead of running away.

"So my girls are not twins? They have different fathers?" All this time. All that pain. The heartache of thinking my girls had come from *him*. The monster. "Are you sure?"

Sam nodded. "I'm sure. I wasn't a match with June. Only May. What happened back then? You can tell me now."

I would never tell him. "I made the whole abduction thing up. It was reckless, but I wasn't thinking. I wanted to punish you *and* be close to you at the same time."

"And the bruises when we found you? Did someone hurt you? Brad?"

"No. I fell over when I was out on that horrible road by myself. It was so dark. I slept in a ditch waiting for someone to find me." The lies came easily when they had to.

"I wish you'd told me. I'm sorry I hurt you." His eyes penetrated mine. "You didn't have to disappear. I would've been there for you. For our child."

I couldn't change a thing now, even if I didn't understand why I did everything I did. All the mistakes I made. The credits on that story had rolled a long time ago.

"I loved you, even if I never proved it." His eyes told me maybe the story wasn't finished after all.

"I guess we were both to blame." If only I could go back in time. "So, what happens now?"

He cleared his throat and played with his hair again. "Nothing happens now. Your case is closed."

Oh.

"I have one final request, if that's okay?"

Stay.

"I want to see her. I want to see May. I have something for her. For both of them."

Sam pulled out two My Little Ponies. Butterscotch and Minty. He remembered what I'd said at the hospital, about them being my favorites.

I didn't cry until after he left. After he had held his daughter.

I didn't know then that I would never see him again.

Chapter Forty-Eight

May was having trouble breathing.

"Okay, so let me get this straight. Mom really did stage her abduction, and you were her secret lover. You're my father, and we have no idea who June's father is." May took a breath. "This definitely wasn't part of the murder board. I mean, how is that even possible?"

Sam's face was serious. "I know it's confusing. It took me a while to understand it myself. I can't remember the name, but if you jump on your phone, I'm sure you'll have no trouble finding what it's called."

She did.

"It's called superfetation." May scrolled through her phone. "Basically, it's when a woman conceives again while she's already pregnant. Mom didn't know she was carrying two children from different fathers."

Sam nodded; his eyes glistened.

May went back to her phone. "It's happened before. Look at this lady. She had one Black baby and one white baby. That'll give it away."

Sam half smiled. "You okay? It's a lot to take in."

"I'm fine. Nothing shocks me anymore, apparently." May tugged down the legs of her jeans as she stood. "I'm glad you told me. I love that you're my real father. If anything has come from the last week, that news makes me happy."

Sam showed his surprise at her response. "It's okay if you're angry with me for not telling you sooner."

The light from the street cast long shadows along the ground. May walked to the tire swing hanging from the tree. A relic from two generations of sisters.

"I don't blame you for not telling me. Mom too. I actually understand. You were protecting me. And June." May didn't know where to look. "And Dad."

"It's okay. He's always going to be your father. I'm happy to be whatever you want me to be."

May sat in the tire and let her feet drag along the ground as the swing moved back and forth. She imagined her mom pushing her, and June complaining she wanted a turn. A smile crept up without her being aware of it.

"Penny for your thoughts? You look . . . happy."

"Weird right? I feel happy. I love my family so much, even with all the secrets. My mom was the best mom anyone could ask for. I guess I wouldn't change a thing about any of this, except Mom dying, of course." May looked at the ground. It wasn't the time to think about that now.

"Should we go in and tell your family? They have a right to know." Sam got up from the steps.

"No. It would just make things more complicated, and right now, we have enough complication. Besides, I like having my own secret . . . for once."

"As long as you're sure. If you change your mind, I understand."

"I'm sure." May caught the detective's eye. "Why did you leave her? If you loved each other so much, why couldn't you be together?"

"Oh, May, if only things were that simple." Sam put his hand up to his hair but stopped himself again. "Love isn't always enough sometimes. I had finally gotten a big break landing the detective gig in Bretford, and Diana was only nineteen. It seems absurd now, but back then it all felt so complicated."

Sam came behind May and pushed her softly. "I was a fool. I thought I knew it all, but I didn't have the first clue."

"You loved her, though, didn't you?"

"I did, but by the time I worked that out, it was too late."

May put her feet to the ground and turned to him. "I finally worked something out that has been bugging me—and don't get mad at me for snooping—there's a photo in your room that's ripped in half. It has a woman's hand around your waist. That was Mom, wasn't it?"

The detective looked away and said quietly, "Yes. Your mom ripped it in half before she went missing, after we had a fight. It was the only photo we took together."

May twisted around in the swing farther so she was facing Sam directly. "So why do you not have her half of the photo?"

"I don't need a photo of Diana to remember her by. I have her right here." He tapped his head. "What I needed was to remember what I looked like. Happy, content, like my life had meaning. I look at that photo of myself every day as a reminder of my bad decisions and everything I lost because of them."

Something tugged at her heart. "You mean Mom."

"I do." He paused. "I also mean you."

May twisted back around. Sam pushed her again.

"You have me now," she whispered.

Sam didn't make any sign he'd heard her. "I can't change the past, but the future is in my hands." He chuckled. "Literally."

May smiled. "You would've been a great father. I want you to know that."

"Thanks. I appreciate that more than you'll ever know."

May put her feet on the ground again, stopping the swing. "My sister's watching from the window. Let's go inside. She has a cunning way of working things out without me saying anything. Pat's the same."

Sam helped May off the tire, and they strolled back to the house. "Your sister is a piece of work."

"That's an understatement." May laughed. "I guess she has her own demons she's dealing with. June has my back, even if it doesn't seem like it. She will always be my twin . . . even if we aren't."

The detective nodded, following behind her.

May put her hand on the front doorknob and stopped. "Did Mom ever tell you where she went? Who June's dad is?"

"No. She never told me." Sam took May's hand in his. "Your mom and I made mistakes. I should've lost my career after Diana went missing because of our relationship, but she never said a word. It must've been so hard for her to be interviewed by me and act as if we were strangers, but she did it. Be careful what you wish for in life, May. All I could think about was a career—and your mom inadvertently fast-tracked mine. Now, I don't have much to show for it."

"You have me." May put her arms around him. It was the least awkward thing she could remember doing in a long time. "Now, let's go and sort out this mess of a family. Whether you like it or not, you're one of us." They broke apart.

"I like the sound of that."

"I do too."

A van with **NEWS** on its side made its way up the street as the screen door slammed behind them.

Hi Mom,

It's me, May.

Thought I'd give this a try. It seemed to work so well for June.

Maybe if I write enough letters to you, I'll believe my own lies. That's how it works, right?

June is getting out of treatment soon, and the doctors reckon she'll make a fresh start. Of course she will. Writing letters to you doesn't seem to be part of her therapy anymore—maybe it never was?

Sorry, Mom, but she has better things to do now. She always wanted to be famous, and you know that June always gets what she wants. She's already famous in that Gone Girl way. Girl turns up alive after everyone thinks she's dead AND is the product of her mother's abduction. There's big money in that story!

The only thing she needs to do now is get her story straight, and she'll be rolling in it. There's even talk of her doing an exclusive with Oprah. I know. Bit much, right?

June explained to me that she doesn't know what she's saying because it's the trauma talking.

What a fucking joke. Am I going to hear that for the rest of my life?

"It's the trauma talking."

Give me a break.

Anyway, I've given enough of my time and energy to June.

Should we talk about me now? Won't find that too boring will you, Mom?

That's all I was really, wasn't it? The reliable one, the consistent one, the one that reminded you of the one who got away?

That's gotta hurt. Seeing his eyes in mine every day. How'd you do it? Just living your life like nothing happened. Damn, Mom. Do you KNOW how fucked up that is?

You wrote about bad blood and obviously sought it out daily, looking for any hint of June being different. Don't lie. I know you did.

Here's the thing about that. Were you seeking out a sickness in her because you saw the same sickness in yourself?

Yep.

Thought so.

Who was the real monster in all this, Mom?

Don't answer that. I already know.

That creepy ghost story you used to tell us about the man who dug graves, was that about you trying to bury all of your mistakes? Your past? Us?

You could have done things so differently, but you didn't. And not once did you try to make it better. Instead you drove June to be just like you.

Because you are the monster, Mom.

YOU.

You took my father away from me. You pitted June and me against each other because both of us were like gaping wounds that you could never heal.

Whatever.

I'm living in Bretford now. Right near your old lover. My father. Going to university there just like you did. How's that for just deserts?

I'm wearing your old necklace too. Guess who had it? I talk to it, too, sometimes, just like you did. I ask it for advice. Ask it for luck.

For forgiveness.

Forgiveness. Something you can never give me. Something that will consume me till the day I die.

I'm sorry about the pool, Mom.

I really am. It was an awful accident. You know that, right?

All I wanted was for you to give me the free-dom you gave June. Was that so hard? I wasn't some delicate flower you had to protect. All I wanted was to get away from Harold. If only you'd just said yes.

I didn't mean to make you fall. I didn't mean to ruin your happy place. It's just so slippery around there, and you were so angry with me, and . . . well you know what happened.

I guess fucking up is what we're good at.

Having secrets too.

Maybe I'm a lot more like you than I thought.

Awesome.

Something to look forward to.

Love, May

Acknowledgments

If you're anything like me, you've started my book here. I've forever been fascinated with who an author thanks and all the people involved in getting a book on a shelf. To be here writing my own acknowledgments is beyond words. Yet, as an author now (!!), I'll try my best.

First, I would like to thank my agent, Gwen Beal, from UTA. You took a chance on me when I needed you the most and have never wavered in your dedication to me and my writing—even when I keep throwing so many projects at you. You're the best! Other special mentions from UTA include Jessica Rios, Geritza Carrasco, and film/TV agent Mary Pender.

To everyone at Thomas & Mercer. Thank you! I'm so lucky to have such a powerhouse team looking after me. Especially my editor, Jessica Tribble Wells, who said yes and made me the happiest girl in the world. Also extra thanks to developmental editor Dee Hudson, copyeditor Alicia Lea, proofreader Jenna Justice, production manager Miranda Gardner, associate rights director Hatty Stiles, marketing manager Andrew George, art director Michael Jantze, and cover designer Jeff Miller.

I have too many friends to thank by name in this fabulous writing community I infiltrated—with imposter syndrome in tow. Here are a few who helped me shape my debut. (If I missed anyone, pizza's on me.)

I start with my first writing group, Fortitude, who've kept me sane for all these years: Jessica Conoley, Lora Senf, and Kellie McVeigh McQueen—Kellie, we love and miss you.

The sharp eyes of these legends: Britney Brouwer, Roselyn Clarke, Megan Davidhizar, Jessica Froberg, Chinelo Chidebe, Carolina Flórez-Cerchiaro, Audrey Henley, and special mention to Sonja J. Kaye for dealing with my erratic messages all the livelong day.

Thanks also to the #2024debuts, Submission Slog Comrades, and Mystery Mavens. Group chats have been my savior over the years, and I am not sure what I would do without you all.

My fab friends who put up with me even when I'm in the writing cave. Christina, Kate, Lucy, Eliza, Carmen, Caroline, Jack, Safwan, Rachel, Emma, Luis, Jim, and especially Catty—you are one of my first readers for a reason.

My family for always believing in me. Dad, BJ, and Lara. Shout out to big bro, Glen, for being such a great sounding board—don't worry, I'll treat you to the audiobook, given you can't stand reading. Ha ha.

And, of course, Mum! Thank you for being my very first reader for everything I've ever written. The journey to get here has been long and hard at times, and you've been through all of it. The celebrations. The commiserations. At every step you believed in me, and for that I am eternally grateful. I couldn't have done this without you.

Pats for the bestest boy, my German shepherd, Atreyu. You make the days better by never leaving my side. Like ever. Pizza, cups of tea, and wine. Thanks for being my emotional support crew. Never leave me. Like ever.

Thank you, kind reader, for picking up my book! I won't ask what you thought of it, unless I've had too much wine, and then all bets are off.

And, finally, to my sister, Kristie. You would've liked this one. One day, when we're together again, we'll read it. In the dark. With our flashlights. Not wearing white, obvs. Miss you with all my heart.

About the Author

Photo © 2020 Larissa Hubbard

Paula Gleeson writes mysteries and thrillers for all ages, usually with complicated females at the helm. She is an award-winning filmmaker and nominated nonfiction writer. She lives just outside Melbourne, Australia, and can often be found in her pj's, drinking tea (wine) and watching horror movies snuggled between her doggo and a large cheese pizza. *Original Twin* is her debut novel.

https://paulagleeson.com